Vengeance

Vengeance

MEGAN MIRANDA

WALKER BOOKS
AN IMPRINT OF BLOOMSBURY
NEW YORK   LONDON   NEW DELHI   SYDNEY

First published in the United States of America in February 2014
by Walker Books for Young Readers, an imprint of Bloomsbury Publishing, Inc.
www.bloomsbury.com

For information about permission to reproduce selections from this book, write to
Permissions, Walker BFYR, 1385 Broadway, New York, New York 10018
Bloomsbury books may be purchased for business or promotional use. For information
on bulk purchases please contact Macmillan Corporate and Premium Sales Department
at specialmarkets@macmillan.com

Library of Congress Cataloging-in-Publication Data
Miranda, Megan.
Vengeance / by Megan Miranda.
pages   cm
Sequel to: Fracture.
Summary: It seems Decker is the only person who does not believe that Falcon Lake,
under a curse, is somehow connected to his best friend, Delaney, but everything changes
when Delaney senses the imminent death of Decker's father and says nothing.
ISBN 978-0-8027-3503-4 (hardcover) • ISBN 978-0-8027-3504-1 (e-book)
[1. Supernatural—Fiction.   2. Death—Fiction.   3. Interpersonal relations—Fiction.
4. Blessing and cursing—Fiction.]   I. Title.
PZ7.M67352Ven 2014   [Fic]—dc23   2013024937

Book design by Nicole Gastonguay
Typeset by Westchester Book Composition
Printed and bound in the U.S.A. by Thomson-Shore, Inc., Dexter, Michigan
2 4 6 8 10 9 7 5 3 1

All papers used by Bloomsbury Publishing, Inc., are natural, recyclable products
made from wood grown in well-managed forests. The manufacturing processes
conform to the environmental regulations of the country of origin.

For my family. All of you.

Vengeance

Prologue

Back when everyone believed Delaney was going to die, I made a bargain with God.

Correction: I made a bargain.

I didn't really believe in a god. I didn't even know how to pray. But I closed my eyes and thought: *Not her.* We were in the hospital. The doctors were talking to her parents. Machines monitored her, breathed for her, lived for her. *Anyone but her*, I thought.

Everyone but her.

Six days later she woke up, and for a little while I forgot about that bargain. She smiled when she saw me. She came home.

Our neighbor was old when she died the next day. I didn't think anything of it. But then Carson died—he was seventeen and probably my best friend, other than her. Then I remembered my words. *Anyone but her.*

Everyone but her.

Someone had been listening.

Chapter

1

The lady in room 2B was about to die. I didn't even need Delaney to tell me that. Her eyes were open, and I was pretty sure she had just blinked, but she wasn't breathing. I leaned over the bedrail, my fingers tightening on the cold metal, and whispered, "Hello?" She sucked in a violent breath, and I tripped over the garbage can at my feet. Her eyes darted around the room, landing on me.

I crouched below the bed and pushed the trash back into the container. Collecting the trash: this was what I was here for, anyway. My hands trembled, like Delaney's would if she was here, but for a very different reason. She should be here—not me. I checked the clock on the far wall. She should really be here.

I stood up, about to leave, about to get help, get anyone, get out of here. The lady's eyes were open, but she wasn't breathing. Again. I watched, waiting for her to blink. Waiting for some sign of life.

Nothing.

"Hey," I said, shaking her by the shoulders. And then she sucked in another giant wheezing breath.

Not dead yet.

But definitely almost dead.

"Hey!" I said, louder, but this time I was calling for someone else. Anyone else. I was not this guy. Not the guy who sat beside people as they died, not the guy who held their hands or promised them everything was going to be okay when everything definitely was not going to be okay. I was not the person who volunteered at the nursing home so I would be there for them when no one else could. *That* was Delaney.

I was the guy who worked at the assisted living facility for the cash, partly, but mostly to be around his girlfriend. So shoot me.

I stared at the empty doorway. Where the hell was Delaney? Her shift started thirty minutes ago, and if she was anywhere in the area, she'd know that this was happening. She'd feel it. She'd be here, because she was a better person than I was.

I jabbed at the buttons on the side of the bed, assuming one of them was to call for help. Though I hoped I hadn't inadvertently given her some lethal dose of morphine or something. Not that it would matter. "I'll be right back," I mumbled, but her fingers gripped onto my wrist as I turned for the door.

Delaney said some people go gently, and some people fight death all the way, like Delaney had, trapped on the other side of the ice. I fought it with her, breathing air into her lungs, forcing her heart to pump blood.

From the feel of this lady's grip on my wrist, she was about to fight it.

"Where . . . ," she whispered, like an exhale, as she stared at the open door.

"I have no idea," I said, realizing we were having two very different conversations.

She turned her head to face me, and I was sure that the effort alone would kill her once and for all, but instead it seemed to make her stronger. Her fingers dug down to the bone in my wrist as she pulled me closer. Her eyes reminded me of Delaney's: hazel; familiar. They were the only parts of her with any color now. White hair, pale face, lips that faded into the skin around them.

"Listen," she said, but it came out like a rasp.

I listened: a ticking clock, a door shutting somewhere down the hall, the air-conditioning rattling the vent. She stared at me, like I had the power to read her mind. She held on tight, as if I had the power to do anything at all.

And then I watched as the blacks at the center of her eyes grew, eating away at the color that remained.

No dying words. She was dead.

"Oh no." My boss, Marlene, stood in the doorway. "Am I too late?" She reminded me of my mom—tall and thin and to the point. Her dark hair was tied back in a bun, and she had a plastic bag in her hand, some sort of tubing. She left it on the counter and walked over to us, looked down at my hand, which was now gripping 2B's wrist, instead of the other way around. She put her fingers to the lady's neck and then pulled my hand away as she folded the woman's arms across her unmoving chest.

"Are you okay?" Marlene asked.

"She just died," I said. What could possibly be okay about the situation?

She looked at me from the corner of her eye. Looked at 2B. Looked at me again. "They're all going to die," she said.

"She was looking for someone."

"Hon, she had Alzheimer's. She was probably looking for someone who doesn't exist anymore." I looked at the empty doorway. The empty hall.

"She was going to tell me something," I said. I stared at my wrist, at the red marks from her fingers, which had force and life and will less than a minute earlier.

Marlene shuffled her feet beside me, put a hand on my back, leading me out of this room. "Hey, let's call it a day. Take the rest of today off, okay? Go home and do something fun. We'll see you Monday."

Fun. I shook my head. "I'm waiting for Delaney."

She looked down the corridor toward the double doors at the end. "She called in sick. I thought you knew."

I nodded. "I forgot," I said. But that was a lie. The door to room 2B was still open. The light was still on. The lady was still in the bed. I felt something rising in my throat. No, something closing it off. I needed out.

"Go on," she said. And then, as I started to go, she said, "Hey, you did good."

But I hadn't done anything at all. And all I was doing now was racing toward the exit, toward the air. I didn't even know her name.

I stood in my driveway, leaning against the hood of my parents' old minivan, my current car. It was hot—hotter than the air around me, and it was record-breaking hot today. Had been all week. My hands were still trembling slightly as I dialed Delaney's home phone. Her cell had gone to voice mail three times straight.

"I thought she was with you," Joanne, Delaney's mother, said after I asked if she was home, and I could feel the growing tension in her voice. Delaney lived next door in a house nearly identical to mine—hers was gray; mine was beige. My eyes drifted up to the window over the door, to the left: her room, same as mine. Her blinds were pulled shut. The front curtains to the living room were open, I was pretty sure—they usually were as soon as Joanne got up in the morning, but I couldn't see in. The reflection of the sun glared back at me instead. I wondered if Delaney's mom was looking out, watching me.

"Decker? Didn't you pick her up for work this morning?" Joanne's voice was higher than normal. Tighter. I felt something inside of me doing the same.

No, I didn't pick her up, because I had to be in at eight, and she had to be in at nine.

It wasn't like Delaney to call in sick if she wasn't sick, and it wasn't like Delaney to lie to her mom about where she was, unless it was with me.

I cleared my throat. Felt everything relax inside me. I knew exactly where to find her. "I called in sick," I said. "I was just making sure she got a ride in." It really wasn't like me to lie to Delaney's mom, either, since she'd been my babysitter and some figure of authority in my life since as long as I could remember. But I wasn't about to tell Joanne where Delaney really was.

I walked down our street—the morning was hazy, as if something was moving across the road, across the grass, across everything. It's like the heat didn't know what to do with itself here in Maine, so it wandered restlessly, looking for somewhere to go. I saw it sliding across the lake in the distance, like fog. I walked toward the crest of the hill—where the sidewalk ended and the ground lowered into a pit, a dirt trail cutting through evergreens, the lake at the center.

Nobody touched Falcon Lake anymore. Not last winter, after Delaney fell through, and not in the spring that followed. Nobody sat on the pebbled shore, watching the sunrise together under a blanket. There were no boats out there now, even though it was summer.

The lake was dead.

Or the lake was alive, depending on whom you asked.

Either way, dead or alive, it's the type of thing best left alone. And alone we left it.

Except for her. I'd find her there, on the days she felt powerless, her feet at the edge of the lake, her toes touching the water, like she was tempting it. This was where I'd find her, I knew it. I closed my eyes before I crested the hill, seeing her in my mind, her bare feet an inch from the water. *Be there*, I thought.

But Delaney wasn't toeing the edge today. She was knee-deep in it, her skin pale above the unmoving surface of the water. Her blond hair tied up, her shirt hanging loose over one shoulder. Her shorts still dry, a few inches above the water.

I knew she heard me as I strode down the embankment, kicking up rocks in my wake, but she didn't so much as flinch. She looked like a ghost, rising up out of Falcon Lake.

No. She was here. She was fine.

"So," I said, walking toward her, "on a scale of one to ten, how sick are we talking? Like too sick to go to work? Too sick for pancakes? Or too sick to tell me you were calling in sick?"

She didn't crack a smile. Didn't even look at me. "Do you believe in reincarnation?" she asked.

"Delaney—"

"Heaven?"

I thought of 2B's fingers on my wrist. Shook the thought. "I'm hungry. Let's get something to eat."

"Some sort of afterlife?"

I thought of dead arms folded against her unmoving chest.

I took my flip-flops off, felt the pebbles slide under the soles of my feet. Heard the splash as my foot hit the surface.

She stared at my foot, like she didn't understand why I was doing this. "I want to know what you believe," she said, raising her eyes to my face. "So that I can believe it, too."

"I don't believe in curses," I said, stepping closer. "I don't believe in this." My arm skimmed the surface of the lake.

"Shhh," she said. I stood still, listening for whatever it was she heard. Or maybe she thought the lake could hear us instead.

Here's the thing about curses: we know they aren't real. Nobody thinks twice about taking a cruise through the Bermuda Triangle. Name one person who would give away the Hope Diamond. Yeah, I didn't think so. Hell, even the Red Sox eventually won the World Series.

Nobody *really* believes in a curse.

Until it has a face.

Until you know the people who disappear. Until you know the person who wore the diamond and died. Until you're the one with the ball rolling between your legs on the final out of the ninth inning.

Too much coincidence, you look for reason.

Too much death, you grasp for something to blame.

They call it the Curse of Falcon Lake, but that's just because they're not completely horrible people. But Delaney knows—I know, we all know—that when people say "Falcon Lake," they're really talking about her. People think it, I can tell. In the way they smile at Delaney. In the way they're too kind. Too polite. Too distant.

Carson helped pull her out of the ice, and he died on the side of the road with her mouth pressed to his. Her air in his body. They said he was soaked when they got to the hospital, like he had drowned in her place. It was the snow he had seized in, melted against his hot skin, they all knew that. But the story held.

Next: Troy. The lake taking him and sparing her. He had found her in the hospital, befriended her when she got home, only to try and kill her—kill both of them actually. Didn't matter. The lake released her, grabbed another.

Correction: *I* had taken her back from the lake. And now it was vengeful.

Delaney tried to put logic to it all. The numbers backed her up. The national death rate, the statistics. According to straight numbers, our town was due to have about fifteen deaths throughout the year. Maybe a suicide every three years. It was just statistics, she had claimed.

"People keep dying," she said now, as if even she had a hard time believing herself. She pulled the elastic from her hair and shook it out, letting it tumble down her back.

I thought of the black pupils, growing wider. "Just statistics," I said. She turned to look at me, her eyes like a storm coming, cloudy and hazel.

She nodded and looked away, toward the rising sun. I watched my reflection waver on the surface as I walked toward her. Then I took her hand—she flinched, then relaxed—and I pulled her deeper. The water rose up over our shorts, our shirts. I heard her gasp as it covered her stomach, rising toward her neck. The lake took her first, her feet leaving the bottom, her weight in the water. I was a step behind. We treaded water, her lips were trembling, and I pulled her close.

I felt her legs tangling with mine below. I felt her arms moving fast, like she was racing against something pulling her down. I felt her breath in the space between our faces. Her lips were trembling, and I kissed her.

And then her arms stopped moving, and her legs grew still, as if she was giving herself over to the lake, to me.

I wanted to move my hands to her back, her face, her hair. But if I stopped moving, we'd start to sink.

Her lips were cold, and I flashed to that other version of her: the one I pressed my mouth to as I exhaled air, watching her chest rise in response, refusing to let go. I pictured her blue, still, and I pulled away.

"It's just water," I said.

"I know," she said, even though I was talking to myself. She arched back, away from me, like she had done it a thousand times, and laid herself flat against the surface of the water, letting it carry her. Her hair spilled out in a fan around her, and with her eyes closed, I saw that other version of her again: lifeless, a deadweight, the one I hauled onto the shore in the snow. The one I pressed my hands down on, keeping count in my head, trying to keep her heart pumping, feeling the crack of her bone underneath as I did.

I closed my eyes, shook the thought, leaned back to float like she did. The water covered my ears, so all I could hear was it rushing in and out, like the ocean. Like air. Like nothingness.

Listen.

I thought of fingers on my wrist, digging down to the bone.

"Delaney?" I jerked upright, but she wasn't in front of me. I spun around, but she wasn't behind me. I felt my throat closing off, heard my heart in my head. *No.*

She broke through the surface of the water right in front

of me, pushing her hair back from her face. She took a deep breath, and I tried to do the same.

"Decker?" she asked. She swam closer, put a hand on my arm. "Is it happening again?"

"No." I shook my head. "I'm fine." *Breathe. From the stomach. Breathe.*

She was pulling me back. Pebbles under my toes. Weight on my feet. "Decker, what happened?"

Water at chest level. Sun reflecting off the surface. Her hand on my elbow. I closed my eyes. Some days I'd wake up in a cold sweat, looking for her. As if the last eight months hadn't happened.

That I hadn't pulled her out of the lake. That she hadn't woken up. That she didn't exist.

But then weeks would go by, and I'd be fine. Months, even. And then she'd slip under the surface of the water for a moment and it would all come rushing back.

I never told her.

I never told anyone.

The doctor my parents dragged me to thought it was because Carson died—he had been healthy, or so we had thought, and then he just . . . died. The idea of being there and then being gone—the doctor said it was my trigger.

I never told him it wasn't the idea of *me* being gone that was my trigger. It was always her. In my head, she was always disappearing.

"Decker?" Water at my waist now. At my knees. "This was a bad idea," she said.

I opened my eyes. "I'm sorry," I said, and I slowly felt something release from my throat. From my lungs. "The lady in 2B died." I shrugged when I said it. I didn't tell her I was there.

"Clarissa Duvall," she said.

Delaney had her arms wrapped around herself. She was shaking. The water was too cold for swimming, even in August.

We were out of the lake. We had just gone for a swim in Falcon Lake, and now we were standing on the shore, and we were fine. There was something empowering about it. Like everyone else, believing in the curse or not, I hadn't touched it. Not until just now, and we didn't die.

Delaney was standing in front of me, her wet clothes clinging to her, and I smiled. She laughed to herself for a second, looking down, a dimple forming on her left cheek. I loved the sound. I loved the smile. It felt like something coming to life.

"Okay, seriously," I said. "I'm starving."

"I'm actually kind of hungry, too," she said, and her smile grew into the one I knew she saved for me.

"I can't take you out like that," I said, pulling at her shirt. "But the offer for pancakes still stands."

"Are you offering to cook for me? Do you even know how to cook?" she asked.

"I'm not promising it will be any good."

"Cook me pancakes," she said, "and I'll love you forever." She was joking when she said it, and she made sure I knew she was joking, in the way she was standing, in the way that her hands were on her hips, and in the way she bit her lower lip. But she also wasn't. She was blushing, like she was nervous to admit how she felt. Even though I knew.

I laughed. "Deal," I said. "Come on." I took her hand, leading her toward home.

The sun was beating on my back. The air was record-breaking hot. But I couldn't shake the cold—Falcon Lake, clinging to my skin, seeping into my bones.

Chapter

2

We snuck into the mudroom in the back of my house. I didn't really need to sneak around—my parents were both at work. And even if they weren't, it's not like I had to clock in and out. But if Delaney's mom saw her out the window, she'd probably freak. First, her daughter wasn't where she said she'd be. Second, her daughter was dripping wet.

Third, she was sneaking over to my house.

We were both dripping water on the linoleum—the rest of the house, through the hall, the kitchen, the stairs, everywhere, was hardwood. "Stay here," I said, even though it didn't look like she had any plans of moving. "I'll get towels."

I ran to the upstairs linen closet, grabbed a set of old towels, grabbed two T-shirts and two pairs of gym shorts from my room before racing down the steps two at a time. I knew I was leaving a trail of water in my wake. I'd clean up later.

I wanted the water off my skin.

I wanted to make her pancakes.

She was in the exact same spot I'd left her in, a puddle gathering around her feet. I slowed when I reached her, when I saw her face. I heard the buzz of the garage door, the hum of a car engine.

"It's okay," I said, handing her a towel.

She took a step toward the door.

"It's my house," I said. "I'm allowed to be here. You're allowed to be here, too." My parents and I operated in a completely different pattern than Delaney and her parents did. And just to show her how okay it was, I reached around her, rubbed a towel over her hair, and kissed her forehead. "I am making you some freaking pancakes," I said. "And then you're stuck with me."

I pulled back from her, expecting to see her smile, but she was looking past me, down the hall. I heard my dad's footsteps first. Probably following the trail of water through the downstairs. Then he turned the corner, coming into view. Still in his work clothes, his work shoes, but his tie was loosened. His top button undone.

"We're cleaning up," I said, holding up the towel to show him. But he was eyeing the ends of Delaney's wet hair, the puddle dripping on the floor.

He walked into the mudroom, stepped into my personal space. He put a finger on my chest. A hand on her shoulder. I could see the fear and logic warring in his face. "Delaney," he said. "Go home."

She was pale. Paler than from the cold water. Paler than

from the fact that she always wore sunscreen. She was pale, and her eyes were huge. *It's just my dad*, I wanted to tell her. *He doesn't believe it.* As she backed away, my dad ran his wet hand through his hair. Then he looked at his palm, at the remnants of Falcon Lake, and wiped it against the side of his pants.

"No," I said. "You don't have to go." But I was looking at my dad when I said it, and I heard the back door creak closed behind her.

Always disappearing.

"Don't talk to her like that," I said.

"Don't talk to *me* like that," he said. People said I was his mirror—in the way we looked, definitely. In the way we acted, according to my mom. Even I could see it—in his dark hair and gray eyes and lean build. Like I could look at him and see my future.

"You're being ridiculous," I said.

"Get changed," he said.

"Why? Am I going to *die* because I went *swimming*? You don't seriously believe that. You don't seriously believe there's a curse."

He stared at the door. Then at his hands again. He wiped them once more, though there was nothing left. "I'm not talking about a curse," he said. "I'm talking about *her.* You need some space. You're becoming too wrapped up—"

"Stop it," I said as I felt my hands clenching into fists. And he was way too late if he thought I was *becoming* too wrapped up. I'd known Delaney for the majority of my life, been wrapped up in her in some way or another for the last ten years. Been in love with her entirely for the last three, at least.

"You can't see it. You're too close. . . ."

"*Stop*," I said, and this time he did.

"Decker," he said, but then he closed his eyes, shook his head, almost smiled. "Clean up this mess," he said. The dark circles under his eyes, permanent fixtures from the last few months, meant he was probably working a headache of a case. And chances are, this conversation was adding to that headache. He disappeared into his office—guess he decided to work the rest of the day from home.

I wiped up the water. Changed, showered, tried calling Delaney, but it went straight to voice mail—figured she was still getting cleaned up. Or getting the third degree from her mother. I could picture Joanne taking the phone from her, powering it off, telling her not to see me for a while. Which would last maybe two hours. Her mother loved me. To be fair, I think she loved me a little less now that I was her daughter's boyfriend—as opposed to her daughter's best friend.

My dad used to love Delaney, too. I'd never pegged him for superstitious. God knows he wasn't religious. He was a lawyer: he loved concrete facts, things that made sense, as Delaney did. But he also liked to argue, like me. I went downstairs and my dad was in the kitchen, hunched over the counter.

Lunch, I figured. I also figured we were done arguing, because that's the way it worked with us. We just pretended it hadn't happened. "What are you making?" I said. "Because I'm famished."

I wanted pancakes. I wanted them with Delaney sitting across the table in my clothes.

"Lasagna," he said, waving his hand over the tomato waiting to be cut. "For tonight. It's your mother's favorite."

"Awesome." I took an apple from a red ceramic bowl and hopped up on the laminate countertop. "Can I invite Delaney?"

His hands paused over the cutting board. I took a bite from the apple, and the sound echoed through the kitchen. "Sure."

Yep, argument done. "Excellent. Then you can apologize to her."

I hopped off the counter and walked away, waiting for him to start yelling again. I reached the stairs. Nothing. And then, "Aren't you supposed to be at work today?" He said it like an accusation, and I could hear all the accusations layered below it: *You ditched work to hang out with your girlfriend. You were here with her because you thought no one would be home.* This was his job—he was a professional at deflecting accusations and framing new ones. He defended people for a living, and he said sometimes the best way to defend someone was to accuse someone else.

"I went to work. They didn't need me. They gave me the rest of the day off." I learned that from my dad, too—how to tell enough of the truth so that people would believe you, how to skip over details without it seeming like you were skipping anything at all.

How to pretend that some parts didn't exist:

A hand, gripping my wrist.

Black pupils, growing wider.

Listen.

The sound of a knife on the cutting board. The clicking of the burner as my dad waited for it to catch. "Want to help?" he asked.

I started to shake my head, but he held up the knife, like an idea. "Girls love a guy who can cook," he said.

"Gross," I said, because he was talking about my mother. But I thought of Delaney, sticking her hip out, leaning into it, telling me she'd love me forever. I owed her a meal. I walked back across the room, took the knife from his outstretched hand, and left the apple on the counter. By the time I reached for another bite, it had already turned brown.

Delaney didn't pick up the phone later that afternoon. It still went straight to voice mail. "Pick up," I said, after her voice told me to leave a message. "I made dinner. I half made dinner. Whatever, I helped. There's lasagna. Come." I even thought about calling the home phone again, but I didn't want Joanne to yell at me, too.

She didn't call back.

I zoned out through dinner, wondering how long she'd be grounded and whether I'd get to see her tomorrow, and then wondering if maybe I should sneak over tonight, and how that would even work if she didn't know I was coming and couldn't leave the back door unlocked for me.

"Decker," my dad said, like he had already said it and was getting annoyed.

"Yeah?"

"Did you hear a word I said?"

I smiled at my mom, then at my dad. "This lasagna," I said, scooping another bite into my mouth. "It's like heaven. It's the

greatest thing ever created in the Phillips kitchen." My mom
threw her napkin at me.

"Tomorrow we're going hiking. Six a.m.," my dad said.

"Pass," I said.

"It's not really optional."

"It's Saturday," I said. "At six a.m."

"Seven," he said.

"*Pass*," I said again. My parents' idea of hiking recently
was more like a leisurely stroll, which would probably eat up at
least half the day—maybe more, depending on how far we
were driving.

"Joe," my mom said, "you're going about this the wrong
way." She turned to me and cleared her throat. "Oh, good, we
can stay home and do one of those SAT prep tests."

"I'll go find my boots," I said, pushing back from the table.
I heard them laughing from my room.

Open the door, I thought. Not that I believed in telepathy or
anything, but I didn't use to believe in a girl who knew when
someone was about to die, either. I didn't use to believe in a
girl surviving eleven minutes trapped under the ice. I didn't
believe she'd ever wake up. Not really.

So I figured this couldn't hurt. We had to be thinking the
same thing. It was after midnight when I snuck out my back
door, the same way we'd snuck in earlier that day. I was barefoot because it made it seem less premeditated if I got caught.
This was definitely premeditated. I'd been meditating about it
for hours.

I'd only done this once before—but it was after this

particularly crappy day where this guy yelled at her at work. He'd grabbed her arm. Made her jump. Called her an *omen*, which I guess she was, standing beside his bed because she had been drawn there. And if she was drawn to him, he was going to die.

Like Marlene said, they were *all* going to die.

But when he grabbed her and she jumped, I hit him in the arm, dying or not. It's a miracle Marlene didn't fire me then, but I think she saw the look on Delaney's face. I think she saw the way he grabbed her wrist. Marlene said his mind was going, that he lost himself. But it wasn't true. He could see more than most. He could see Delaney, like a sign. Like a warning.

I told Delaney to leave the back door unlocked that night because I didn't want her thinking she was an omen. I didn't want her thinking of that man dying a few hours later.

The grass was shorter in her backyard, and cooler. Damp. Her house had these motion-detector lights in the backyard and off the front porch, and the only way to avoid them going off was to press myself against the siding of the house and creep along it until I reached the back door. Like I was a stalker. I held my breath and tested the handle. Locked. They didn't keep a spare key under a mat or a rock in the side yard, like we did. I crept back to the front of the house and stared up at her dark window. Guess we weren't thinking the same thing after all.

The air felt thick with humidity, even though the grass was cool, like maybe it would rain. Good. Then maybe the hike would be canceled and I'd get out of waking up in less than six hours.

I wasn't as quiet as I should've been coming back inside my own house, and the kitchen light flicked on down the hall. Crap. I froze but figured I was already caught. I looked down at my bare feet. *I was just out back.* True. *I didn't go anywhere.* True.

Then I heard a clatter, like furniture being pushed around. I walked into the kitchen. My dad stood hunched over the counter, like he had earlier today. But there was a chair toppled over beside him. "Dad?" I asked.

He spun around too quickly, knocking a glass of water off the counter. It shattered into pieces beside him, and I was trying to focus on the pieces, trying to figure out what was happening after midnight in this room with a chair on the floor and a glass in pieces and water pooling on the hardwood next to my dad's bare feet.

"Something's not right," he said. He clutched at his chest for a heartbeat, maybe two, and I watched as his knees hit the pieces of glass on the floor.

I felt something closing off my windpipe. Felt terror growing in my chest. "Mom!" I yelled.

I slid to the ground beside him, holding him up by the shoulders, looking anywhere but at his eyes, at the black centers. I looked at his mouth, instead. At the way it formed a word, but no sound came out. My mom was in the room, gripping the phone already. "Decker?" she asked, and I realized she couldn't tell which of us was hurt. We were both struggling to breathe. My arms were shaking as I tried to keep him up. They were shaking, still, as we both sunk farther onto the floor.

The ambulance took my dad away, took my mom away, too. She said, "I'll call you" as they closed the double doors. I'd ridden in the back of the ambulance with Delaney. There was barely any room, and it felt like a coffin. It felt like hell.

I didn't fight to ride in one now. I'd meet them there with my own car. It was smart.

We'd all have a ride home later.

Then I saw Delaney standing between her parents on the front porch, her arms folded across her chest, her hands tucked up under her shoulders, like she was hiding something. Her mouth was open but she didn't have to say anything. She closed her eyes, and in that stupid motion-detector light, I could see the tear trailing down her cheek, and I knew.

I knew with every cell in my body—now paralyzed, nauseous—the same way she knew with hers.

Sometime between here and there, he wasn't going to make it.

When death is close, she hides her hands. They shake. They give her away.

The engine of the ambulance turned over, the red and blue lights lighting up the night. Delaney was racing across my yard, and that jerked me into motion. I was back-peddling toward my house, like if I could just get away from her, if I could pretend I didn't see, it wouldn't be true. I held up my hands. She stopped dead in her tracks. And then I looked at her hands, which were hanging still beside her, and for the briefest second I thought that he was going to be okay.

Then she looked at them too, and she clenched them into fists.

"No," I said, talking to her, talking to myself.

But she didn't listen. She walked up the steps and followed me into the house.

"Decker," she said, nearly whispering, "I am so, so—"

"*What?*" I spun around as I said it, and she cringed.

"Sorry," she said, and I could see her mouth moving, but I couldn't hear anything else.

"I have to go," I said, fumbling for the car keys. My mom would be there, alone. Alone because Delaney's hands were still as the ambulance drove away. Death wasn't coming anymore. It was done.

His work shoes were beside the door. And the house still smelled like lasagna, still felt like him—I could hear him, walking down the stairs, all some big trick, like how I'd keep imagining Delaney gone, see her still body, and then she'd appear, full of life, right in front of me.

I ran into the office. The kitchen. Watched the stairs, my breath coming too fast, my vision going hazy from it.

"Decker," she said. And she was crying. Shaking her head at me.

Like I was that lady in 2B. Looking for someone who didn't exist anymore.

I shook my head at her. Like she had the power to change this. *Change this,* I thought, turning away from her, watching the stairs again.

"Delaney? Decker?" Joanne stood in the open doorway, her curly hair a mess, a bathrobe pulled around her pajamas, sneakers over bare feet. "Hon? Do you want to go or wait for your mom to call?"

"I'm going," I said, holding up my keys. They trembled. My hand trembled.

"Ron will drive you," she said.

"I need my car," I whispered. But I didn't know how to say no to Joanne.

"I got it," Delaney said, reaching for the keys over my shoulder.

I couldn't stop my hands from shaking. Couldn't take a breath. I pressed the keys into her hands and heard her exhale.

"Mom," she whispered as we brushed by her.

"Be right there," she said, and she squeezed my shoulder as I passed. Delaney ran for the car. I couldn't figure out why we were running. Why were we running?

And she drove fast, like that might change anything. I remembered that it could. I ran for her on the ice. I found her. She lived.

Delaney had died under that lake—her heart had stopped, her brain had gone without oxygen for eleven minutes—she was blue and cold and painfully still when I pulled her out of the ice, and I didn't let her go. She came back. She was sitting beside me this very second.

Not him, I thought—I thought it all the way to the same place I'd begged for Delaney's life.

We were halfway to the hospital when I realized she

didn't have any shoes on. I realized that I didn't either. Her toenails were painted a pale purple that I hadn't seen on her before. I was still staring at them when she jerked her foot to the brake and put the car in park.

She handed me the keys in the parking lot, but she didn't follow me. Just stood in the parking lot, staring at the moon. I wondered if she was just waiting for her ride. I wondered if maybe she was praying. I wondered if she was making a bargain with someone. "Thank you," I said, and then she turned and clung to me, her face buried in my neck, like she knew that everything was about to change. I left her there, pretending I didn't know what she meant.

I found my mom in the waiting room a half hour later, after racing from floor to floor, room to room, with no idea where I was going. But it seemed like there was a clock, something I was racing against. As long as I kept moving, as long as we all kept moving . . .

But there she was, with her back to me, perfectly still. Also missing shoes. It was almost comical. She had these blue gauze things on her feet that surgeons wore over their shoes in the operating room or something. She was staring at her phone. Just staring at it. It was trembling slightly as I walked up behind her. "Mom," I said.

She stared at the phone, then stared at me. "I was going to call," she said.

But she couldn't. She didn't have to say why.

*   *   *

It was almost light when we made it back home. Not morning yet, not to me. "You should sleep," my mom said, tossing my car keys on the dining room table, which seemed like the most ridiculous idea in the world. There were a million things more important than sleep. A million things to do. Except there weren't. Not really. "Your grandmother will be here after lunch, so . . ." And then she disappeared into my dad's office.

I wandered past the kitchen and noticed the glass was off the floor. The water was gone. The chair was upright, back beside the table, like last night had never happened. I wondered if Delaney had cleaned up—she knew about the spare key, knew where to find it, had the guts to use it.

I wandered up the stairs and stood in my doorway. Yep, definitely Delaney, seeing as she was sprawled facedown on my bed. I took a step into the room, wanting to fall down beside her. Lie there while she rubbed my back and told me I'd be okay. I stepped toward her, the floorboard creaking, and she jerked upright to standing, sucking in a breath, a hand against the wall to steady herself.

She was looking at me like she wasn't sure where she was or what I was doing here.

It felt like I was supposed to tell her something, but she already knew. She'd known it before we left this house, racing toward the hospital for no reason. I stared at the hiking boots in the corner, the bottoms covered in mud. "The doctors said he had a heart condition," I said to her, because I couldn't think of anything else to say. I had nothing else to say. There *was* nothing else to say.

"I'm sorry," she said. She was walking toward me, and I was thinking she was the only person in the world I wanted to see right now. She knew me, she knew him, she knew us.

I was reaching for her, and then I wasn't.

"He had a heart condition," I said again, and it was like things were falling into place inside my head as I was speaking them. She had stopped moving, one foot in front of the other, halfway across the room. "Something building up inside of him," I said, repeating the words my mom had spoken when I found her in the waiting room.

Delaney was looking somewhere past me, somewhere beyond this room, and she wasn't speaking at all.

"Delaney," I said, slowly, each syllable of her name a question, and she was looking at the floor, like she had just been caught in the biggest lie of her life.

Please, no, I thought. *Let me be wrong.* But she still wouldn't look at me.

Because now I understood the reason she had paled and backed out of my house. Why she ignored my calls for the rest of the day. *She knew.* She stood in the mudroom and my dad walked up to us and she *knew.* She knew and stood there, lying in her silence. She went home and painted her nails. She knew and backed away and never said a word.

"Tell me you didn't know," I said. "Yesterday. In my house. Tell me you didn't know." And I meant it. If she would just say it, I would believe her.

She stared at the wall behind me. At the space above me. At the floor between us.

There is this saying that you need to know sadness to know happiness. I thought it was a load of crap when I first heard it, and I thought it was a load of crap now.

But the truth is that the only reason I could understand what I was feeling in that moment was because I had spent years loving her.

"*Tell me,*" I said, only I yelled it. She jumped. I made her jump.

"Decker . . ."

I circled around her, switching places, trying to force her out of my room with my will alone.

"*Leave.*"

She jumped again. Back. Toward the door.

Her fingers gripped the sides of the entrance as she stumbled out into the hall. I could see her thinking, pausing, her brain working through how to fix this, how to make this right.

My dad's hand on her shoulder.

The chair on its side.

The glass on the floor.

"Wait," she said, leaning against the hallway wall. "Listen . . ." Her eyes searched the space between us in desperation.

I waited. I waited. I wanted to hear her. I wanted there to be some other explanation. But she just stood there, like she was begging me for something.

Fifteen deaths. Statistically speaking.

I could forgive her pretty much anything.

She could forgive me pretty much anything.

We had both done it to get to where we were right then.

But not this. *Not this.*

She was staring at me, willing me to listen. But she didn't make a sound.

I closed the door in her face. Slouched down with my back against it, my head in my hands. Held my breath until I heard her feet racing down the hall.

No dying words.

Chapter

3

She was everywhere.

She was all tied up in my memory of that night. She was everything I was thinking about during my last conversation with my dad. She was who I'd been trying to get to while I was losing him instead. I couldn't think of any of it without seeing her face, looking innocent. Her face, looking like she didn't know. I felt the rage fighting its way out.

And now, she was downstairs. In my house. *Everyone* was in my house.

My grandmother was cooking like the survival of our species depended on it, even though half the neighbors had dropped off some sort of baked dish. There wasn't even enough room in the freezer.

I ordered pizza from my room.

My mother brought it up, leaning her hip against the door. She looked tired. She looked skinny. She'd been a robot, thanking people like she was grateful, accepting condolences like we were saving them up for something. Like we wanted them. "I take it this is your doing?"

I shrugged. "I was hungry."

She slid it onto my dresser and said, "Delaney's downstairs."

"I heard." I didn't really. There were so many people down there, it sounded like a low hum of sameness. But I'd seen her walk across the yard with her parents. She wore a black skirt that I knew her grandmother had gotten her for Christmas.

I hated that she wore it.

I hated that she walked over with her parents.

I hated that she thought she had any right to be here.

"I told her she could come up, but she wouldn't. So . . ." She opened the pizza box and pulled out a slice, sniffing it. She took a bite, closing her eyes.

"I don't want to see her," I said.

"I see," she said. She put the slice back in the box. Sat on the edge of my bed. Took a deep breath, then another, like she was steeling herself for something. She shook her head to herself, brushed her hands over her blouse.

"Some of your other friends are downstairs," she said. "Sure you won't come down?"

I looked out my window and saw Kevin's black Explorer at the curb. Behind it was Tara's red sports car, which never used to bother me—it just seemed like an extension of her, demanding attention. But now it seemed so wrong, so out of place. Justin didn't have a car, but if Kevin was here, he probably was too. I'd known them all for almost as long as I'd known Delaney. Not counting Delaney, Kevin and Justin were the closest friends I had now. We grew up together. We'd gone through the hell of last year together.

"Delaney's still here," I said. "So no thanks."

She stood in the doorway, her eyes wide. "Don't be this guy," she said. And before I could ask her what guy she meant, before I could tell her not to think too highly of the innocent girl next door, she stepped into the hall.

"Good call on the pizza," she said, backing out of the room. "You should've seen your grandma's face. Priceless." She pulled my door shut behind her.

The scent of pizza was overwhelming, sickening really, and I was opening my window when there was another knock. "Yes, take a piece," I said. But it wasn't my mother who stepped into the room. It was Delaney. Guess she changed her mind about not coming up.

"I know you're mad," she said, her hands held up, like she was surrendering.

"Really," I said, staring at the box of pizza. "How observant of you."

"But yesterday," she said. And then she shook her head. "That's not how we leave things."

I looked at her then, and everything twisted inside of me. "You didn't even turn on your phone," I said through my teeth.

She shifted her lower jaw around and whispered, "You saved my life, and I didn't save his." It's why everyone turned on her last year at Carson's funeral.

"No," I said. "*No.*" I stuck my finger out at her. "You didn't say *anything.* Like, 'Hey, Decker, don't be a jerk to your dad.' Or, 'Hey, Decker, *call 911.*'"

"No," she said, waving her hand at me from across the room. "Listen. It wouldn't—"

"Don't," I yelled. "This is the part where you stop talking."

Delaney's eyes went wide, and she narrowed them a fraction of a second later. "No, this is the part where I remember that nobody, not even you, and not even now, gets to treat me like this." And then she waited for me to apologize or agree or argue. Anything. But I gestured toward the door behind her.

It was a small miracle she didn't slam it on the way out.

It stayed closed until my mother knocked on it the next morning. Or maybe not. I looked around the room, and the pizza box was gone, including the uneaten pizza. I bolted upright in bed. I didn't remember falling asleep. I didn't remember waking up. "Wear the blue shirt," she called through the door. "The one with the stripes." Which was really unnecessary. It was the only dress shirt I owned.

I stared at the double doors at the back of the service, waiting for Delaney to show so I could be furious, but she didn't. Which somehow made me even more furious. Her parents sat directly behind us, and Joanne squeezed my shoulder. I looked away before I could demand to know where the hell Delaney was.

Everyone else was there: Kevin, in his designer suit, with his parents, in their designer clothes—looking somehow completely out of place and perfectly in place at the same time; Justin, looking like a knockoff of Kevin in every way, from the clothes to the haircut—but his hair was curly, so it didn't fall right; Tara, in a dress cut way too low for a funeral, but I thought that was probably for Kevin's benefit and not mine. It also looked like she brought friends. To my dad's memorial. She was also trying to look happy. *At my dad's memorial.* Kevin had unceremoniously dumped her earlier this summer, and she did not seem to be taking it well. Still.

Next came the part where I was supposed to stand next to my mother and grandmother and let people walk by and shake my hand or pat my back or kiss my cheek and tell me how sorry they were. I was planning to hide out with Justin and Kevin until I was dragged away. But Kevin was consoling his new girlfriend, Maya, who was *sobbing* even though I was 99 percent sure she had never met my father, and as I approached, I heard Justin say, "I'm getting really fucking sick of funerals." And instead of hiding out with them, I sat on the floor of the bathroom, trying to remember how to breathe.

I kept picturing my dad saying, *"Something's not right,"* the second before he fell. And Delaney's face as she backed away. And I couldn't separate the two. It was like his death was stretched out, filling the hours between those moments, filling every memory in between—dying over lasagna, dying while I snuck out, dying over a glass of water.

His mouth had formed a word, my name, as he sunk to the floor. Like I had the power to save him.

I had my head between my knees, and I was slouched in the corner of the handicapped stall. A couple of people came in and out, and if they noticed me in the corner, gasping for air, they didn't say anything.

And then I saw designer shoes turn toward the stall. Another person hop up on the sink. "I can't stand this part,"

Justin said. Because we'd all been here for Carson's funeral—had to walk through the line, look his parents in the eye, look his sister, Janna, in the eye, and tell them how sorry we were, which seemed completely insulting. "And no offense, but you need to get Maya out of here. She's making a goddamn scene."

Kevin didn't respond at first. I heard the faucet turn on, imagined him splashing water on his face. "Probably thinking of her mom," he mumbled. "I'll get her out." Maya's mom was sick—no, she was *dying*. It's how Delaney and I met Maya in the first place—caught staring at her house, wandering her yard. This should've been *her* funeral, Maya's mother's. Not my dad's.

I wasn't breathing. No, I was breathing too fast. Couldn't catch my breath. The lines of the tiled floor grew wavy, fading in and out of focus.

The door to the stall shook and then gave way as Kevin forced the door open, even though it was locked.

"Oh, crap," Justin said, looking at me over Kevin's shoulder.

Kevin half pushed, half shoved him away. "Go find Delaney," he said. Then he rolled his neck and pulled me by the shoulders, and at first I thought he was trying to pull me up, but he wasn't. He knelt on the bathroom floor beside me and was pulling me forward, toward him. Toward his shoulder. He wrapped his arms around my back and stayed there.

Justin came back in, a second or a minute or an hour later. "Can't find her."

"Then get *someone*," he said.

"I can't breathe," I said into his shoulder.

"You're breathing," he said. And the weird thing was that as soon as he said it, I felt it, the air in my lungs, the oxygen moving, my heart pumping.

But I was still gasping for air. No, I was crying. And I was ruining his jacket.

I stood up quickly, wiped my sleeve across my face. "Sorry," I said. "I'm fine. God. I really fucking hate funerals, too." I looked around the bathroom, thinking there was no way this was really happening. Caught sight of myself in the mirror, in the same clothes I'd worn to Carson's funeral eight months ago. Carson, who was gone, but still existed in the awkward gaps in our conversation—like we were waiting for him to say something. I could almost imagine what he'd say. But he never did.

"I can't stay here," I said. "Tell my mom I took the car." She could get a ride with my uncle. With anyone.

"I'll drive you," Kevin said. Sad thing was that in the last year, we'd had enough experience with hospitals and funerals and grief to understand each other, even now.

"I want to be alone," I said. He'd understand that, too.

I pushed through the double doors, and Maya was sitting on the bottom step, the heels of her black shoes scraping at the concrete. She looked up at me as I passed, but I pretended not to notice. "Decker?" she called. "Where are you going?"

"Home," I said, moving toward the parking lot, but she had already stood and was walking toward me.

"Wait," she said. She had this perfectly straight, long brown hair and perfectly shaped big brown eyes. They looked even larger because she had been crying. I didn't want to wait, and it must've looked pretty obvious because she gripped my wrist like she needed to hold me there. She scanned the packed parking lot, then looked back at me with glassy eyes. "I'm sorry," she said. And then she hugged me, awkwardly and unexpectedly—her forehead resting against my shoulder for a second before she released me. She cleared her throat. "You have a lot of people," she said.

But I didn't know what to say to that, because I was thinking of the one person who wasn't there instead. "Kevin's looking for you," I said, already walking away.

I pulled into my driveway and barely had the car in park before I was stripping out of the suit jacket, throwing the tie on the front seat. God, it was sweltering. I unbuttoned the blue shirt with the stripes, tore that off too. Would've stripped off the undershirt, too, except I saw Delaney standing on my front porch.

I slammed the car door and marched up the front steps, not even looking at her.

She held her phone out between us, like a shield. "Kevin called me," she said.

"Kevin called you," I said slowly. So much for him understanding me. "Did he also tell you I wanted to be alone?" I ran a hand through my hair. Looked at her nails, which were cut extra short. At her jean shorts, which were probably pants at some point, because they were frayed at the bottom. At her white tank top, which was loose and had buttons, but the top

ones were undone. Her hair was twisted off her neck, held up
by a clip.

"No, he just . . . He said you left and he wanted me to
know and I said I'd make sure you were okay, because he was
worried. So here I am."

I brushed past her, up the front steps, not looking at her
face. Opened the front door, felt the blast of cold air through my
undershirt. Saw Delaney's long legs still standing on my front
porch while I was sweltering in black dress pants. "Why are you
dressed like that?" Accusations layered under accusations.

She looked down at her outfit, like she was confused.
"Because it's nine thousand degrees?"

"Why weren't you there?" And when she didn't respond,
didn't even let the air out of her lungs, I said, louder, "Even
Maya was there." Which had nothing to do with Delaney at
all, and she knew it. What I really meant was that Delaney
had done more for Maya than she'd done for me. That Maya
wouldn't know any of us yet if it hadn't been for Delaney
twisting her frown into a lie, saying, "Welcome to town,"
when Maya stood in her backyard, watching us, watching her
house. Everything for a stranger who had a parent who was
about to die. Nothing for me. I gritted my teeth and asked her
again. Demanding she tell me. *"Why?"*

"So you could yell at me? So you could kick me out of a
room again?"

"It was my father's funeral."

"You made it perfectly clear that you didn't want me—"

"How the hell do you know what I want?"

I felt her pause. Everything pause. "Do you want me to

come in?" she asked, and everything shifted in her face. It was painful, how much I could hear in her question. Questions layered under questions.

I didn't answer. I wanted part of her to come in, I wanted to scream at a different part of her. She stepped onto the hardwood, barefoot, like she had been the night he died. Her toenails were still purple. Too close.

I put a hand up. Tried to think. Tried to clear the anger. Tried to remember all the fights we'd had, and recovered from, our entire lives. "You were right not to come," I said. I would've done to her what Janna had done to her at her brother's funeral. I would've blamed her. I would've hated her.

"I need some space," I said. An empty house. An empty head. I needed not to think of her, I needed to have a memory without her in it.

I saw her spin on her toes, turning to leave. She put her hands on the doorjamb and paused for a second. "I need to tell you something," she said.

I wanted silence. An empty house. I didn't want to hear her. I couldn't even look at her. She didn't get to stand here in cute summer clothes while I was at my dad's service. She didn't get to stand here trying to make things right when she'd completely betrayed me. She didn't get to stand here at all.

"No. No, you don't. You *needed* to tell me something. *Before.* Right now, you need to get the hell out of my house before I throw something against the wall."

She didn't look at me. She walked away. No, she ran.

She ran with a hand over her mouth, and she slammed

the front door of her house, and it took me a second to realize what had just happened. She had asked to come in. I had said no. No, I had just threatened to throw something at the wall.

We weren't arguing. We'd spent half our lives arguing about everything and nothing—I loved it, and I'm pretty sure she did, too. But I'd never told her she couldn't come in. I'd never threatened to throw something against the wall. We weren't arguing now.

We were done.

I took a blue vase off the mantel above the fireplace—it was a gift from my father to my mother, years ago. It held flowers back then. The flowers died, but she kept the vase. I turned it over, tossed it up in the air like a baseball, caught it against the palm of my hand. Then I pulled back my arm and hurled it against the wall.

Honestly, I felt a little better.

I heard Delaney leave for work the next morning. I stood at my bedroom window, and she didn't even look up. Didn't even pause in the driveway before opening her dad's car door. I was in my room where time had stopped, but she kept moving. Everyone kept moving. I didn't go to work. Didn't call in to explain or ask for time off or anything. I just stopped going. There were only two weeks left until school started anyway.

Delaney kept going, every morning. I heard her car door close, every morning, at the same time, a second after her father's. I saw Maya eating dinner at her house, night after night. I saw them sitting on the porch swing together after, Maya's voice carrying across the yard while Delaney rocked in silence. In the beginning of the summer, when I had been not so subtle about wanting more time with just Delaney, and less with Maya, Delaney told me to cut her some slack. Her brother was spending half his time in Portland, where they moved from. Her mother needed full-time care. Delaney said Maya needed someone.

Joanne, for once, took my side. "What happens after?" she'd asked Delaney. "Where's her dad? Where will she go?" But Delaney said she wasn't about to bring that up, and Joanne kept making the poor girl—her words, not mine—food and sending the leftovers home for her mom.

Funny how I'd been so scared of losing her.

I'd spent six days in the hospital with Delaney, waiting for her to wake up.

I'd spent eight months after, scared she'd disappear.

But in the end, I was the one who told her to go. She listened. And she went to work, on time, the very next day.

I hadn't left the house in nearly two weeks, and I was not looking forward to setting my alarm tomorrow and going to school, pretending everything was normal.

"Decker?" my mom called from somewhere in the house.

"Yeah," I said. She didn't let me stay in my room all day. Not after the first week. I wandered down the stairs and fell onto the sofa, remote in hand.

She was searching through the drawers in the foyer. "Getting out of the house today?"

"School starts tomorrow. I'll be out of the house all the time."

She sighed. "I'm leaving," she said, pulling her hair back into a ponytail.

These are the things that are supposed to happen on Labor Day—the things that happened last year and the year before that: One, Main Street gets blocked off and people hand out free food and paint kids' faces and Delaney and I share a whole pizza before noon, because it's free, but only before noon. Two, we meet up with our friends and Tara's grandmother tells fortunes, and we all crowd around, listening to what she says about the lines in our hands and the rings in our eyes. Three, we go to Justin's lake house to celebrate the end of summer. Which in hindsight makes no sense anyway.

"You sure you're not going out?"

"Yep," I said. One, I wasn't hungry. Two, I didn't want to hear any more lies about my future. Three, Maya's family had moved into Justin's lake house over the summer. Permanently.

And four, it was the first time I'd had the house to myself.

After the funeral, we had visitors come visit us and mourners come mourn with us. And now our fridge was full of food and Mom was antsy to leave and I was antsy to get my house back.

"Okay," she said, smoothing back the sides of her hair again. "If you change your mind, I'll be at the Graysons'. Otherwise, I'll bring you back some dinner." The Graysons were my parents' best friends. My dad worked with them both, which meant they were probably all going over paperwork with my mom. Wills or whatever. No thanks.

I turned on the television the second she was out the door. My phone buzzed sometime around lunch, but it was on the other side of the couch. I'd have to get up. Then it rang—I could see Kevin's name glowing from the display. I focused back on the television, but this red banner scrolled across the bottom, a weather alert, ruining the movie. It cut off the gun in some guy's hand, so I couldn't tell where it was pointed.

Flash flood warning. I looked out the window. Not a cloud in the sky. Liars.

The doorbell rang, followed by persistent knocking before I'd even have time to get to the door, which I wasn't doing. But that's how I knew it was Kevin. Then his face was in the living room window, hands cupped around his eyes as he squinted. He saw me looking and waved vigorously, ignoring the fact that I was obviously ignoring him.

I opened the front door and he ran his fingers through his even-shorter-than-normal hair. "So," he said. "Funny story."

"I can't wait."

"I heard you're not talking to Delaney."

Yes, because that was the most important thing to happen recently. "What did she—"

"Maya told me."

I rolled my eyes before I could stop myself. I mean, I get what Kevin saw. What every guy saw. And I got what Delaney saw—what she felt—as we drove by and saw a girl unloading the back of a car, balancing a crate on her hip as she walked into Justin's lake house. Delaney had been worried it was her—we had to get closer to be sure. We had to get too close to be sure. Close enough to see the guy carrying a wheelchair over his head as he walked up the makeshift ramp that hadn't been there the week before. Close enough for Maya to see us watching.

But their whole friendship was based on a lie: that Delaney was friendly, when really she'd just been drawn to her house. And to me, Maya was just another reminder of what I'd done to Delaney.

Part of me thought Delaney liked having her around, despite what she said, because Maya didn't know anything about her. Didn't know the history here, never knew Carson or Troy. Never understood why everyone, except me, kept a little distance.

"Is it because she didn't show at the funeral?" Kevin asked. "Because, not that I'm going Team Delaney or anything, but she doesn't have the best history with funerals. . . ." The last funeral she'd been to, Janna had jabbed a finger at her chest and blamed her for Carson's death. In front of everyone. Nobody stood up for her. Nobody told Janna to stop. Not even me.

I cringed just thinking about it.

"Nope," I said, swinging the door closed.

Kevin jammed his foot against the door frame to block the door as I was swinging it shut. "Funnier story," he said. "Janna's back." He seized on the fact that I'd paused. "So. We're going to Justin's. I'm here to kidnap you. It will be easier if you don't resist."

Kevin would follow through. He would drag me there.

He'd think it was hilarious. If he wanted to, he'd win. I could probably take Justin. I used to be able to take Carson. I couldn't take Kevin. I learned that lesson in eighth grade when he held my face in the mud after I told his then-girlfriend about his other then-girlfriend. I'd since learned to keep my mouth shut in all things related to Kevin and girlfriends.

I'd also learned not to resist when he tells me not to. So I didn't.

There wasn't any history in Justin's basement. Not like at his lake house. Here, we couldn't see the lake or the trees. We couldn't look at all the places Carson should've been. We couldn't see the ghost of him running through the kitchen and straight out the back door, cannonballing into the freezing water.

Janna stood up from the couch when I reached the bottom of the stairs. She was tan. Skinny. Her blond curly hair was longer, past her shoulders now. So not like I remembered her, as Carson's shadow. I walked over and gave her a one-armed hug. "Hey," I said. "How was Arizona?"

"Hot," she said. "Oh, and turns out my brother's dead there, too."

She fell back onto the cushions and cut her eyes away from me. "Heard about your dad. Sucks."

"Yeah," I said. I liked the way she talked about death. Like you could be mad at it.

"You guys back for good?" I asked. Their house had sat

empty—deserted—since February. Honestly, I wasn't sure if she was gone for a while or gone for good.

"Me and my mom, anyway." She tapped her foot on the coffee table.

Tara strode over to the couch and leaned down to give Janna a hug. "I missed you," she said. Then, to me, "You okay?"

Then Janna scanned the room—we were all there: Kevin, Justin, Tara, me. Everyone except Carson. And . . .

"Where's Delaney?" she asked.

"He dumped her," Tara said.

Janna tilted her head to me. Raised her eyebrows.

"Sitting right here, Tara," I said. Like that made any difference to her. "Any more gossip you'd like to fill us in on? *Oh.* Kevin and Tara were together until he dumped her for the girl living in the lake house."

There was a moment of silence—I wasn't sure if it was because I'd mentioned the lake, or the house, or just the fact that I was being an ass to Tara.

"Screw you, Decker," she said. She got up, then looked over her shoulder. "And he didn't dump me." But she had to whisper it since Kevin was on the other side of the room and he did, actually, dump her. I was there. I didn't hear what he said, but I heard Tara say, "You're such a dick," and saw her walk away.

I mouthed the words, *He totally dumped her,* at Janna.

"God, I missed you guys," she said. Guess she didn't remember not calling. Not answering her phone. Not telling anyone she was leaving a month after Carson's funeral. She looked around the room, at all the places she didn't see him. I did the same thing. Last year at our Labor Day party, he'd said, *"This'll be the best year ever."* And then Delaney almost died. Carson did die. So did Troy. So did my dad. I thought of Delaney's bullshit statistics.

"I want to do something," Janna said. "For Carson."

I pretended I hadn't heard. Was that what happened? You got over someone's death and held some memorial and then you moved on?

And then the room grew quiet. "Who's that?" Janna asked.

We saw her legs first: skinny and tan. Next, her brown skirt; white shirt; long, straight brown hair. Brown eyes, maroon nails. "That," I said, "is Kevin's new girlfriend. Maya."

"Nice skirt," Tara said to Maya, fake smile. Like she wasn't upset about getting dumped. Like she wasn't terrified of being replaced by the new girl who was definitely hotter than her and didn't even have to try. And Maya didn't try. She knew she didn't have to. Probably had known it forever.

She said, "Thanks," caught Kevin's eye, and smiled. Kevin looked past her as I heard someone else walking down the stairs.

I saw her sneakers first—with the blue stripe and the frayed laces. Then the dark jeans above them. I turned to Janna. Watched as she raised a hand in greeting, forced her mouth to grin as she held her breath.

Delaney.

"Wanna get out of here?" I asked.

"I would like nothing more," Janna said.

I bumped Kevin's shoulder as I passed. "It was Maya's idea," he mumbled.

Right. Get them in the same room. Obviously they'll get back together. I wondered if Delaney put Maya up to it, but from the way her feet froze at the bottom of the steps, I knew she was surprised to see me here too. Her feet moved to the side as Janna and I approached the steps.

A breeze blew down the street, and Janna rubbed her hands over the goose bumps on her arms. "I never realized how cold it was until I left," she said. But it wasn't cold at all.

We stood on Justin's porch, shaded by a row of evergreens on the side of his yard. The sky behind us was a heavy gray, almost black. Storms were rolling in.

"He's dead everywhere, you know."

"I know," I said.

"My dad thinks that as long as we lived in a place where Carson never had a room, he never left it."

"Hence Arizona."

"Hence."

"We missed you," I said.

She pulled at a curl, stretching it down past her collarbone, and it was so achingly familiar. I could see her sitting beside Carson—always with him—doing the same. She shrugged, like she was clearing a thought. "So . . . are you gonna tell me what happened? Or do I have to consult the rumor mill?"

I almost told her right then. Told her how Delaney's brain

was damaged, like the doctors said. That she could tell when someone was sick—going to die. That she knew Carson was going to die and that's why she was driving him down the highway to her doctor. That she was trying to save him and couldn't. That she knew when she walked into my house that my dad was sick, that he was going to die, and she said nothing. Didn't try to save him. Didn't even tell me. I almost told her because she would understand. She was furious with Delaney, and she would understand.

I shrugged. "Nothing to it. We're not together."

She tilted her head back and laughed. "I gathered. Not that I object or anything. I'm just wondering why you can't even look at her."

"I can look—"

The door swung open behind us and Delaney barged out, just as I was turning to look. She bumped my shoulder. Stumbled back. Looked at the ground. "Sorry," she said as I grabbed her elbow to steady her. And then I looked away. Problem with looking at her, with being this close, is I couldn't remember why I was angry. What I was mad about. Not till I stepped away and felt the rage clawing its way to the surface again.

Maya walked down the steps after her, not even looking in Janna's direction. "Okay, so I'm sorry," Maya said. "I was trying to help."

"I need to go," Delaney said, looking at Janna, who wasn't saying anything.

Maya turned and finally realized they weren't alone. She

ignored us and turned back to Delaney. "Please don't be mad," she said.

Delaney's eyes grazed mine for a heartbeat as she turned away, walking toward her mom's car. And then I felt it: the tightness in my throat, the inability to take a breath. Cold hands on my throat. Janna was saying something, but I was clawing at my neck. And for a second it had a face, the thing cutting off my air. It had gray eyes and hands of ice and a hazy cloud of mist. And it tightened those fingers while it leaned closer, like it was furious with me. *Panic*, I thought. If I gave it a name, it stopped having power. That's what the doctor told us. *Panic*.

I took a breath.

Janna's hands were on mine, pulling them away from my neck. "Decker?" she was yelling. She was pale, like Delaney had been in my house that day when she knew the truth and said nothing. But Janna was probably thinking of Carson.

"Something stuck in my throat," I said. I coughed into my fist and pounded twice on my chest. "I'm gonna leave," I said.

"God, do you ever think of anything besides her?" It reminded me of my dad telling me I was too close. Too wrapped up.

I shook my head. "Told my mom I'd meet her at her friends' place. But you should stay. Catch up on all the gossip and stuff. I only came to say hi."

"Okay," she said, narrowing her eyes. "Hi, then."

"See you tomorrow."

"Senior year. Best year ever." She twirled her finger in the air and went back into the house.

I started walking. I didn't live too far from Justin's—hell, I didn't live too far from *anything* here—and it's not like I'd never walked it before. Two miles. Maybe two and a half. Better than going back in and asking Kevin for a ride home. Having him list all the reasons I shouldn't leave. Hearing Tara tell everyone I wasn't speaking to Delaney.

Knowing Janna was smiling about it.

The clouds were blocking half the sky now, and by the time I made it to Main Street, the vendors were packing up and clearing out. A few kids with painted faces weaved across the deserted street, and a stack of napkins blew down the center of it, scattering in every direction. Six blocks from here to the lake, one block from the lake to home. The thunder rumbled in the distance. I wasn't sure I'd make it before the storm.

By the time I reached the lake, the wind gave it current. The surface moved and broke and swirled. I jogged the last block home.

The key wouldn't turn in the front door. Already unlocked. I stuck my head inside and called, "Mom?" My voice echoed through the wood-floored rooms and off the bare walls and back again. I was pretty sure I had locked the door. I looked at the tree on the side of the yard where we kept the spare key, the wind bending the branches under the dark sky. Delaney knew where we kept it, and her car was back in her driveway. But she wouldn't. I cleared my throat. "Delaney?" I said, listening to the syllables of her name bounce back too loudly.

I walked inside and locked the front door behind me. I heard the steady drip of rain on the roof. It sounded off, somehow. Closer. The house was in shadows, gray, like the dark clouds outside. I flipped the light switch on the wall, heard a faint buzz, a pop, then nothing. No light.

"Hello?" I called again. I took another step and heard a splash of water, like stepping into Falcon Lake. I took another step, heard another splash. Looked down. Something was moving across the floor. Like the lake was in my house, taunting me. Seeping across the hardwood, looking to claim me.

A curse. A trade. I bent over and put my hand against the floor. Cold water. What the hell? I took out my phone and shone the screen on the floor, saw the water moving across, inching farther and farther throughout the downstairs. I moved the light around, saw dark trails of water down the walls, saw it dripping from the light fixture in the center of the room.

Closing in around me.

It was coming for me.

Maybe it was coming for her, too.

I backed out of my house, raced across the yard in the rain. A bolt of lightning lit up the sky, and I pressed and pressed and repressed Delaney's doorbell. She opened the door, freezing at the sight of me. I looked past her, at the carpet through her house. Dry. At the lights turned on. At the walls, untouched.

"Hi," she said, like a question. One syllable, but I could hear everything inside of it.

"Something's happening," I said. I looked over my shoulder. I'd left the front door wide open. The rain was getting in. "My house," I said, shaking my head. "Something's happening to my house."

I must've looked as confused as I sounded, because she didn't ask me to explain. She put a hand on my arm as she passed, ducking her head as she raced through the rain. I almost crashed into her back as she stood, frozen, in my front entrance.

There was still water everywhere. I hadn't imagined it. Seeping up, dripping down—it was real. It was happening. "Do you hear that?" she asked.

I heard rain. I heard water.

She ran to the kitchen, where the faucet was turned on high. Water ran over the basin, onto the counters, down the cabinets, onto the floor. She pulled out two dish towels that had been stuffed into the drain, and we heard the water gurgle down. She looked at the walls. The light fixture. The rain coming in.

"The bathtub," she said, her voice wavering, just like my breathing.

I followed her as she raced up the steps; they creaked—they *gave*—unnaturally. There was water everywhere, a thin coating over the wood floor. And there was more coming. She raced to my bathroom, and I went to my parents' room. My *mom's* room. The bathtub was plugged, and the drain near the top was stopped up with a towel, and water was pouring out. I turned the handles. Delaney must've turned the ones in my bathroom. All I heard was the rain on the roof. The thunder, coming closer. Then I heard her steps coming closer, splashing through the water.

"It's not safe," she said. "The electricity. The water . . ."

I followed her down the stairs. Slipped on the third step from the bottom, collided into her, knocked her to the floor. "Shit," I said. "Sorry." I held my hand out to her, and in the dark, she took it. "I didn't mean . . ."

"I *know*," she said. Her clothes were wet, like they had been that day in the lake. I could tell her eyes were wide, even in the dark. She looked around my house, at all of it, one last time, and backed out the front door. "Call your mom. I'm going to call the police." I followed her out of the house, stood on the porch, watching her walk away.

"I—" A bolt of lightning lit the dark sky. We looked up, both of us, as the thunder rattled the air.

I waited for lightning to strike. It felt like something that would logically happen right now. My house was flooded. Nothing made sense.

I reached into my pocket for my phone, scrolled to my mom's number. Couldn't press the button to make a call. Couldn't tell her what else was lost.

Delaney shivered and ran across our yards. She disappeared inside for just a moment but came back to the open doorway with her phone pressed to her ear while I was still staring at mine. I watched her profile as she stood in her doorway, like she was waiting for me. She fell through the ice and almost died. I took her back from the lake and here she was, perfect. Like in order to keep her here, breathing, perfect and living, the world around us had to die.

Seizing on the side of the road.

Drowning in the middle of Falcon Lake.

That a heart had to stop, and the water was here to remind me. Carson was soaking when they brought him to the hospital. Like he had drowned in her place. The lake had taken Troy.

We took something from the lake, and it took something from us. It was coming for us all.

Janna's brother.

My father.

I stared at Delaney, standing under the light on her front porch, untouched, under the darkening sky.

And I believed.

Chapter

4

"No," I said.

We were sitting in Delaney's kitchen, and I'm sure they could all hear us through the thin swinging door to the living room, but I didn't care.

"Shh," my mom said, because she did care. "Decker . . ."

"I can stay with Kevin. Or Justin." Or a complete stranger for all I cared. Hell, I'd sleep in the back of my minivan.

"They are offering to take us in. I don't want to stay in some hotel. Please. I don't want us to be apart." It was so unlike my mother to say something like that. "They're converting the upstairs library into a spare room. And you can use the office."

Delaney's house had the same layout as mine. But the spare bedroom upstairs was basically just a room of books. And, true, her dad didn't use the office downstairs much, but it didn't have a bed. When I used to stay over, when I was younger—and then after—I'd sleep on the pull-out couch in the living room. "I don't want to stay with her," I said. Which was more than I'd said to my mother about the situation since it happened. She knew enough not to ask. And we had bigger things to think about.

"I know . . . I know you guys are fighting about something. But they're practically family."

I looked at the kitchen ceiling and laughed. "We're not fighting, Mom."

She paused. "Please, Decker. It won't be long. You'll have your own space. I just want to know where you are. I've already spoken with the insurance company. They need to assess the damage before we can start repairs. But until they tell us otherwise, it's . . ." She put her fingers in the air, in makeshift quotes, and rolled her eyes. "Uninhabitable."

Delaney's mom knocked on the door, which caused it to open, and she gave us a pained grin and whispered, "Sorry to interrupt. The police want to speak with Decker."

Excellent.

My mom was waiting, still leaning toward me. Asking me. I shrugged at her with one shoulder, and she mouthed, *Thank you.*

The cop was sitting on Delaney's couch, chewing gum, hair buzzed short, watching me. Everyone was standing but him. "Your mom says your front door was unlocked when you returned home. Are you sure it was locked when you left?"

"Pretty sure," I said. Everything that happened in the first half of the day was kind of a blur. When Kevin came for me, I grabbed my cell and pulled the door shut behind me. . . .

"Yes, I'm sure." I turned the lock and Kevin looked over his shoulder to make sure I was coming.

"And the spare key," he said, pointing to where it sat on the coffee table, sealed in a sandwich bag. "Does anyone else know where you keep it?"

"No," my mom said.

Delaney used that key all the time. "No," I said. "No one," I added. Just anyone who ever dropped me off at home. Probably all my friends by now.

"I did," Delaney said. She kept her eyes on the cop, but she must've felt everyone else's on her. "I've used it," she added. Then she looked at me, like she could feel me staring at the side of her face. "What?" she asked. "It's true. My fingerprints would be all over that."

Before Delaney could say any more, before Delaney's parents could ask anything at all, my mom said, "She and Decker grew up together." And then there was this perfectly awkward gap of silence where none of us knew what to say after that.

The cop shifted on the sofa, positioning himself toward Delaney. He turned the key over in his hand. "Okay. But just to cross you off the list, is there any reason . . . that *anyone else* . . . ," he said, choosing his words carefully, "might think you had a motive to target the Phillips's house?"

"No," I said. And I said it fast.

I was lying. Other than the cop, the whole room knew I was lying. And the entire room stayed silent for my lie.

"All right," he said as he moved the gum from one side of his mouth to the other. He held the bag with the spare key in his hand, narrowing his eyes at it, like he could almost see the answer. "Such an odd thing to do, is all. What's the point?"

I caught Delaney's eye from across the room. Looked away. Hard to put that into words without sounding ridiculous. But apparently he didn't expect us to answer, because he was talking to my mom again. "Mrs. Phillips," he said, even though they were probably the same age.

"Allison," she corrected. I didn't like the way she relaxed against the wall as she said it, or the way he nodded at her when she did.

"Allison," he repeated. He put the key on the coffee table, rested his elbows on his knees. "We'll be looking into your late husband's cases," he said. *Late husband.* "Like you suggested. But I'm not sure we'll find a connection."

My dad was a lifelong public defender. He had wanted to be a prosecutor, but my mom convinced him otherwise. Said it wasn't safe for our family, which was kind of funny. He still got hate mail, occasionally a threatening visit. Ironically, not from the criminals. From the victims. From the victims' families.

My mom cleared her throat. "Any timeline you can give us?" she asked. "It's just that the insurance company won't pay until they hear from you."

"Why not?" I asked, wondering how long I'd be stuck sleeping on the floor of Ron's office.

My mom didn't respond, so the cop spoke instead. "Just that, given the recent changes in your life . . ." Meaning death. "Your insurance company is going to take a hard look at you."

"I was out," my mom said, pushing off the wall, her eyes wide. "Since this morning. Everything was fine when I left. You can check."

"I know," he said, holding out his hands like he was showing us *he* didn't think she had anything to do with it. "I meant the both of you." It took a second for his words to sink in. Me. They'd be looking at me.

"I was out with friends. I was walking home."

"Could've done it before," he said. I could've. It's true. Then, to my mother, "Not that that's what I think happened here. But . . ."

"But my dad's work . . . ," I said, much louder than I meant to.

"We know," he said.

"Maybe someone didn't know he died." The cop nodded. Gave me a tight smile. But all I was doing was deflecting accusations with new accusations.

The rain was still falling when the cop put on his hat, shook my mom's hand, and left. I went into the downstairs office so I wouldn't have to sit across the room from Delaney while my mom made phone calls and Delaney's parents shot each other looks across the room, like they were communicating telepathically.

There was a mattress next to the desk in the office, and

someone had tucked the sheets up around it like it was a real bed. My mom had packed a suitcase of my clothes—I wasn't sure how it was safe for her to go upstairs in our house and not me, but I figured this wasn't the best time to argue. They were the clothes I never wore, too. The ones hanging in my closet that I mostly ignored. But I guess it was better than her searching through my drawers.

I didn't sleep that night, staying in someone else's house, in someone else's bed. I was thinking of Delaney sleeping peacefully upstairs, with her intact family and her intact house.

I was thinking of the sound of the water dripping down the steps, sliding down the walls, spilling over the tub. Coming for me.

I felt fingers circling my wrist. Kept picturing the way 2B turned to face me, gripping so tightly, like I could keep her here. The way she looked at me, looked into me, as she said, *"Listen."*

My car was still in my driveway the next morning, and I paused for a second as I backed out. I'd always driven Delaney to school. Who would take her? My mom was in their driveway, and she had her phone pressed between her ear and her shoulder as she got into her car. She raised her hand at me in a wave, or like she wanted me to wait.

Delaney wasn't my problem.

I sped down the street without another glance at their house.

The thing about living in a small town is that there are

very few—if any—secrets. Everyone knew that Janna was back. And everyone knew that my house was flooded, that it was now, as declared, *uninhabitable*. And they knew where I was staying.

"Dude," Kevin said. "You can stay with me."

"I know. Thanks. My mom wants me to stay with her. So, I'm stuck."

Kevin looked somewhere beyond my shoulder. I turned to see Delaney walking by, walking down the hall next to Maya, like she wasn't annoyed about her attempt to reunite us. She had to be annoyed at her. I knew Delaney. Of course she was annoyed.

"Maya's mad at me," Kevin said. Because obviously that was more interesting than someone flooding my house. "I think. I'm not sure."

"So go find out."

"Not my style." He shook his head. "I mean, I'm not a goddamn bus. So I pick her up after getting Justin, who first of all was eating in my car, so I'm already not in a great mood. And I'm not a morning person, which everyone else knows. And she says, 'Aren't you getting Delaney?' No, I don't get Delaney. Decker gets Delaney. And if Decker doesn't want to get Delaney, that's his business. She really doesn't get how things work here. At all."

I took it that this was his apology for yesterday, for setting us up in the same house together. But all I could picture was Delaney alone. I left her alone. Again. "I don't care if you get Delaney," I said.

"Dude. Not a bus. Like I said." He shook his head at me, like I was being ridiculous. "Anyway, I called her, just to check, you know? I mean, could you imagine if she got an unexcused tardy?" He smiled, then saw that I wasn't, and stopped. "She was already on the bus. So the whole argument was a freaking waste. Maya doesn't get to be pissed." Then he looked down at the creased paper in his hand. "Who do you have for English?" he asked. And just like that, school had begun. The summer, and everything that had happened in it, was gone.

"Home sweet home," Janna said, stepping between me and Kevin.

"Little Levine!" some guy called as he walked down the hall. Janna frowned. *Dead there, too,* she had said. But at least *there,* people didn't see her first as an extension of someone else. Someone gone.

I closed my eyes and felt the hands of ice reaching for my neck.

And then the weight of solid hands on my shoulders. "Please," Janna whispered, her minty breath in my face, her fingers pressing down to my bones. "For the love of God. Get me the hell out of this place."

"Dead everywhere."

We skipped first period of the first day of our last year. We were in the woods behind the school—past the sports fields but still in view of the field house. "Okay," Kevin said, crouched down beside me, "Ready?"

"Please explain to me once again why I'm the one who has to do this?"

"You won't get in trouble," Janna said. "Dead dad." She said it so matter-of-factly, it actually didn't sting. "Dead brother got me fifteen unexcused absences before they started calling my parents." She looked at me from the corner of her eye. "I wouldn't push it that far if I were you, though."

"Brother trumps dad?"

"Every time," she said.

The twigs snapped behind us, and I jumped. I think I even gasped. Justin swung his pocket knife back and forth as he walked toward us. "Jumpy much?"

"Excuse me for being on edge. Someone flooded my house. *Yesterday.* Not that anyone seems to care."

There was a moment of silence, and I realized people hadn't processed the fact that someone did it. It was just a thing that happened, part of the curse. My house, drenched with water, uninhabitable, while Delaney's was perfect next door. A trade.

"What do you mean *someone*," Justin said.

"I *mean* someone broke into my house and flooded it."

"A pipe burst in our basement once," Justin said. "Nobody's fault."

A chill ran down my neck. They had no idea. Only got half the rumor, I guess. "No, *someone* turned on all the faucets. Blocked the drains. *On purpose.*"

"That is seriously creepy," Kevin said.

Justin cleared his throat. Nobody wanted to talk about this. Not the curse.

"Am I the only one wondering why?" I looked from Kevin to Justin and realized that, yes, I was definitely the only one wondering why.

"Asking why doesn't help anything," Janna said, in this monotone voice. "So says the Arizona shrink." She stood up straight, like she was pretending to be someone else. "Look forward. Move forward," she recited, pointing her arm in front of her like an arrow. Then she broke down in laughter.

Justin pulled her down and put a hand over her mouth. "How about not drawing more attention to ourselves, huh?"

She shrugged but crouched back down with the rest of us.

"Maybe because of your dad?" Kevin asked.

I nodded, because he was doing the same thing I was doing. Trying to make sense of it. Make it fit. Take away its power. "Maybe," I said.

Justin handed me the pocketknife. "We should really come back and do this at night," I said. "You know, when there's not five hundred people in the giant brick building with windows across the field."

"A premeditated act will carry more punishment," Kevin said, his hand on the nearest trunk, scanning the fields. And suddenly I was back in my house, sneaking out the back door, barefoot, so it wouldn't seem premeditated, while my dad was dying a few rooms away.

"Godspeed," Justin said as he pushed me forward, into the clearing.

Janna was smiling—the first time I'd seen a real smile on her since she came back. She had Carson's smile, only there was a gap between her front teeth. But if you didn't look closely, you could see him there.

"Screw you all," I said, and I took off running across the baseball field.

The field house was painted gold and blue, but the gold had faded in the sun to kind of a sad yellow. And the blue had gotten grayish. Weathered. I was hoping if anyone from the science wing looked out the window, they'd think I was maintenance or something, just doing work on the long wall. I hoped they wouldn't look for too long, or too closely. I hoped they didn't see the sun catch off the blade in my hand as I carved the giant letters into the paint.

It took much longer than I'd thought, and the adrenaline wore off when I was on the third letter. I jerked my hand down, cutting boxy lines into the wood, thinking of Janna and Justin and Kevin watching me. Thinking there was no way Delaney would be out here watching me. No way she'd skip class or sneak around campus or vandalize school property. Even for this.

I didn't stop to admire my work when I finished, just took off across the fields again, toward the woods.

Kevin patted my back. Janna had that same smile—part mischief, part happiness. I passed the knife to her and said, "You're welcome," as my palm connected with hers.

Her smile disappeared. "It's not for *me*, Decker."

I rolled my eyes before I could stop myself. Of course it was. Carson was gone. And it sure as hell wasn't for *me*.

It wasn't until fourth period, in science class, that I risked a look out the window. Smiled to myself as I saw the words: CARSON WAS HERE.

Janna wanted to do something for Carson. Like a memorial or something. A reminder. This was Kevin's idea. He thought it would adequately freak people out. Janna agreed. She said if people were going to talk about him, might as well make it big. And it was so perfectly literal as well—Carson had been in that field house. Many times. With many different girls.

It was perfect.

I walked into my house after school. It was instinct, and I was already inside before I realized I wasn't supposed to be here. Cleanup definitely hadn't started, despite what my mom had said. Nobody had changed anything.

The wood floor throughout was dark, soaked. Stained by water. And the walls were streaked, so the paint was bubbling in sections. It felt humid inside. Stifling.

I tested the first step. It creaked but seemed solid. My mom said the drywall was damaged, that the flooring had to be assessed, but everything seemed fine. It's just water, anyway.

Just water.

I tiptoed up the rest of the steps. The hall seemed fine. My room seemed fine, everything exactly as I'd left it. Everything was just damp and streaked with water. I took a bag out of the top of my closet and started emptying drawers into it.

I scanned the surfaces of my desk, my dresser. After losing people, I didn't care so much about things. But I couldn't stop myself from pulling out the top drawer, seeing Delaney's notebook wedged under a bunch of school crap I never used. She kept it here because she thought it was safer in the mess of my room. She'd kept it since January, trying to find the patterns. Each page had a name. Or an address. Or a location—maybe a description. What she felt and when she felt it. And then . . . the obituary. Like she could quantify it. Find an answer in the passage of time. There was math in the margins. Her trying to assign what she felt on a scale of one to ten. Her comparing it to the time until death. It didn't belong here anymore. I grabbed it before closing the drawer again.

The front door creaked open. "Decker? Hello?"

She must be kidding.

"Seriously?" I tossed my duffel bag down the stairs and saw it land at her feet. Delaney stood in the open doorway, blocking the sun.

I noticed Maya standing behind her. "Whoa," Maya said. Delaney sent her a look. And then Maya looked past her, at me. "She's just *helping*," she said.

Delaney rolled her eyes at Maya, and I kind of wanted to smile. "I'm helping *your mom*," she added.

Delaney held out the key ring on her hand—my mom's—and said, "My mom sent me over to let in the cleaning crew. The door was already open." She was already backing away. "I didn't know you'd be here."

"You can't be in here." A man pushed past both Maya and Delaney into the foyer of my house. One man—so much for a crew. He wore thick black boots and rubber gloves, like the kind my mom used to clean the bathrooms, and he was pulling an industrial-looking vacuum behind him. He had a hospital mask hanging around his neck, and he pulled it up over his mouth as he stepped inside, like this place was contagious.

"I'll just be a sec," I said, backing down the hall to my dad's office.

The office was rancid. Mildewed. The water had come through the ceiling fan, saturating everything. I felt like I should take something. Save something. Do something.

All of it just things. The man watched me rummage around. There was probably some rule against this. My mom said we couldn't go in until it was declared safe. Something about insurance. "I live here," I said, just so he knew I wasn't some thief, and he nodded at me.

Nothing left to save.

"I'm done anyway," I said as I walked out the front door of what used to be my home.

Maya was standing on my porch—I looked around for Delaney, but it looked like it was just us. She eyed my bag. "What's that?"

None of her business.

"Clothes," I said.

"Planning on going somewhere?" She asked it like it was so out of the realm of possibility. Like people didn't head out on vacation every day. She asked it like she had any right to know about my life. She stepped closer, leaned closer, smiled closer. "Running away?" she asked.

Which implied there was something worth running from.

"Uh, no. I need the clothes. And I need a suitcase. I'm going to Boston. On that college trip," I said.

Our school offered it every year—a bunch of seniors flew to Boston with a few teachers and we toured all the colleges. Delaney had signed up back in June.

"You want to go to school in Boston?" I had asked her as she held the permission form out to me.

"I want *us* to go to Boston," she had said. I knew what she was thinking—I wouldn't get into the same schools as her, there was no way. But there were a lot of schools in Boston. We could still be close.

It was the first time she had talked about something that far away. That she'd want to plan something that far in the future. I kissed her while she was still talking about the form and the cost. I kissed her until we heard her mom walking down the hall.

"There's a lot of people in Boston," I said, my voice low as her mom passed the open door (which was a new rule).

She knew exactly what I was worried about. Lots of people meant more people dying, statistically speaking. I knew what it did to her, the way she couldn't quite focus on anything else. The way she constantly wondered if there was something more she should be doing.

We listened to her mom's footsteps walk down the stairs, and she leaned closer to me. An inch, maybe less, from my face. "That many people, it's hard to tell who it is," she said, and her lips brushed mine. She hated knowing. I didn't realize how much until that moment. But then she was kissing me, and I was thinking of only that, and then Boston, and then her and Boston, and the future stretching out before me, like the vision in her head transferred to my own until I wanted it as much as I wanted to close the door to her bedroom.

I had filled out that form and asked my dad for a check the second I'd walked into my house.

Boston was Delaney's dream, and I wasn't sure if I had one separate from hers. But Kevin and Justin were going, and we got excused from classes, so I was going.

"You overpacked," Maya said, almost like she was trying to be cute—it was something she would say to Kevin, tossing her hair over her shoulder, leaning into him. But with me, she didn't move. Didn't smile. Didn't blink. So unlike the girl who hugged me in the parking lot.

"Don't you have somewhere to be? Kevin's, maybe?"

"You're being a dick," she said.

I stared at her. "Yeah, you don't get to talk to me like that."

Before she got together with Kevin, Maya was always around. It drove me crazy through the summer, when all I wanted was time alone with Delaney. But her mom was basically in some sort of hospice care, and her brother bounced back and forth between college and home. Delaney said it seemed like she just needed to get out of the house, so I was a jerk if I said anything. Honestly, I was thrilled when she hooked up with Kevin, because she hung out here a lot less.

She narrowed her eyes, scanned me slowly. "I don't get what she sees, anyway," she said. She shrugged, turned to go.

"Get off my porch," I said, even though she was already on her way.

"Oh, poor Decker," she said. She strode over to me, and I was completely taken aback. I'd never seen this side of her. She stood too close, way too close, and tilted her head to the side, like she was lining up to kiss me. "Your dad dies and that gives you free reign to be a complete ass?" Her breath smelled like cinnamon gum. She put her hand on my chin—I looked past her, wondering if anyone else was seeing this. "Grow up," she said. Then she wandered back to Delaney's.

Chapter
5

I drove up the winding road cut into the side of the mountain overlooking Falcon Lake. The only place you'd find enormous homes and fancy cars. The place you'd find Kevin's house. His family had money for generations and generations, and half the original establishments carried his last name. All the money in the world, and he was still here with the rest of us.

I pulled into his circular driveway, but he was walking down the front steps. "Hey, Deck," he said, "you coming with?"

My master plan was to stay here, bum a meal off him so I wouldn't have to sit around the dinner table with Delaney and Maya.

Kevin continued, "I'm supposed to be in the dunk tank in thirty minutes."

"For what?" The dunk tank was exactly what it sounded like—a plastic box that our school owned. Every group or club used it for fund-raisers. Kevin wasn't in any clubs.

He looked at me like I was a moron. "That PTA barbecue. Favor to my mom."

His mom was the head of the PTA. His mom was the head of everything. His family practically owned this town. This was another thing that happened every year, one of those things I could keep time with. Labor Day equals free pizza and fortunes and Justin's lake house. First day of school equals PTA barbecue—*not* vandalizing school property and scouring what used to be my home for clothes.

Kevin was in jeans. Nice sneakers. A collared shirt that the rest of us would've looked ridiculous in. "Bathing suit?" I asked.

"No way. Then I'll have no excuse to leave. Come on. Free food."

Which was, after all, what I came for.

Half the school was here. There were grills set up in stations around the parking lot, and there were raffles, and, of course, there was the dunk tank. I got in line for a burger and saw Delaney's mom when I reached the front. "Hi, honey," she said. "Your mom is at the hot dog station." She pointed her finger across the parking lot. "Have you seen Ron? He was supposed to come straight from work. His shift at the grill starts in ten." God. Everyone was here. Even Delaney's dad. I would've thought that my dad dying and our house being flooded might've changed my mom's plans. But no.

"No, sorry," I said as I walked toward the ketchup station.

Everyone was going through the motions of their normal lives. My mom was handing out hot dogs for a fund-raiser. Joanne was worried about scheduling.

Kevin was climbing into the dunk tank like he was genuinely looking forward to this.

"It's supposed to be Carson." I spun around in line, and Janna was holding a hamburger down at her side, watching as Kevin launched himself over the plastic wall of the dunk tank while people applauded. Her eyes were wide and bloodshot. "This was always his thing."

It was true. Everyone wanted to take a shot at Carson, who was all too willing to go along with it. Saluting as the principal wound up to throw, taunting the guys, teasing the girls. But it had been eight months. Eight months.

I couldn't hear Kevin from across the lot, but he was smiling, and he was yelling something at the guy with the ball in his hand. Even the way he was sitting reminded me of Carson. "Kev is doing the job just fine," I said.

His whole act was like one big CARSON WAS HERE. You couldn't look at him without seeing Carson. Without remembering. I couldn't *not* remember, especially with her standing this close.

She tossed her barely eaten burger into the trash. "When I talk to you," she said, "I feel like you're not even hearing me." She was staring me down, and I was staring back at her, and then Justin was walking toward us. "I thought you of all people would understand."

"I'm sorry," I said.

"Me too," she whispered. Then she wrinkled her nose at me. "Can we skip the hugging-it-out part?"

I left her with Justin. Patted her on the head as I passed, messing up her curls, like I'd done for years.

One of the teachers was pulling a hose toward the dunk tank. He turned on the nozzle, spraying several unsuspecting seniors. Their screams turned to laughter, their clothes dripping wet, and I lost my appetite. Everyone here was acting like everything was normal.

I saw Justin near the dunk tank, with his elbow resting on Janna's shoulder. She shrugged him off but didn't resist when he hung an arm over her shoulder instead. I saw Kevin push himself out of the churning water, shaking his head, flinging the water on everyone nearby. They shrieked as they backed away. Except for Maya. She was close to the tank still, like she didn't mind at all. And she had this smile—the kind that was meant for only him.

I wondered if Kevin ever saw the other side of her—the side that stood on my porch and turned cold. Or if I was even meant to see the smile she gave him now. If there are sides to everyone that you never know, that they save for different people.

The principal drew back his arm, winding up to pitch. He smiled as he said, "I'm going to enjoy this more than you know." He threw a strike at the bull's-eye, sending Kevin deep into the water again. You could hear him yelling, or maybe laughing, under the water, as bubbles rose to the surface. He stayed near the bottom, his hands pressed to the plastic, smiling at us all.

Delaney, dripping wet as I pulled her from the ice.

My dad, staring at the lake water on his hand.

The water pooling around the broken glass.

Water, seeping across my floor.

I felt nauseous, walked to the nearest trash can, and rested my forearms on the black plastic ledge. I dropped my burger inside and tried to think of anything else. Instead I pictured the trash can in 2B's room as I righted it. As I stood. As she grabbed my wrist and dug her fingers to the bone.

Black pupils, growing wider.

Listen.

Footsteps. Laughter. A horn blaring somewhere on the other side of the parking lot. Water splashing.

Breathe.

I pushed off the trash can and walked back toward the dunk tank. Kevin was climbing out, dripping wet. Maya leaned into him, like she didn't even notice. They started walking away, back toward the parked cars, like the rest of us didn't exist.

"Kevin!" His mother stood with her hands on her hips near the dunk tank, her high heels on a dry spot of pavement, like even the water knew enough to obey her. "Where are you going?"

He gestured toward his clothes. "To get a change of clothes."

She looked at Maya beside him. Then at the rest of us. I wondered if she was about to ask one of us to strip. I bet someone would listen. But she just shook her head. "Straight there, straight back."

He smiled wide. "Obviously."

He took off across the parking lot, Maya chasing after him, so obviously not intending to return.

I scanned the parking lot. Janna and Justin were debating the merits of mayonnaise on burgers. My mom handed someone a hot dog. Tara raised her hand at me from across the way, surrounded by a group of girls. I raised my hand in return, started backing away before I could accidentally spot Delaney. I wished it was this easy to stop seeing someone. Tara and I had stopped seeing each other by just . . . stopping seeing each other. Though I guess we weren't ever really together. Not seriously. I guess I wasn't really together with anyone, *really*, until Delaney.

And then I heard her name. Someone asking for her. Coming closer. He was vaguely familiar but I couldn't place him. He stopped in front of a group of freshman girls and asked, "Do you know a girl named Delaney?"

"What do you want with Delaney?" I asked, and he moved through their circle, a look of relief on his face.

"I'm looking for my sister," he said. "She said she was coming with her friend Delaney, and I left her a message that I would meet her here, but she's not answering her phone . . . and I'm not having much luck asking for Maya." And then his features clicked into place. Maya's eyes. Maya's hair color. The shape of her face. The same slim build.

"Maya?" I asked. "You just missed her. She left with Kevin."

"Who's Kevin?" he asked slowly.

"Her boyfriend," I answered, and from the look on his face, I knew I shouldn't have.

"Her *boyfriend*?" he repeated.

Last thing I wanted was to get in the middle of someone else's drama, so I started walking toward the parking lot. "Yeah. Sorry, I gotta go."

"Do you have any idea *where* they were going?" he asked.

I had plenty of ideas where they were going, none of which I was about to tell her brother. "Nope."

He scanned the crowd, his jaw clenched. "How about Delaney then?"

"She's around here somewhere," I said. And I left before he could ask me to find her for him.

I wandered back toward my car. The streetlights were just starting to flicker on. One glowed right above my car, and I sensed movement from somewhere behind me. I froze, listening, waiting for the feeling again. The sounds from the barbecue were blocked by the school. "Delaney?" I said. And then I hated that I said it. That she was my first thought, always, even now.

Someone was there, between the rows of cars, I could feel it. Or maybe I was panicking again.

"Decker?" I heard. And then Tara rounded the corner, coming from between a minivan and a pickup truck. "Hey," she said. "I saw you leaving. . . ."

I was leaving because I didn't want to see Delaney here. Didn't want to talk about mayonnaise or burgers. Didn't want to think about Kevin off with Maya. And if everyone was here, Delaney's house was empty. I missed having a house to myself.

When I didn't respond, Tara bit her bottom lip. "You okay?"

I didn't know whether she was referring to right this second or in general. "Sure," I said.

She grinned. "I just meant . . . with everything going on. And you're alone. . . ."

"I kinda want to be." I didn't want to be rude to her— most people didn't know this other side of her. That she knew when someone was hurting, and she reached out. She wasn't like most people who pretend it doesn't exist, like that makes it better.

She nodded, then smiled. "By the way, the field house? Not so smart."

I wondered if she had seen me do it. Or if someone had told her. "Can't prove anything."

She shook her head. "Well. You still have my number," she said as she turned to leave. Funny. I'd never not had her number since we were old enough to have numbers.

"Hey, Tara?" I called after her.

She glanced over her shoulder. "Kevin's loss," I said.

She smiled and twisted her dark hair over her shoulder, and as the streetlight flickered off again, all that remained was cherry lips and chocolate hair and the realization that Kevin was a moron. Tara trumped Maya any day.

"Right?" she said, and strode back to the barbecue.

*   *   *

I parked the minivan in my driveway and walked across the yard. The Maxwell home was perfectly, gloriously silent. I found myself walking carefully and slowly through the downstairs, not wanting to disturb it. I opened the duffel bag from earlier today, pulling out the clothes from my room. And then I pulled out Delaney's notebook, one of those black-and-white composition books.

I opened the notebook now to see if my dad was in it. But he wasn't. She knew, she had to have known, but she never wrote it down.

But there was never a page for Carson, either. Like putting pen to paper made the whole thing too final. She didn't write anything about Troy, either, but there was an article folded and crammed into the front of the journal. I didn't have to read it—I had read it a hundred times already. It's the article that started everything.

It has a black-and-white picture—the lake, frozen over. You can't see the other people running for the ice, for Troy, because they were already down the embankment. You can see my back and the lake and my arm, reaching off the page. I was holding Delaney's hand, but you can't see her. In the picture it looks like I'm reaching for something that doesn't exist.

This was the trade. I was staring at the hole in the center of the ice as the lake took another. My hand on Delaney, claiming her instead.

The picture said everything.

The article said nothing. The article said that nineteen-year-old Troy Varga fell through the ice at Falcon Lake. The article said that this was the second accident this winter. It said he was dead, but a girl survived. The article said nothing about the guy staring on, like an innocent bystander. It didn't name the girl just outside of the photo. It didn't say that Troy committed suicide or that he tried to take her with him. It didn't say that the girl ran for the shore—for me—while the lake swallowed up Troy.

The picture didn't show that she was soaking wet. That we turned and ran for home a second after that. Or that the police came later that day to take our statements.

I lied first. Said we were both out walking, saw him standing there, and Delaney went out to get him because she knew him.

Delaney said she was almost there when he fell, and the ice started breaking, and she ran back.

This was the article that set everything else in motion. That gave the lake power. That tied it all together. After this, people started whispering about a curse. Delaney out on the ice again, and it split open, trying to claim her. When it couldn't, it took another.

I wondered if it would've made a difference if they'd known the truth—that Troy committed suicide and tried to kill Delaney in the process—if they would've thought the same thing. But the lie shook something free. The curse was born from it. From us.

We gave it power, and now it lived.

I couldn't stand to look at this. Maybe that's why she kept it at my house. But it wasn't mine, and I didn't want it.

I ran up the steps and stood before her closed door, thinking it was creepy to go in her room if she wasn't there. Wondering if she would think I was snooping. Whatever. I opened the door quickly, before I could talk myself out if.

Only she was in it, and she was changing, and the whole thing happened so quickly.

How quickly she held her shirt in front of her. How quickly I looked away.

How suddenly you're not allowed to see things you've seen a hundred times before. Do things you've done a hundred times before. Say things you've said a hundred times before.

Truth is, transitioning from friends to something more was slow and awkward and terrifying. Were we supposed to kiss good-bye, even though we usually didn't? And should I hold her hand when we were walking, even though we never did before? And was I supposed to look away if I walked into her room while she was getting changed, or was I not supposed to hide that I was checking her out, or was that totally creepy, either way?

It took a month to figure out I should just kiss her when I felt like it. Hold her hand if I wanted to. Look every time I got the chance.

But it took a second to fall out of it. There was nothing gradual about breaking up. Everything undid itself in a heartbeat. Cut and severed and clean.

I was in her room, definitely not looking at her. I didn't know where to look or what to do or what to say. "I thought you were at the barbecue," I said.

She scrambled to get her shirt on. "I hate crowds," she said, as if I didn't know anything about her.

"I didn't know you were here," I said. "I just . . ." I held up her notebook. "I was leaving this for you."

It was almost comical. Funny how something so small can carry such finality.

I put the notebook on her desk, still not looking at her, and turned to leave.

Walk away, walk away, walk away.

"Why isn't my dad in there?" I asked, pointing to the journal. Sad thing, how desperate I was, too. Maybe she'd tell me she didn't know until later that night, and her mom took the phone and she was locked in her room. I'd let her lie. I would.

She didn't answer.

"Was it because it hurt too much to write in there?" That's what happened with Carson. "Or because you didn't want me to see? Or did you just not have enough time?" I said through my teeth.

"Because I didn't want it to be true," she said, and the simple honesty of it made me nauseous. And furious. There should be nothing simple about my dad dying.

"You're serious," I said. "That's all you've got?"

"I don't want to know, Decker." This was her big, illogical defense. It reeked of desperation.

"But you do," I said, turning back around. "You *did* know. I don't get you, Delaney. You knew I was going to find out. You knew. You're supposed to be the smart one. Didn't you realize what I'd think?"

"Your dad was *dying*. I didn't spend a whole lot of time wondering what you'd think of *me*." I couldn't look at her. Couldn't focus on what she was saying. "I mean, you can't get any madder, right?" she continued. "You already hate me. So what's the point in lying?"

"I want you to tell me why," I said. "Because I don't understand. I don't understand how we could be like that . . ." Everything that we were, which I couldn't even put into words. . . . "And you would lie to me."

She didn't say anything. "Seriously," I said, stepping closer. "What's the point of it all? You knowing and doing nothing!" I felt the anger bubbling to the surface. Bubbling over. "Don't you think you're meant to do something with that information?"

Her head whipped to the side, like I had slapped her. We never talked about this. I always just deferred to her since it *was* her. And since it was also very solidly my fault in the first place. *I* was the reason she was out on the lake that day. *I* was the one who left her standing there. So whatever she chose or didn't choose to do, she had every right to it. I figured she had her reasons, but now that it was my dad, I thought of all the things she could've done to prevent it. "You let him die!" I yelled.

Her fingers were pressed to the sides of her forehead, and her face was streaked with tears. I couldn't remember when she started crying—whether it was before or after I started yelling. She was staring at the carpet, breathing heavily, and she yelled, "I couldn't do anything!"

"You didn't even try! You didn't give him a chance!"

"I *did* try. I *told* him." I felt all the air getting sucked out of the room. I felt the room stretch out and hollow. I felt my heart sink into the pit of my stomach. "I told him," she repeated, and then she looked up at me. "But he already knew."

Chapter
6

Everything inside of me froze. "No," I said, and I thought about time. "Don't lie to me. There was no time." I pictured that day again. Her, in the lake. Us, in the house. She left. Her phone was off. I was home the whole day. I cooked with him. She didn't have the time. "When?" It wasn't possible.

She crossed the room and put her hand around my wrist, and I looked at her fingers, wondering in what universe she thought it would be okay to touch me right now. "I told him," she whispered, "in July."

I had this moment where I felt like everything inside of me was about to break open. Understood that this was a differ-ent side of her holding my wrist. July. *July.* Dying for months. *Lying* for months. I thought about all the ways this didn't make any sense. I thought about my dad most of all. "He wouldn't believe you." He wouldn't.

"*You* did," she said. But that was different. My dad didn't believe in things that didn't make sense. He believed in justice. Facts. Without facts, in life, like in the court room, it didn't count.

"He *didn't* believe you," I said. He did nothing about it. Nothing.

"He knew, Decker. He asked if you told me. He asked me if *you* knew. And when I said you didn't, he asked me not to tell you."

He would've told me.

Her fingers were still around my wrist, like she was my friend, telling me I'd been betrayed by someone other than her. And in that moment, with time standing still, I felt her stepping closer. Felt her thumb rub across my cheek. Heard her shaky breath. Wondered where this part of Delaney ended and the next began. If there was a line between the person I'd known forever and the girl I couldn't look at. Whether I was mad at them both.

I felt her arms around my back, felt myself sinking into her. "Decker," she whispered, like she was scared of breaking some trance. "Please."

And it doesn't matter how mad I was after that because she was too close—too close to push away. Too close to remember why I wanted to, even. I rested my forehead on her shoulder and felt us sinking slowly to the ground.

I was numb.

So I sat there, with Delaney an inch away, sitting cross-legged in front of me. "Let me say it," she said, but it's not like I was doing anything to stop her. It's not like I could do anything to stop her right then. All I could do was lean back against the carpeted floor and pretend to be somewhere else. But I heard her say it all. That she went to my dad's office. That he asked her how she knew, and she flat-out told him that she could sense illness, like pheromones or something. And he looked at her funny but didn't say anything for a while.

And then her voice was closer, and I realized she was lying on the floor beside me, and her hands were hovering just over her body as she spoke, as if she were illustrating a point, except they were palms up. She looked like she was pressing against some invisible barrier, like she was back under the ice. I wondered if she had any clue she was doing it.

She kept speaking even though I had practically stopped breathing, seeing her that way again. She said that my dad told her he was seeing a doctor already. That they were doing what they could.

We sat in silence for a long time. Long enough for me to put together the pieces that if my dad was already seeing a doctor, my mom knew, too. The only way she'd know about some heart condition in the hospital so quickly is if she had known about it before. We lay there long enough for me to think of all the signs I'd missed, or ignored, at home. All the moments I'd spent with Delaney between July and the time he died. All the times she'd smiled at me, laughed with me, kissed me.

She rolled onto her side, pushed herself up on her elbow, watching me. "Say something," she said.

I thought of the Fourth of July and that fireworks show

we went to, and then skipped, sneaking back to my house. My room. I wondered if she knew back then. If she was already atoning for something that hadn't happened yet.

I thought of the fact that she chose my dad over me.

I thought of how she had hidden a part of her from me, and I hadn't even realized it.

I closed my eyes and shook my head at her, and I heard her sigh.

Everything was building up inside me until I felt like if I spoke, the room would implode from my anger.

She was wrong. I could get madder. I was. I just wasn't sure who I was the maddest at.

My eyes were still closed but I felt Delaney pushing herself up. Away from me. And I heard something shattering, far away, like an old echo of my dad knocking the glass off the counter. It couldn't be real.

Delaney scrambled to her feet and raced across the floor on the way out of the room. "What the . . . ?"

Glass breaking, again. *Downstairs.* We were alone. I jumped up, my head cloudy, and checked her window quickly—no cars. "Wait," I said. But she was halfway down the stairs. We were supposed to be alone.

I was five steps behind her, too far to reach her, too far to stop her. Too far to do anything when she reached the bottom step and immediately curled back toward me, covering her face, as another spray of glass sounded throughout the downstairs. I could hear the outside. Feel the outside. See the back motion-detector light on from movement.

I pulled her back up the stairwell, leaning against the wall, until a whole minute passed without any more breaking glass. I felt it in her hair as she cowered into my shoulder. I saw blood on the backs of her hands, from where she had blocked her face as she dove back into the stairwell.

She was staring at her hands. I pulled them away from her face and ran my fingers quickly along her cheeks, her neck, her skin. I peered around the corner and saw the glass covering the carpeting, the living room windows only partially remaining, the night air rushing in.

"Stay here," I said, and I ran for Ron's office. Found my phone. Called 911. Again.

When I came back out, Delaney had a broom. Her hands were shaking as she tried to sweep up the mess. "Don't," I said. "You need to leave it."

So instead, she sat on the bottom step, running her fingers through her hair, shaking out the fragments of glass. I stood on the back porch, staring off into the distance, like time wasn't real and if I stayed still enough, I'd be able to see what had just happened.

I called Joanne's cell, and the noise from the barbecue came through the line before her worried voice. "Decker?" she said.

"Delaney's okay," I said. Figured I'd lead with that. "But something happened at the house. The police are on the way." I heard wind rushing through the phone, and I realized she was already coming.

* * *

That same cop showed up—the one who told me I could've destroyed my own house. I felt unreasonably vindicated by this, by the broken windows, by having an alibi in the form of the girl sitting on the couch, staring at the backs of her hands.

"Are you sure you're okay?" the cop asked Delaney. Other than her hands, which weren't too bad, she looked physically okay. Except she had this vacant expression. Not okay. I wanted to sit next to her. Put my arm around her. I wanted to find the person who'd done this to her and put my fist in his face.

She focused her eyes on the cop. Nodded. Looked at me. "Ice," she said.

The cop cleared his throat and said, "Uh, I'll check the freezer."

But that's not what she meant. I leaned against the far wall, felt the cold drywall against my back. Dropped my head, saw the pieces of glass everywhere, littering the floor between us. Like shards of ice, floating on the surface of a lake.

Water. Ice. *Us.*

"Are *you* okay?" she asked. Damn her. I was walking. I was going to sit next to her. I was going to put my arm around her.

The front door flew open, and Delaney's mom covered her mouth with her hand. "What the hell?" she said, which struck me, inappropriately, as hilarious.

My mom stepped around her, surveying the scene. Glass on the carpet. Glass on the table. Empty window frames. Me, standing in the center of the room, halfway to Delaney.

Joanne rushed to Delaney on the couch, lifted her arm, flipped it back and forth, assessing the damage. "What happened?" she yelled, even though she was an inch from Delaney's face. Delaney winced but not from the glass. Ron assessed the room, his eyes lingering on everything, piece by piece, like he could put the whole scene together in reverse.

The cop came back into the room carrying a bag of frozen peas that he handed to Delaney. She stared at the bag, totally confused. He flipped a page on his notepad and said, "Sorry to be meeting like this again." Then he cleared his throat and said, "The kids were upstairs when they heard the sound of breaking glass. Delaney came down the stairs first, entered the living room"—he gestured to the glass everywhere—"just as another window was shattered. Decker was still in the stairwell."

"I was almost down." The way he explained it, I sounded like a freaking coward, sending Delaney out first.

"What were you doing in her room?" Ron asked, forgetting about the broken window and the cop and the room full of people. And then he turned red, like he realized he didn't really want to know the answer to that.

"*Nothing*. I had to give her something."

"Ron. Later," Joanne said. He must've known we weren't together. *Everyone* knew.

The cop cleared his throat. "The vandalism?" he said. And we all fell silent.

"Who would do this?" Joanne asked. "First your house, now ours," she said to my mom.

"Whoever's doing it isn't trying to hurt anyone," the cop said.

I stared at Delaney's hands. At the dried blood.

"So far, the only target seems to be property."

"Delaney isn't *property*," I said.

She stared at me. I looked away.

"I didn't mean . . . Look. She got hurt, but that wasn't the intent. You understand?" And now he was talking to me like I was a moron. A cowardly moron.

He turned to my mom. "We have to acknowledge," the cop was saying, "that the target may not have been your late husband."

He kept calling my dad her late husband, and I hated the way that sounded, like he might still be on his way.

"Can you think of anyone who might want to target *you*?" he asked. My mom had her thumbs pressed to her eyes. She worked in social services. Both my parents, lifelong do-gooders. And look what it got us. It could've been anyone. Joanne had Delaney lie back on the couch and started combing her fingers through her hair. She dropped the fragments of glass into the ceramic bowl on the coffee table. Delaney's eyes were closed, and her hair was splayed out, like she was floating on the water. Under the water.

I heard the sound of another piece of glass landing in the bowl.

"Or maybe it's me," I said, and my mom frowned at me, the line appearing between her eyes.

"Who would be after *you*?" she asked. Delaney's eyes were open now. She knew. I knew. But neither of us could say: we let a curse loose. We lived. I saved her. It all sounded so ridiculous.

"I need to leave," my mom said.

"Don't be silly," Joanne said.

"I'm bringing you and your family into danger. I'm . . . I'll check into a hotel."

Thank God, I thought.

"Will you keep Decker?" she asked.

"What? You're the one who said you didn't want us separated. That's the only reason I'm even here!"

My mom blushed, I guess on my behalf. I was embarrassing myself. Us. I was being rude. I didn't give a shit.

"This isn't a request," she said, not involving me in this at all, like I was a child, incapable of making decisions. I had pulled Delaney from the lake. Gone to the funeral of one of my best friends. Watched someone try to kill Delaney. Held my father as his heart gave out. And still, she treated me like this.

Delaney's eyes were closed. Squeezed shut. Her chest wasn't moving. She was almost lifelessly still.

My hands, pushing down on her chest. My mouth, breathing air into her lungs. Wake up.

I had spent months living in terror of Delaney disappearing. But everyone was disappearing except her. *Everyone but her.*

Joanne said, "Of course, Decker will stay here. And so will you."

Ron looked at his wife. Then at the cop. "It's a window. Kids, probably. Nothing to do with anything."

The cop nodded, but he seemed to sense there was something more—water and ice, maybe a story he'd heard that he couldn't quite put his finger on. A girl who lived. A curse.

"Mom?" I asked, after the cop put his card on the table and left the house. My mom was walking toward the empty window with a box of garbage bags and a roll of tape. "Was Dad sick?" She stopped walking, in that same way Delaney had, as I put the pieces together in my room. "I mean, did you know *before* that Dad was sick?"

She made her hands keep moving, lining up the plastic against the window. Joanne cleared her throat and left the room. I wanted Delaney to leave, too, but she was watching. Leaning toward us. Waiting. My mom didn't look at me as she said, "This isn't the time . . ."

Which was all the answer I needed. I slammed the door to the office. Paced the room, waiting for the adrenaline to wear off. I put on my sneakers and went for a run, pounding the pavement until I had nothing left. When I got back, I stopped in front of my empty house. I wanted to tear the place apart. Find my dad and push him into a wall. I wanted to set this house on fire.

Kevin had his arm slung across Maya in the hall, and she smiled at me like she hadn't been a total bitch to me half a day earlier. "Did your brother find you guys?"

Her face fell. "Oh, that was *you*." She laughed. "Well, at least now I know how he found out."

"What?" Kevin asked.

"I don't think her brother is thrilled with the idea of you," I said.

"No," she said. "I'd say that's about right."

"That's only because he hasn't met me yet," Kevin said, a huge cheesy smile on his face.

She put a hand on his cheek. "Not gonna happen, babe."

"Hey," he said, bending down to kiss her. "I'll see you later, okay?" Really, he might as well have just said "Dismissed."

She blinked three times, rapidly, and said, "I need to go and make up a quiz. After school?" And she left before he had the chance to respond.

"So . . . problem," Kevin said as I pulled my books from my locker. "The field house."

Problem: someone had flooded my house; someone had broken three windows in the house I was living at.

Problem: nobody told me my dad was sick. Not Delaney. Not my mom. Not even him.

"Huh?" I responded. Kind of a mumble, kind of an I-don't-care.

"I'm going to assume you didn't sign your name?"

"Sign my name? What the hell are you talking about?" Please tell me there wasn't a camera. Please tell me security doesn't have me on tape somewhere.

Kevin leaned against my locker and rubbed his chin with his free hand as he scanned the hallway. "Okay, yeah, we'll find out who did it."

"Did what?" I asked. Kevin raised his hand to Justin, who was walking toward us.

"I got nothing," Justin said. "Where's Janna?"

Kevin laughed. "Abandoning ship." The warning bell rang and everyone in the hallway scattered.

"What the hell?" I said. I was going to be late. Screw it. I ran down the science wing, found an open classroom where people were still milling around, not yet in their seats. The teacher was talking to someone in the hall. I pushed past a bunch of freshmen, pressed my face to the glass window, and cupped my hands around my eyes.

I could see the words glaring back: CARSON WAS HERE.

And right below it, in letters so thick it must've taken an hour: SO WAS DECKER.

Kevin and Justin were pissed—they kept talking about this code of pranks or whatever, but Kevin said, "It's clever, I'll give him that. A prank within a prank." And Justin nodded. "We'll find out who did it," Kevin assured me. Someone had seen me and called me out, that was their assumption. No big deal. They'd find out who did it. They'd get revenge. Justin narrowed his eyes as he scanned the tables in the cafeteria.

Delaney walked by our table with her bagged lunch in her hand. I hadn't seen her in the cafeteria yesterday, but if she had the same lunch period, I guessed she'd eaten in the library. She sent a quick glance in our direction, a quick glance away. Kevin put his foot on the chair next to him and pushed it out without making eye contact, in an invitation. She paused for half a second before sitting.

Janna stopped eating. I stopped eating. We both stared at Kevin.

Delaney put down her lunch and walked toward the napkin dispenser. "What?" he said. "It's her table, too.

Always has been." He finished the rest of his lunch in one bite and talked through his chewing. "If you want me to hate her, Decker, better give me a good reason. *I* didn't break up with her. And, honestly, I have no freaking clue why *you* did."

Delaney returned with a stack of napkins. "What's up, Maxwell?" Kevin asked, eyeing the food she pulled out of her bag. "Gonna eat that whole sandwich?"

She elbowed his hand away. "Hands off, Kevin. I have math next period. I need the brain power."

"Maxwell," Kevin said, his chin in his hand as he assessed her. "I don't know how to say this. You're kind of a nerd."

Janna slammed her hand down on the table. Everyone stopped talking. "What? There was a fly." She bit a french fry in half. "Did you see the field house, Delaney?"

Delaney shifted in her seat and shook her head. Oh yes, she had seen the field house.

Kevin grabbed for her sandwich again. "Hey," he said as she elbowed him again. "I played a very small, but incredibly dramatic, role in saving your life. I'd say worth at least an eighth of that sandwich."

Janna was watching me as she sipped her soda. She pulled the straw from her mouth and said, "Do you believe in ghosts, Decker?"

"Ha-ha," I said.

"No?" She grinned at me, whispered so nobody else could hear. "How about curses, then?" She took another sip of soda, then burst out laughing. "Oh my God, you should see your face right now."

Justin leaned over to Janna and whispered, "Boo," in her ear. She swatted him away, and then they both started laughing.

Nobody seemed to be reading the words on the field house like I was, and with Janna sitting with us at lunch, I wasn't about to say it either.

Carson was here, and now he's not.

Was.

Past tense.

SO WAS DECKER.

Flood. Glass. A warning.

The vice principal called me out of last period. For a second I thought maybe the whole thing would be ignored. Maybe stand as a tribute to Carson. And maybe it would have, if my name wasn't carved in right below.

I walked into the front office, sat in a chair in front of the glass window that separated the office lobby from the front hall. The secretary was busy talking to the same guy I ran into at the barbecue—Maya's brother. I knew he was older—in college—but I mistook him for a student when I first walked into the office. There were several papers flattened against the counter between them. "These are the documents you requested," he said.

The secretary ran her fingers along each one while Maya's brother scanned the class photos on the far wall. "Birth certificate, transcript . . . Seems like we're still missing her immunization record."

"I know," he said, running his hand through his hair. "I called the doctor's office. It should be coming."

The secretary raised her eyes to him over her glasses. "How old are you, hon?" she asked. He was probably my height, my build. And, like I said, he looked like a student.

He stacked the papers together and handed them to her and said, "Old enough to be taking care of this." I guess since his mom needed full-time care, he had to take care of this kind of stuff on her behalf.

She handed him one last paper and said, "We'll need your mother's signature on this one."

"I'll get it," he said. He drummed his fingers on the counter. "Since I'm here, figured I'd take her home with me."

"Sure," she said. The secretary picked up a phone and said, "Maya Johnson to the main office for early dismissal."

The secretary waved her fingers at me. "She'll be right with you, Decker."

He turned around, and I realized it was the features he shared with Maya that made him seem younger. But he had dark circles under his brown eyes, and his skin was paler, which made him seem older. He blinked heavily in my direction. "Hey," he said. "Last night. I didn't know . . ." He shook his head. "Decker. Of Decker and Delaney." He quirked his mouth. "Sorry, I didn't realize you were a friend of Maya's."

"Friend" was kind of an overstatement. "Right," I said, and I stuck out my hand to shake his. He was stronger than I expected. He gripped my hand like my dad's lawyer friends would. Trying to show authority in the work place. An adult handshake. Guess he had to, since he was pretty much filling that role.

"Holden," he said. "Brother of Maya's." Then he dropped his voice lower and said, "Sorry to hear about your dad, by the way."

"Thanks," I said. *Should've been your mom, but thanks.*

"Decker?" Mrs. Woolworth was standing halfway out of her office, motioning for me to enter.

I saw Maya sprinting down the hall, her backpack bobbing on her back with each step, like a little kid, as I turned to go. She threw open the door and whispered, "Score one for the brother!" Then, lower, "I thought you had to leave this morning."

He laughed. "I'm drowning in paperwork. *Your* paperwork," he said.

She bit the inside of her mouth. "I thought you had a test you couldn't miss."

He hooked an arm around her neck, pulling her out the door. "Turns out, I didn't want to miss dinner with my pain-in-the-ass sister."

"Come on, Decker," Mrs. Woolworth said. I waved to Maya, but she was already leaving. If she'd seen me, she'd forgotten about me a fraction of a second later. So I turned for the office, my punishment waiting on the other side.

Her desk was pristine. The entire office was pristine. Not a paper in sight, not a speck of dust. She was in charge of discipline at the school. Carson used to say her stare alone could break you.

But right now, sitting across from me, she was trying to look kind. Caring. It didn't quite translate.

"I know it's been a rough month for you," she said.

Guess Janna was right. Dead dad cuts me some slack. "A rough *year*, really," she continued. "And part of me understands what you're trying to do."

She hadn't seen Janna's face in the woods. She didn't see all the places Carson should've been.

"But I can't let this go, you understand. What kind of message would that send?" She tapped the eraser of a pencil against the desk blotter. "But I see no reason to involve your mother. Or your record. Are you in any sport?"

"Not in the fall." I ran track in the spring. Hoped she wouldn't kick me off the team.

"Clubs?"

"Nope."

"Good. Then I'll see you after school until it's fixed—you can see Mr. Hayes at the athletic center. He'll set you up with everything you need. You start today."

I was in the parking lot with Justin and Janna. Justin was asking Janna who she was trying to impress with her skirt, and Janna was telling Justin to fuck off in every iteration possible. I saw Kevin from across the parking lot and waved him over.

"I'm not in trouble—"

"See?" Janna said. "Told you." She ruffled my hair, like I was a pet she was proud of.

"—but I have to fix it."

"What do you mean, *fix it*?" Janna asked, arms folded across her chest.

"Sand it and paint over it, I guess."

She leaned toward me, stuck a finger in my chest. "You're not going to, right?"

"I pretty much have to," I said.

"Carson would never paint over your name," she said, and it stung. Because it was true. But I wasn't him. Neither was Kevin, who put a hand on her shoulder and said, "Sorry, Janna."

She shrugged him off.

"So," I said. "Work detail. Starts today. I figure we could get it done in a couple of days if we all do it."

Kevin cringed. "Dude, yeah, that's kind of like an admission of guilt on our part."

Janna nodded. "I've run through dead brother goodwill."

I eyed Justin.

"I . . . have a test to study for."

"I hate you all," I said.

And as I left, I heard Kevin yell, "Go, Decker!" like a baseball chant, and then they all clapped and cheered as I walked away. It was hard to hate them. Really.

Chapter
7

There were worse ways to watch September slip by. I spent the afternoons scraping off paint, and not just over the letters—over the entire field house. Guess they figured it was a good time to repaint the whole thing, and I was free labor. A week of scraping off paint and sanding. A week of painting. So far, two weeks of avoiding just about everyone. The field house doors were usually locked—though that had never stopped Carson, who'd flip the lock on the window during afternoon practices whenever he was planning to use the field house after—but Mr. Hayes had to leave the doors open for me while I was working so I could paint the trim up to the hinges.

I'd spent three days pretending to do just that, but mostly I was just passing time. There was a riding mower in the back corner. Football equipment along the wall, nets and balls and hurdles in various states of wear. The floor was wood, finished enough to protect from the weather but not finished enough to make it comfortable. It was cool inside—cooler than the air outside, turning to fall. I spent three days lying there, in the center of it all, with an open container of paint, with my hands under my head, smelling sawdust and sweat and paint and the faint odor of gasoline from the containers next to the riding mower.

I'd stay until practices were over and people started dragging equipment back inside, then drive to my mom's office, where we ate by ourselves and didn't talk about the fact that she'd been lying to me.

Then we'd go to Delaney's, where I'd say meaningless things like *it's raining* or *the phone is ringing* or *where do you keep the laundry detergent* and also *I don't know how to work the dryer*, and didn't talk about the fact that she'd been lying to me.

Except for one night, she cornered me while I had my math homework spread out on the dining room table and said, "How long are we gonna keep doing this, Decker?" And I said, "Doing what?" like an asshole. "You're being an asshole," she said. And then I laughed because I knew it. She stomped up the stairs, and Ron, whom Delaney hadn't seen on the sofa, glared at me from the living room couch until I opted to do my homework in the office instead.

And that night, I found a note under my door. It said, *"To clarify, I didn't mean you ARE an asshole. Just that you're acting like one. Also, #2 is wrong. Good night."*

God, if I had no memory, I'd fall for her all over again.

But most of the time, I didn't say anything at all. Delaney would either be working in her room, or if she was downstairs, I'd sit out back, or if she was out back, I'd sit inside.

Turns out, it's not so hard to not see someone. Even in the same house. I thought of how many times I'd waited for my dad to leave a room before going in. How many times I'd pretended to sleep until they both left for work because I wasn't in the mood to talk.

How easy it is to become strangers.

On my fourth day of not finishing the field house, a shadow stood over me as I lay on the bare wood. "Waiting for someone, Deck?"

Tara was grinning and breathing heavily, her dark hair in a high ponytail. Her cheeks were pink, like she'd just finished a run. She bent over to pull her socks up over her shin guards. She winked at me while crouched down. "Don't worry, I won't tell."

I pushed myself onto my elbows. "No, I'm not."

"Hey, you don't have to explain to *me*." She shrugged, but it felt like I did have to explain it to her.

"I'm painting the field house."

She raised her eyebrow.

"I'm *supposed* to be painting the field house."

She started stretching in front of me, sitting on the wood floor, legs straight in front of her, reaching for her toes. "I'm supposed to be getting cones," she said, but it looked like she was about as interested in getting the cones as I was in painting the field house.

She switched positions, tucking one leg underneath her,

and leaned toward her other shoe. "Heard about Delaney," she said. "Scary."

I stood up, turned away so she couldn't see me. "You heard *what* about Delaney?"

"That someone tried to break in last week while she was home."

"I was there," I said. And that's not exactly what happened.

"Lucky for her, I guess."

Her home. Her windows. My mom thought she was the target. I thought *I* was. But it was Delaney's house, and she was home. She was home alone, as far as anyone could tell. Maybe it was her. I started rummaging through the equipment mindlessly. "I don't see any cones," I said.

I heard her sigh from somewhere behind me. "Behind the nets," she said.

I shifted the nets to the side, careful not to knock over any of the gasoline containers, and pulled out three stacks of cones—same ones we used in drivers ed, judging from the tire marks and the way half of them were misshapen.

I grabbed two stacks and nodded toward the third. "I'll help," I said.

She stood and brushed the dust from her soccer shorts. She picked up the stack of cones and bumped her hip into mine playfully as she passed. "Ah, Decker Phillips. Always the hero."

She talked the whole way, past the baseball fields, the football field, to the girls' soccer field. She talked and talked and I didn't have to say anything. She talked about people, about everything, about nothing, and I remembered why it was so great to hang out with Tara. You forget about everything else. There's no room in your head for anything else.

But a few of the girls on the team stopped running drills as we approached. They were watching us. Watching me. With her. I imagined rumors of *Tara and Decker* starting right then, circulating around school, through everyone, around everyone, straight to Delaney. I dropped the cones at the far corner, waved to the team in general. I lifted my hand as Tara called her thanks, but I was already halfway across the football field, and I didn't turn back around.

I opened the door to the field house. My eyes took a second to focus from the shift in light. I flicked the light switch, ready to pop open the can of paint and be done with this. But the room smelled off. Too much like gasoline, not enough like sawdust and sweat and paint. The floor was darker, like my house's when the water had seeped across the wood floors.

But this was gasoline.

One of the red containers was on its side, the nozzle lay beside it, and the floor was soaked in gasoline. The container was near the nets, which I had moved to get the cones, but I had been careful. I had checked. When I left, they were upright and sealed; I was sure of it.

And now this whole place was charged and waiting, seconds from going up in flames. The whole room, waiting for me.

Waiting for a spark.

I raced across the field, like it was chasing me.

* * *

Mr. Hayes said it was an accident, but I think he really assumed it was *my* accident. "It's all right," he said. "Appreciate you telling me. Could've ended badly."

"It was like that when I walked in," I said. Coming for me. Waiting for me.

"Sure, sure. Probably one of the coaches knocked it over on the way out and didn't notice."

"But the lid. Shouldn't that be *on*? Isn't that the point of it?" *Water dripping down the walls. Glass shattered on the floor. Gasoline clinging to the insides of my lungs.*

"Yeah, it is. Probably somebody forgot to tighten it." An uncapped top. An accidental nudge while I was out. A string of small mistakes that could've ended in disaster.

Or one event. One person, unscrewing the top, watching as the gasoline spread across the floor. Waiting for me.

But nobody knew I was still in there. To anyone else, it probably looked like I'd finished four days ago, like I was supposed to. I was just avoiding everything now. Going through the motions. Counting the days until they became weeks, the weeks until they became months, until all of them disappeared—to schools all over the country, to jobs with long hours, to apartments with friends.

Or they'd disappear from school, becoming lifelong fixtures in this town. Not the same people. Like the alumni who stuck around and put their old jerseys on during homecoming, becoming the people they'd once been. We never noticed them around town any other time of year. Just that one day, when they became who we remembered.

Everyone would disappear. I knew that now.

But not Delaney. She'd always be here. Or the ghost of her would always be here. The legend of her. An image of her, floating under the ice, clawing to get out. She'd live in the stories, the warnings, that generation after generation would tell. *Don't touch Falcon Lake. It wants you. It wants.*

I never did finish painting the field house. Mr. Hayes had to clean up the spill. He said he'd finish up. I knew, next time I went back, the doors would be locked.

I checked my car. Around my car. Checked the streets at each intersection, even if the light was green. I checked her house. Ran my fingers along the window frames, making sure they were locked.

I shouldn't stay here. Whatever was happening—the water, the windows, the gasoline—it was targeted at me. I was sure of it now. I was the only one tying it all together. When I got home from Boston, I'd figure out a way to convince my mom to let me leave. Though from the activity going on in our house—there'd been an electrician yesterday, a dry-wall company today—I figured it wouldn't be much longer, anyway.

"Some help with the groceries, Decker?" Joanne was watching me from the hall with two paper grocery bags in her arms. I hadn't heard her come in. *"Listen,"* the lady in 2B had told me. I hadn't even heard the garage door.

"Yeah, sorry," I said, backing away from the front window. I went to the garage and pulled a few bags from the trunk.

"I see you less now that you're actually living here," she said when I got back to the kitchen.

"Yeah," I said, emptying the bag. I knew where everything went in this kitchen. I practically grew up here.

Joanne cleared her throat. "And don't worry about those windows. . . ."

"I wasn't," I said, even though of course I was.

"Well, anyway, we just had an alarm system installed." She pointed to the keypad on the wall. "So no need to worry, if you had been."

"I wasn't," I said again.

"Two-five-four-three," she said.

"Huh?"

"The code," she said.

"Oh, that's okay, we'll be moving out soon."

"Decker, don't be ridiculous. Two-five-four-three," she repeated.

I pulled out three containers of hamburgers. "Sale on burgers," I mumbled as I searched for space in the freezer.

Joanne put a hand on her hip. "We're having a barbecue tomorrow. It's on the calendar." She pointed at the calendar stuck to the side of the fridge, then shook her head to herself. "Am I the only one in this family who checks the family calendar?" I didn't want to point out I wasn't actually a member of this family, and once I moved out, I wouldn't be here much at all anymore. "Seriously, you're worse than Delaney," she said.

*   *   *

We were leaving for Boston in two days, and I was supposed to be at that barbecue at Delaney's house in less than an hour. So was Maya, I guess, because when I showed up at Justin's basement after school, she said, "Oh good, you can drive me," like we were friends.

I wanted to tell them about the gasoline, about the feeling of something after me, but not with Maya there. None of us knew how to talk with Maya there. Kevin kept having to pause and explain things in the middle of a conversation.

"We need to do something bigger," Janna said, resting her head back on the couch.

"Bigger than what?" Maya asked, and Kevin had to explain about the field house again.

"I'm thinking Johnny's," Janna said, which made sense since we'd all eaten there since we could do anything by ourselves.

"Who's Johnny?" Maya asked, and Kevin had to explain that it was the pizza place in town.

"Oh," Kevin said. "My parents own that building, Janna. So no."

"Your parents own the *building*?" Maya asked, but this time Kevin didn't respond.

Janna narrowed her eyes at him. "And they have the money to handle it."

"What's the point?" Justin asked. "If they just paint over it again?"

"You could talk to your parents," she said to Kevin. "Get them to leave it."

"Yeah, no. A creepy message on a sign would be bad for business, which would be bad for my parents. See how that works?"

"Yes, I see how that works," she said, her words short and snipped. "So then you come up with an idea."

This would be the time when Carson would butt in and tell his sister to chill out, to stop being so bossy, and he'd hook an arm around her and say something like, *"Don't mind her, she's pissed about a math test. A-minus. Such a disappointment."* And smile at her. She'd roll her eyes. It would be over. But now, the silence just sat there.

"I'm gonna go," Janna said, and I said good-bye louder than I needed to, trying to shake off the awkwardness.

"Decker," Kevin said. "Whatever's going on with Delaney, fix it already. You look like shit. It's messing with my mood."

"Enough," I said.

"No," he said. "Enough from you. Break up, fine. But the moping and gloom and angry eyes, it stops. It's awkward. Every lunch I get, like, a tension headache or something," he said. He rolled his shoulders back. "I think it's giving me neck pain." For a second, I thought Maya whispered that speech in Kevin's ear. But Maya was staring just beyond me. At a silent, frozen Janna.

"You're blocking me in, Kevin." She was irritated, like something was forcing us all to be together. He tossed her the keys from the couch.

"Sexist, much?" she asked.

"How the hell is that sexist? I'm trusting you with my car. That's the opposite of sexist."

I needed out. I hated the gaps of silence. The way Carson's absence could fill this room. The way it was pushing us apart, instead of the other way around. "Let's go, Maya," I said. She tried to lean into Kevin, to say good-bye in the way she always said good-bye to him, but his arm stiffened and he pulled away.

Kevin was looking at me like Janna's attitude was also somehow my fault.

"What?" I said.

He leaned his head back on the couch, like Janna had done when she was thinking. "I just want everything back how it used to be." But I didn't see how that was possible when one of us didn't exist anymore.

Janna came back in while Maya was getting her bag. She held the keys on her finger in Kevin's direction, but she didn't step closer. He held his hand out, palm up, still sitting on the couch. The room was silent. Even Maya stopped rummaging through her bag to watch. Janna slowly tilted her hand down, and the key slid off her finger in slow motion. It collided with the hard basement floor, shattering the silence.

The car alarm was going off in the distance. Must've hit the panic button when it fell. But Janna left it there. Kevin left it there. The alarm blared in our ears. I went to pick them up, to silence the damn noise, to put an end to the standoff.

"Wait," Kevin said as he got up off the couch. Walked over to Janna. Bent to pick up the keys. He pressed a button, silencing the alarm, as he stood. And as he stood, he circled his arms around Janna, pulling her toward him. He whispered something in her ear, and she started sobbing into his chest, like Carson had just died all over again. And Kevin had his other hand over his eyes, his face resting on her shoulder.

Justin said, "Shit," and he bent in half on the couch, his forehead resting in his hands.

I felt my insides bend in half. Felt him die again. Right now.

I heard Maya start to speak beside me. Half a word. "Wh—"

I dragged her by the arm and pulled her up the stairs. Out the door. Out from where she didn't belong. "Don't talk," I said. We drove in tense silence to Delaney's.

"I get it, you know," she said as we pulled into our street. "If my brother . . . Well. I get it."

But she didn't get that Carson had been one of my closest friends or that he had helped save Delaney's life, and then he had died on the side of the road from a rare, sudden seizure disorder, with Delaney by his side. And Delaney had never told Janna why they were in the car, headed down the highway together. And Maya didn't get all the steps that led up to that, when you looked in reverse.

"Delaney told you about falling through the ice, right?"

"No. I mean, I *know*, but she never told me."

Everyone knew. The town practically breathed it. "Then I guess she never told you why she was out there in the first place. I was pissed at her. It was before we were together. I walked in on her and Carson a few days before. On my couch." I tightened my grip on the steering wheel. "And Carson *knew* that I . . . he knew. *Everyone* knew. So I was jealous and I made her do it because I knew she didn't want to. And when she stopped in the middle, I saw Carson waiting for us, and I gave her shit about it, and then I left her there."

I pulled into my driveway, but Maya didn't move to unbuckle her seat belt. "And then she fell," I said as I turned off the engine.

"Why are you telling me this?"

I had no idea. But it felt like something I had to say. That Carson wasn't perfect, that none of us were, but it didn't matter. That everything, every horrible thing that happened over the last year could be traced back to me. "Because you *don't* understand," I said.

"You think I'm such an idiot," she said. "That I'm just some girl your friend is screwing around with. That I'm incapable of thought."

"I don't," I said.

"And now," she said, unbuckling her belt and flinging open the door. "You're lying."

Everyone was too cheerful, too loud, at Delaney's. Maya transitioned just fine, smiling and saying, "Thanks for having me," and going to join the crowd out back where Ron was grilling burgers while Joanne manned the kitchen. A few of our neighbors were over. My mom was here. Everyone was eating out back or had finished eating and was now sitting around. The windows were all open. Probably one of the last days they'd be able to be open. I brought my food inside and picked at it over the kitchen counter before relocating to the empty living room, listening to the conversation through the open window.

"Are you going on the trip, Maya?" Ron asked.

"Nope. I've got another year left," she said.

"How's your mom doing?" Joanne asked.

"Fine," Maya said. There was an awkward pause, and then Maya started talking again. "Anyway, I'm going to visit my brother this weekend."

"Where is he in school?" Ron asked.

"Portland," she said. "Not too far."

Southern Maine. At least three hours away. Might as well have been Boston or New York or Florida. But at least it was close enough for her brother to hop in a car if he needed to.

"At least you can drive," Joanne said. "You sure you don't want to go somewhere you can drive, Delaney?"

Delaney didn't answer.

"She's not the best flyer," Joanne said, I guess to the rest of the group. That was an understatement.

I was listening from the living room couch with a can of soda in my hand and my homework on my lap, though I wasn't really concentrating. "Drink some tea," my mom was saying to Delaney. Drinking tea was her go-to cure for nerves.

"I'll be fine," Delaney said. Delaney would not be fine. She hated to fly. Hated it but did it. She'd told me that mentally she knew she'd be fine, but she couldn't convince her body.

"Oh," Maya said, "have you tried Xanax? Works wonders."

There was a beat of silence before her mother said, "Delaney would prefer not to take medicine." Yeah, she'd preferred that ever since her mother kept forcing drugs on her, trying to turn her back to the person she thought she knew before the accident.

"Maybe you outgrew it? You did great over spring break," Joanne said.

I choked on the soda. Had to wipe it off my notebook. Spring break she'd had to visit her grandmother in Florida. She got antsy the whole week before, but at least she had school to distract her. The morning of her flight, the first day of spring break, she let herself in my front door. "I'm leaving in fifteen," she said, pacing the living room absently. She had on a black skirt that hit just above her knees and gray tights underneath. The skirt was flowy and pretty but definitely not her. "Nice skirt," I said, trying to catch her as she paced back and forth.

"My grandma gave it to me for Christmas. So." She plopped onto the sofa, and her skirt rode up an inch, and I could see that her tights weren't tights at all, but something that stopped at her thigh.

"This, too?" I asked, pulling at the top of her stocking.

"No, these are all mine." She stood up and said, "Look. Maine-weather-appropriate." She gestured toward her covered legs. Then bent over and pushed down the socks. "Florida-weather-appropriate. Totally practical. I can do it on the airplane."

It was so logical and ridiculous and so totally Delaney.

She sat down again, and her fingers shook as she pulled the sock up her left leg. I knelt in front of her. "Okay, you have to breathe." I pulled up the right one for her. I actually found it kind of adorable that airplanes freaked her out. Of all the things that happened to her in the last few months, *this* still scared her. I was smiling and had my hand on her leg, about to stand up.

And she was definitely still not breathing.

Then I felt her bare skin under her skirt, under my hands, where I had frozen. Her skin was hot. The room was hot. I didn't want to back away. I looked up at her, and she was watching me, and her mouth was kind of open, and I said, "Okay, seriously, breathe."

She smiled for a second, and she didn't pull away from me or say anything clever or tell me she had to go, which she did. I could hear the clock ticking from the mantel.

There was an eternal span of seconds, I heard them ticking away, where neither of us moved. Neither of us breathed.

"Hey, Delaney? I love you, you know." I'd said it to her before, more than once, but never kneeling between her legs with my hand halfway up her skirt, where I could feel her pulse coming fast. She nodded and I kissed her mouth and moved my hand and almost lost it when she closed her eyes and leaned into me. Lost it completely when she whispered my name and pulled me close, breathing into my ear.

I didn't tell her that it was time to go after. But I pulled her up to standing, watched as her skirt fluttered down. She kissed me good-bye, pressing every part of her to every part of me.

She walked across the room, and I smiled—or I was still smiling—and said, "Have a good flight."

She opened the front door, looked over her shoulder, and smiled like she knew a secret. A side of her I'd never seen before.

And of all the moments that happened between that day and this one, that's the one I remember the most. The one that made me feel like I hadn't known all of her until that day. That every side of her—the ones she showed and the ones she didn't—were mine. And some were mine alone.

Even now, I got a thrill knowing she was thinking of that moment hours later, on the plane. That she was distracted from her fear of flying by thinking of *that*. That she was thinking about it this very second as she walked behind the couch, on the way to the bathroom.

"So, guess you must really miss me right about now," I said. The words tasted vile on the way out, felt like acid in the air. They burned her skin. Burned her eyes. Burned everything between us.

"What did you say?" she asked, coming around the couch. She stared at me, but I couldn't look at her. Felt the words burning me, too. "Of course I miss you. I miss you all the time. But don't do that," she said, and I watched her feet shuffle down the hall. She let me hate her. She let me be angry. But not this. "Don't," she said again, the second before she slammed the door.

Don't make us cheap.

Don't make us not matter.

Don't give us up.

Maya was standing by the couch when Delaney walked back through. "My mom just texted," she said, holding up her phone. "She needs me home. Any chance I can get a ride?"

Joanne came out of the kitchen with a Tupperware container of potato salad. "How about a burger for the road? For your mom?"

"Hold on," Maya said, intently typing on her phone. "No thanks," she said.

"You don't have to go," Delaney said. "Come on, my mom makes a killer apple pie."

But Maya waved her phone again. "Yes," she said, "I *do* have to go."

Joanne said, "Delaney, drive her home." Joanne didn't always get Delaney. Didn't understand every turn of her thoughts, every tone of her voice. But I did.

Delaney plastered on a fake grin and headed for the front door, but I knew. Maya just wanted an excuse to get out of here. Honestly, today I couldn't blame her.

After dinner, I walked with my mom over to our house. She opened the garage, which had remained perfectly functional, no water damage. A separate light, battery powered and not connected to the rest of the house, hung from the ceiling with its own switch. She turned it on, and the room was filled with a yellow glow.

"I could camp out in here," I said. She laughed. I was only half-kidding.

She had these books and papers spread out on top of the hood of my dad's gray car, which sat, unused, taunting me. Like he was still here, in this house. I wondered if she was planning on selling it. I wondered whether she'd give it to me if I asked for it. If I wanted it at all.

"I want your opinion on the floors," she said.

"The floors?" I asked, trying to figure out what she was talking about.

"Yeah, the color. We have to replace them, so I'm trying to decide what I want."

"What you want," I said. I couldn't process that. What she wanted, like this was all an excuse to do things around the house. I could see why insurance said they'd be taking a hard look at us. "What was wrong with the floors we had?"

"Nothing," she said, but she shrugged. "They weren't in the best shape. Before. They were on my list of things to fix anyway."

"You're not serious," I said. She froze under the light in the garage, knowing exactly what I meant. "You want my opinion on the goddamn floors. You want to change the *goddamn floors*."

She put her palm flat on the hood of the car, bracing herself. "We have to put new floors in anyway."

"And you think I care."

She set her mouth, like she did when she was disappointed

in me. Or like she did when she didn't want to give anything away. "I'm trying to include you."

"Oh, *now* you want to include me? That's funny. That's *hilarious*. Yeah, let's talk about the floors. That's important." I had my hands on the trunk, and we stood like that, looking over the top of the car at each other. "Do you honestly care?" I asked.

"I don't know, Decker. But don't you think I'm entitled to something good? Even if it's just the damn floors?"

"What about me?" I asked.

"What *about* you?" she asked. "What would you like? Would you like to go to Boston? Oh, good, you are. Would you like me to pay your way to college, even though you have no clue what you want to do? Because I am. I'm trying. So tell me, what is it, exactly, that you *want*?"

I stared at her. She stared at me.

Listen. The buzz from the light. Her breathing. My breathing.

She lowered her voice and said, "I mean, something I can actually give you."

I dropped my head and closed my eyes. I hated looking at her like this. She came around the car and pulled me toward her. I wrapped my arms around her back and buried my face in her shoulder. I realized today that we'd never get over Carson. I'd never get over this. "I'm sorry," she whispered as I swallowed back the urge to cry. I was losing.

I hated that she was apologizing, like everyone else with their useless condolences.

"I'm sorry we didn't tell you," she said.

I wondered why Delaney couldn't say the same thing.

"Why didn't they *do* something?" I mumbled into her shoulder. "Isn't that the whole point of being a cardiologist? To fix the freaking heart?"

She let out a slow breath. "It's a condition that can affect your whole body, but it went after his heart the hardest. There were deposits all over it by the time he had any symptoms. They were keeping an eye on it . . . doing what they could. But Decker, we knew there wasn't a cure for cardiac amyloidosis. I'm so sorry."

It was like she was apologizing because nobody else could.

"Couldn't they just give him a new heart?"

I could feel her shaking her head. She whispered, "No, they couldn't. It would just come back. It was a part of him."

I gritted my teeth. Shook my head. Felt the anger coursing through me again. "And that was *it*?" I hated feeling like he went gently. I wanted him to be the kind who fights death, all the way.

"He was taking medicine, Decker. He was trying to slow it down. We were keeping an eye on it . . . we *were*. We didn't think it would be so soon." I felt her weight, like I felt my dad's as he fell to the floor. And I realized we had shifted positions. I was holding her up.

Delaney was blocking the door to the office/my bedroom when I was trying to leave for school the next morning. She must've been waiting there, because as soon as I opened it, dressed and ready to leave, she put her hands on either side and leaned toward me.

"Shit," I said as I dropped my bag in shock. I stared at it on the floor.

"This is my house," she said. If I was looking at her, my guess is that she'd be scowling. "You don't get to make me feel like crap anymore in my own house. You don't get to make me feel like . . . *trash*—"

I winced.

"—in my own house."

"Sorry," I said, even though I hated that I was the one apologizing. I felt the guilt stirring inside of me, where it sat permanently, like a lung. Easy to forget about until you can't breathe.

Guilt for leaving her on the lake. Guilt for everything that followed. She stood in my house after and said, "I forgive you," like it was the easiest thing in the world. And then she did. She never mentioned it. Not once.

Everyone else acted like I was a hero because I'd saved her. Nobody remembered what happened the moment before, when I left her.

She just . . . forgave me. I wondered whether I could do the same. If I could force the words out and they'd gather meaning on the way from my lungs to my lips. If they'd become real.

I opened my mouth, but she put up her hand. "And I know I'm not supposed to say this because your dad died and you hate me and you can't even go to your own house. And now you're stuck here with a girl you can't even look at in a place you don't want to live, and it sucks. But this is my house. So pretend. It's not that hard. Look. I'm pretending right now."

I actually smiled because it was so ridiculous. She wasn't pretending anything; she was saying exactly what she was thinking. "What, exactly, are you pretending?" I asked.

"I'm pretending that this"—she waved her hands in the empty space between us—"isn't *killing* me."

I swallowed the knot at the base of my throat. "Anything else?"

"Yes," she said. And that was just like Delaney. Ignoring my sarcasm. "When you finish the goddamn milk, don't put it back in the goddamn fridge."

I looked at her then, as she walked away, her hair trailing halfway down her back. And the truth is, I'd trade her again. I'd make the same bargain. Her for anyone.

Even now.

It made me sick to my stomach, knowing that.

"Do I get a turn to talk now?" I asked.

"Sorry," she said. "The guy living at my house is too pissed at me to let me ride with him to school, so I have to catch the bus."

Point: Delaney.

"I never said you couldn't."

"No, you just left without me. Good thing I'm smart enough to read between the lines."

I heard Maya's voice in my head, telling me to grow up. "Just give me a sec." I tossed her the keys, and by the time I got outside, she was sitting in the passenger seat with the engine running, reading a book.

I heard her flipping the pages as we drove. I could set a clock to it. But every few minutes she'd stop and make a note in the margin. For school. For a grade. I didn't apologize. I didn't say I forgave her as she sat beside me, planning for her future like none of this mattered in the long run.

I didn't say anything at all.

Chapter
8

"You didn't pick up your phone this morning," Kevin said as I rifled through my locker.

"Sorry," I said. I'd been not picking up my phone for a while now. Not on purpose, but I kept the ringer way down. It made me jump.

"I needed a ride," he said, and his eyes were wide, like I was missing something important. "My car wouldn't start, and my parents had already left and I couldn't find the keys to the spare." I grinned. Kevin's expression didn't change. He had no idea how he sounded. A spare car. He had a *spare car.* Like the rest of us kept a spare tire in the trunk for emergencies. They kept a whole car.

"Sorry," I said. "Looks like you got here okay."

"Dude," he said, leaning forward, lowering his voice. "I took. The bus."

I laughed. I couldn't help myself. Couldn't remember a

time Kevin had ever taken the bus. Before he got his license, Justin's older brothers would drive them both. Then they left for college and took the car with them, but by then Kevin had his license and a car, and, apparently, a spare.

"But that's not the worst part," he said. "I was supposed to pick Maya up." He made this exaggerated *oh shit* expression. Held his palm out. "Keys to the minivan. Please. I'll be back in twenty."

"Uh-uh. No way. You're not taking my car."

"The girl is waiting at home. With her dying mother. Are you serious?"

I spun the key on my finger. "Think I've got any dead dad goodwill left?"

Maya was pacing the front yard when we arrived. She kept looking at her cell phone and then looking at the road. Maya was the only thing that reminded me that Justin's lake house wasn't just Justin's lake house anymore. Honestly, it looked pretty much the same.

No cars in the driveway, unless they were ours. The same cheap, generic shades pulled down over the front windows. I wondered if they used the same furniture that was always there, or if they had brought their own. I wondered how sick her mother must've been, that the house had no touch of them to it, other than the wheelchair ramp in place of the front steps.

Kevin had told me he never went in. Not even to pick her up. He said they spent most of their time in the backseat of his car. He wasn't complaining.

Maya saw us coming and swung her bag up onto her

shoulder. Not her backpack. Something bigger. She stared at her feet as she walked toward the van but stopped when she saw Kevin get out of the passenger seat.

"I thought you said you were borrowing a car," she said.

"I did," he said. "I even borrowed a driver." He was going for levity. She didn't bite.

She frowned at me, sitting in the driver's seat.

"Maya, get in the car," Kevin said. "We're already late. Next time, take the damn bus."

She crossed her arms over her chest and yelled to me in the car. "Isn't my boyfriend the sweetest?" she asked.

"Seriously?" Kevin said, and he crossed his arms back. "Want to get some other guy you can try to boss around? See if someone will walk over here and give you a damn piggy-back ride?" I knew where this was going. How it always inevitably turned. Kevin wouldn't budge. He'd get stubborn and cocky and he wouldn't cave, and the girl would get pissed and threaten to leave, and Kevin wouldn't do anything to stop her.

I was about to witness a breakup. I looked at my watch, shook my head.

I got out of the car. "Come on," I said. "I need to get back to class."

"I'm sorry to ruin everyone's morning," she said. "But the reason I needed a ride, Kevin, is because I need to get to the *bus station*. Which you would know if you listened to *half* of what I said."

She swallowed back tears and dropped her oversize bag on the ground.

I picked up her bag before we could find out whether Kevin was going to leave it there. Leave her there. Before this went downhill really fast.

"Skipping school?" I asked. We were getting excused for missing a day for the Boston trip. She wasn't, I assumed.

"I hate to be alone," she said. She brushed Kevin as she passed him. He tilted his head back and made an exasperated face at the sky. He reached around her waist and pulled her toward him and kissed her. I didn't mean to stand there staring; I'd just never seen Kevin cave like that before.

"I'm sorry," he said. "I got here as fast as I could. I'd take you with me if I could."

I slammed the car door. I wondered how sick her mother was that Maya already thought she was alone.

I half expected Kevin to slide into the backseat with Maya, that's how much they were ignoring my existence. But Kevin took the seat beside mine, and we settled into a completely awkward silence. I cleared my throat. "I don't know where the bus station is."

Kevin sighed. Loudly. Like this whole situation was seventeen layers of obnoxious.

"Couple miles down the highway. Behind the Burger King," Maya said.

"That's, like, ten miles," I said.

"I didn't mean to make you miss class," she said, in this light voice. I would've believed it if I hadn't heard the other side of her once.

"That's okay," Kevin said. "Sorry I didn't get here sooner.

And anyway, I asked to just borrow the car. Not the driver. He doesn't trust me with his baby."

"Oh, I trust you just fine to *drive* it," I said. "I just didn't know what else you planned to do in it."

Kevin laughed, and I cast a glance in the rearview mirror to see whether she would too, but she wasn't paying attention. She was thumbing through her wallet as I pulled out onto the highway.

"Okay, this is embarrassing," she said. "Any chance you could lend me some money for my ticket?"

Kevin pulled out his wallet and handed her the solitary twenty-dollar bill.

She held it between her fingers and said, "Do you have any more?"

"Sorry, I don't."

"Seriously? You're filthy rich. We all know it."

Kevin's eyes went wide. It's true. He was. We all knew it. He had a freaking spare car. His parents owned *buildings*. But nobody said that to him, nobody asked him for cash, nobody expected him to pay our way because of it. He was here, in the middle of nowhere, just like the rest of us.

"No," he said. "My *parents* are filthy rich. *I* have to work if I want money."

"Right," she said. "I'm sure you bought that car yourself."

"No, I didn't. Which is why it's in my parents' name."

"Okay, okay," she said, "I don't mean to be a bitch or anything, but I've got to see my brother, and I've got no cash, so can you please loan it to me? Please."

"Maya, I would. I have a credit card for emergencies, but that's pretty much it right now. Until my next paycheck. I'm not so good with the money thing."

"Kevin. My mother is dying. This *is* a goddamn emergency." Her eyes welled up, and I took out my own wallet. Girl tears were like freaking kryptonite. I pulled out the forty-three dollars I had to my name, passed them to the backseat.

Kevin put a hand on my arm. "No, she's right. I got this."

Maya didn't talk for the remaining eight miles, but every once in a while I heard her take in a short gasp of air. Kevin leaned his head against the window. I wondered when we'd ever stop thinking about death. If that was even a possibility if I had a girlfriend who was drawn to it.

Listen. The van shifting gears as we went up a hill; Kevin drumming his fingers along the base of the window; the blinker clicking as we got ready to turn into the bus station.

"I'm going to miss you," she whispered as she slid out of the backseat.

"It's three days, babe," Kevin said.

Kevin paid for her ticket at the station. Ran his hands through her long hair. Bent down to kiss her. I looked away. Waited outside. Kicked a rock across the barren parking lot.

"Shit," he said when we got back in the car. "Now I feel like an ass."

"Not your fault her mom is sick."

He shrugged. "Guess not."

But I got what he was saying. There's a weird sort of guilt that comes with helplessness. Because there was nothing we could do except hand her twenty-dollar bills, like condolences, and that wasn't going to change the fact that her mom would be dead soon.

We were almost back to school when I said, "I was pretty sure I was about to witness the epic breakup of Kevin and Maya when we picked her up."

He grinned. Almost. "She didn't use to be like this, you know. You remember? God, she was so . . . *perfect* this summer." I didn't exactly agree with that assessment, but I chose to keep that to myself. "Whatever," he said, "it's not like I can break up with her *now*." I knew why. But still.

"She's not exactly nice." I probably shouldn't have said that. If somebody had said that about Delaney, I would've been pissed. But I also didn't think the thing with Maya went anywhere below the surface. Or, like he said, the back of his car.

"I'm not exactly nice either," he said. "You know what happened with Tara?"

"You dumped her."

"Ha. That would've been the nice thing to do. No, I made her do it. Asked her if she minded that I was taking Maya out the next night." He grimaced. Shook his head to himself. "She minded."

I thought about Kevin at my dad's funeral. Kevin at my house, with his face pressed up against the window, not letting me stay alone. Kevin pushing the chair out at lunch for Delaney. "You're nice," I said. "You're just also an ass."

We got back to school in the middle of second period. The halls were empty. "I owe you one," he said before slipping into his classroom and waving at his teacher. "Sorry," I could hear him saying. "Girl problems."

I walked down the hall to the English/History wing but stopped at the class before mine. I saw Delaney in the front of the room, her eyes following the teacher as he walked back and forth across the classroom, the bottom of her pen resting on her lower lip.

I circled back before reaching my class, turned around, and walked by again—she was looking out the window, her head resting on her hand. Thinking about something.

I walked by again, and she was writing. The light from outside hit her desk, and she had one hand cupped around the paper, shading the words as she created them.

One more time. I'd go one more time and then get to class. But as I spun around, circling back, the door flew open, and she was racing down the hall in the other direction, searching through her bag as she walked. She jumped into the alcove leading to the girls' bathroom, put her hand over one ear, pressed her phone to the other, and whispered, "Hello?"

I was close. Closer than I should've been. Just outside the alcove. If she wasn't listening so intently to the person on the other end of the phone, she'd have heard me by now. I stepped inside, into the hall leading to the stalls.

She was nodding, and she said, "Yes. Ten? Yes, I can make it." She hung up, and I could see her mouth reciting something, trying to commit it to memory.

"Who was that?" I asked before I could stop myself.

She jumped. Put her hand over her heart. Paused a second

too long before saying, "A friend." Maya was gone. Everyone was in class. I was standing right in front of her.

A friend.

She was lying. She was hiding. How much of herself did she keep from me?

I was staring her down, which I had no real right to do, and she said, "What are you doing here?"

I shrugged and said, "I was late for class." Then realized she was referring to the fact that I was technically in the girls' bathroom, and added, "You looked . . . like something was wrong."

She looked down at her phone. Back at me. Pressed her lips together and nodded. But before I had a chance to figure out whether or not she was going to keep it a secret, before I had a chance to know for sure that she wouldn't tell me, I said, "It's okay. You don't have to tell me. I mean, what you do now isn't really my business anyway, right?"

She put one hand on the wall. "Do you want to know or not, Decker?" she asked. Meaning layered under meaning.

We heard footsteps coming, and I stepped closer into the space with her. So our breath was sharing the same place.

Listen. Footsteps in the hall; her holding her breath. Hope.

Black pupils, growing wider.

The weight of my father as he slid to the floor.

Her pale face as she backed out of my house.

Her pale face as I dragged her out of Falcon Lake.

I felt my lungs try for air, felt them fight for it, felt nothing coming in. I backed out of the hall as soon as I heard the footsteps disappear, ran across the hall to the boys' bathroom and splashed cold water on my face, trying to wash that image away.

I opened my eyes and saw her reflection in the distorted mirror above the sink, like she was floating, drowning. I ran my fingers along the image. "You okay?" she asked. I spun around. She was right behind me. In the boys' room.

"In my head, I see you die. All the time." She turned pale, like she did in my vision. "In my mind, you're still dead."

It was a horrible thing to say, which is why I never told her before. It was a horrible thing to have her know. It was a horrible thing to think.

"Is it . . . is that one of the reasons for the panic?"

I kept things from her, and she kept things from me, and I wondered if there was something—something *before*—that was already broken between us. Some lack of trust that started the day I left her on the lake. If my dad was just the thing that gave it a name.

"It's the only reason," I said. "Every time."

It was easier to be honest with her when we weren't together. When I wasn't worried about hurting her feelings— I'd already done that. Figured it couldn't really get any worse. I was wrong. She nodded at me and backed away, very slowly. Her footsteps were silent as she walked out of the bathroom. By the time I got to the hall, she was gone.

I was packing for Boston after everyone had gone to their rooms when I heard the front door squeak closed. But I didn't hear any engine. I went to the window in time to see Delaney's blond ponytail bobbing around a corner and out of sight. It looked like she was in a hurry.

What the hell.

In my pursuit to avoid her for the past few weeks, I had no idea what she'd been up to. What she'd been doing. Who she'd been with. Who had called her on the phone. Who she planned to meet at ten.

I went outside and sat on her porch swing. The night was crisp, almost October now, which meant almost winter for us. I checked my watch—9:32. There are really only so many things you can be doing after nine p.m. on a Thursday night. She was meeting someone at ten.

What the hell?

I watched the far corner, willing her to come back. I had to know. I didn't want to know, but the not knowing was driving me mad. I broke up with her and she moved on, which is what most people did. It's what was supposed to happen. No. *I* broke up with her. *I* was supposed to move on. I couldn't even move the goddamn swing I was sitting on, scared I'd miss the sound of her coming. Or the sound of her whispering to someone in the distance. In my mind, I didn't see her dying. I saw her in someone else's room, in someone else's bed, with the smile she always saved for me.

But less than a half hour later, I heard footsteps coming from the other direction. Delaney was coming up the street. Correction: she was *running* up the street. I stood and checked behind her, seeing if someone was following her, but it looked like she was alone. Her head was down, so she didn't notice me until she was at the front steps. Where I was waiting.

She looked at my shoes first. Her cheeks were flushed, and she was practically gasping for air. She stumbled onto the steps and sat down, close to where I was standing. I leaned onto the porch railing, going for calm indifference.

"What the hell are you doing?" I asked. So much for calm indifference.

She leaned back on her elbows, tilted her head up. I watched the cloud form as she exhaled, still catching her breath. "Running," she said. Guess her plans to meet someone weren't for tonight.

And then I looked closer: gray sweatpants, long sleeved T-shirt, sneakers. I felt her watching me take her in. I looked out at the night. "You hate running."

"Yeah," she said. She stood up and brushed off her pants. "But the only thing I think about when I'm running is how much I hate running."

And I thought, *You're perfect.*

"It's supposed to rain," she said. "In Boston."

"Huh?"

"Umbrella," she said. "Pack one. There's a stash in the coat closet."

And then she was back in the house, presumably in her room, and I was left wondering how she could be talking about umbrellas when I was trying to figure out how not to want to smile at her even though I was furious with her.

Chapter
9

We rode in one of those planes where there are actual propellers. Which made it loud. Even louder because I was sitting over the wing. Even louder because I was sitting between Kevin and the wing. Justin stuck his face over the back of our seats. "When do you think this plane was built? World War One?"

"Sir, please take your seat." The flight attendant tapped him on the shoulder, pushing him down gently. She smiled, but you could tell she was not looking forward to this flight with twenty unparented seniors. None of the other passengers looked amused, either.

Justin turned to ask her a question instead. "What if a bird gets sucked into one of those propeller things? I saw that on the news once. . . ."

"The bird dies," she said, stone-faced. Kevin got this look on his face that meant he was totally into the flight attendant now. I put on my headphones. She leaned across Kevin and pulled one ear bud from my ear. "The door is closed. Until we reach ten thousand feet, all electronics must be stowed and in the off position."

Kevin mumbled, loud enough for her to hear, "I am totally turned on right now."

Loud enough for Janna to hear, next to Justin. "Seriously, how does Maya put up with you? How does anyone put up with you?"

"Janna," I heard Justin say, "explain it to me again. How does the airplane stay up?"

"Oh my God, someone, please switch seats with Justin before my brain explodes."

"Gladly," I said, stepping across Kevin.

"Seats!" the flight attendant shouted from the back of the plane.

I sent her my most apologetic smile, but it wasn't really working. Instead, I saw Delaney. She was sitting near the back, and she had this death grip on her armrest already, and the plane hadn't even started taxiing. I couldn't tell who was beside her. Didn't look long enough to find out. When her mom dropped us off, we walked in opposite directions. Me, toward Kevin. Her, toward a bunch of kids in her classes. Classes that I definitely wasn't in.

I slid into the aisle seat next to Janna as Justin took mine. "He's going to crash the plane with his thoughts alone," she said as I tightened my seat belt.

Once we'd reached ten thousand feet, music was blaring in my ears, and Janna was sleeping with her head against the window. The plane shook, loudly, and Janna jerked her head up. She smiled at me, like she was making fun of her nerves.

It jerked again, and all the luggage shifted in the compartment above us. Then we dropped. Suddenly and quickly. And briefly, thankfully. Must've hit an air pocket.

"What was that?" Justin asked. And when Kevin didn't respond, his face filled the gap between the seats. I pulled off my headphones. "What the hell was that?" he asked.

"Turbulence," Janna said. "Can you stop freaking out *please*?" she asked.

"I've never been on a plane before," he said. "I'm just curious. I'm curious whether a plane is *supposed* to fall like that." And just as he said it, we hit another air pocket, and Janna instinctively grabbed onto my hand on the armrest.

"Yeah, well, I would appreciate *not* picturing the plane crashing," she said, and he turned back around. But then the plane started shaking again, like we were driving over boulders at sixty miles an hour.

"It's just physics, right?" I said.

She nodded and leaned forward and spoke in Justin's ear. "Just physics," she said. "You're fine."

I looked at her hand in mine and wondered if maybe this was how things happened. You cling to the person closest to you. And Delaney was always the person closest to me. I was the person closest to her. Proximity.

I cast a quick glance down the aisle. Her head was back, and her eyes were closed, and I could tell even from here that her knuckles were white on the armrests. I was thinking of all the ways I could take her mind off it. I let go of Janna and unbuckled my seat belt.

She gripped my arm. "What the hell are you doing?"

"Have to pee," I said.

Janna arched around the seat to look. "Right."

"Sir," the flight attendant called from her seat in the back. "Sit down. Now."

Delaney opened her eyes, saw me standing. Sat up straight. We hit another patch of turbulence, and I fell sideways, back into my seat.

"God, boys are dumb." Then she twisted in her seat so she was facing me. "What do you think, Decker?" Janna asked as the plane kept shaking. "Are we far enough away?" And a chill ran up my spine. "Or can it reach us, even here?"

"Stop," I said, and I put the headphones back on and turned the music up louder.

She pulled an earbud out and said, "It's not a joke," and I nodded. It wasn't. I understood. And then she balled up her jacket and used it as a pillow as she rested her head on my shoulder. I may have been dumb, but I was the closest thing to her.

As soon as we landed, safe and sound, someone shoved Justin in the shoulder. "Thanks, man."

"What?"

"Way to almost get us killed." Like his words, his fear, had created the turbulence.

Kevin smacked the back of Justin's head halfheartedly. He shook out his arms, like he was clearing himself of the last few hours. "Keep your thoughts to yourself next time," he said. Then shook one last time.

We all understood. It felt much better to blame the things we can't control on something real.

They'd been doing it for months. They were experts at it now.

Kevin stood up and reached for his luggage, and suddenly, I wanted to say something. I wanted to stand up for Justin. But I thought of what Janna had said, what she had been thinking. And as long as everyone was focused on Justin, nobody would remember Delaney, sitting on the back of the plane. The trade. The curse. So in the end, I let him take it. Turns out I was a coward after all.

We rode the T at rush hour in Boston. The subway car was crammed with people—college students and people on their way home from work—and we were all scattered throughout the car, gripping any free gap on the overhead bar or the standing poles.

Delaney's hair was in a long braid right in front of me. Between me and the pole. The subway car lurched, metal screaming against metal underneath us, and I grabbed for the pole in front of her, brushing her hair in the process. I felt her tense beside my arm. Guess she knew it was me. I heard Kevin laughing from the other end of the car. Janna, too. Delaney's hair was practically in my face. "Rough flight," I said.

"Yeah," she said, not turning around.

Wow. Profound, the both of us. I stared at the back of her head. Each part of her braid was a different shade of blond—one strand was almost white, the part the sun hit—and I wondered if she had done that on purpose. It didn't seem like something she would do, but it also seemed impossible for it to happen randomly. It was too perfect. And there was a chain around her neck. The clasp was off-center. I wanted to straighten it. I wanted to see what hung from the other end. Wanted to trace the chain around her neck, under the collar of her shirt.

"I . . ." I felt her whole body tense. Felt her holding her breath. The subway screeched, and we lurched forward together, and suddenly I was pressed against her back, and my free arm was around her waist. I wanted to be able to talk to her. The problem with having your girlfriend be your best friend is that you could lose both in an instant. I wondered if I could get one back. Problem was, I couldn't separate the parts of her, never could.

The doors separated, a gust of stale, cold air billowed in, and Mrs. Adams's loud voice carried over the crowd. "Anderville High, this is us!"

Not embarrassing at all.

"It's alphabetical," Janna said as we crammed into the elevator together. Which is why Justin was rooming with Parker Banyon.

"Come on," Justin said. "Fifty bucks to whoever trades with me."

"No can do," Kevin said. "Decker is my favorite."

"Ass," Justin said.

"I'll trade," Janna said, looking down at the key in her hand. "Room 521."

Justin raised an eyebrow at her. "Something about Parker I don't know? Who do I get to room with?"

"Delaney," she said. And the elevator went suddenly silent.

The doors opened on the fifth floor, and Janna stepped out. She saluted us. "Gentlemen," she said as the door slid across her face, sealing us in.

"Sometimes," Kevin said, "she reminds me so much of him."

Which is why it was both comforting and painful to have her around.

After we had dropped our bags and had dinner, and after we'd gone back to our room—with Justin, because he said his room smelled like ass—there was a knock on the door. Janna made this face at me as I opened the door. It was a face I recognized, just not from her. A glimpse of Carson as she raised one corner of her mouth, and then it was gone. She put a finger on my chest. "Let me in," she said.

"Room checks are in an hour. Come back after," Justin said.

"You're here," she said, sticking her hip out.

"Male genitalia, my friend," he said.

"Ugh." She covered her ears and sent me a pleading look.

"Okay, hey," I said. "I'll be back."

Nobody asked where I was going. Probably because I was

so freaking obvious it was pathetic. If Janna was here, then Delaney was alone. And there was something about being away from Falcon Lake that made this easier. Like maybe I could look at her. Talk to her.

I took the stairwell down two flights and saw the elevator doors shutting. Half her mouth, a hazel eye, looking down through the sliding door. Disappearing. Always.

Shit.

I raced down the stairwell, taking the steps two or three at a time, and exited at the main lobby. I saw her back, leaving through the revolving door. I thought maybe she was going running again, but she was in jeans, and her hair was loose.

Sometimes I felt like I was following a ghost, the way she lived on the outskirts of my vision. Like I was aware of her existence but tried to ignore it, but then some days ended up following it into the basement, where nothing good could ever happen.

Like now.

I followed her through the crowd of people—she walked with single-minded focus, like she knew exactly where she was headed, which was weird because she didn't know the area. And then I panicked that she was drawn to someone and was following them, and I started walking faster to keep up.

She stopped abruptly a few blocks later, at the edge of Boston. She stood in the grass, staring out at the river, like it had called to her. Or like it was drawing her in—maybe she could never escape the pull of the water, wanting her back.

She sat cross-legged on the edge, as if she was imagining her future here. But this time, I couldn't picture it.

My legs carried me forward, boldly, because of the crowd. The way I could disappear in it, become invisible. Until I was standing a few feet behind her, watching the wind kick up the water.

"What are you doing?" she asked, and I felt exposed.

"What are *you* doing?" I replied.

Her back stiffened, and I realized she hadn't been talking to me. She looked flustered as she stood up—about as flustered as I felt. She wasn't a ghost. She was a drug I couldn't stop taking. A habit I couldn't quite kick. I didn't understand why I couldn't stay away. Even now.

"Are you following me?"

Of course I was following her. "I was out for a walk."

Everything was different away from the lake. Like we were people with no history. Maybe this was our future— maybe we'd come here and we'd meet up, a year from now, two maybe, and we'd just . . . talk. Like the past didn't matter. Like I hadn't left her on the ice. Like she hadn't completely betrayed me. Delaney wanted me to pretend. I pretended. I sat down in the grass, and she sat down beside me, a few body lengths away. "What schools are you touring tomorrow?"

There was a list, and we were supposed to meet up tomorrow in the lobby with a specified teacher. I was still mostly undecided. Would probably go wherever Kevin ended up going.

Delaney kicked at the grass on the ground. Looked at the streetlight overhead, like she was buying time.

"I'm not gonna stalk you or anything," I said.

"That's a given."

And now I was getting irritated. I was making an effort and she wouldn't even go along with it. "It's not really a trick question," I said.

"I'm not going to any of them," she said.

Not what I was expecting.

"You change your mind about Boston?" Because of me? I wanted it to be because of me.

"No. I just have other plans."

Other plans. "Because . . ."

"Because I have an appointment with this guy." She unfolded and refolded her legs. "This guy doing his post-grad work. He's doing research. About, you know . . ."

No, I didn't know. And then I understood. "Brains?"

"More like . . . pheromones. But related to brains. So, yeah."

That's what she'd told my dad. She'd said it was like pheromones. I wondered if she'd been studying up on it for a while. But she'd never said anything to me.

"I don't understand . . . why you need to talk to this guy." When what I meant was, I don't understand why you need to tell this guy about you. It felt private. Fragile.

"Because I don't understand, don't you get it?" I thought of her notebook. The numbers, meaning nothing. "Sometimes, everything makes sense: somebody is sick and they are going to die. But sometimes, I can't tell. Like with Maya's mom . . ."

My stomach turned. Her, still alive. My dad, gone. "Because she's still alive?"

"No, because I can't feel anything. I used to get pulled right there. And I saw her once, sitting with Maya out by the lake, in a wheelchair. And I went back home, because I remember thinking . . . I remember thinking they wouldn't have a lot of these moments left." I wondered if she knew what she was saying. "But now when I go by her house to pick her up . . . there's nothing. I feel nothing. I thought maybe it was fading. I asked Maya if her mom was better, because I hadn't seen her, I kept asking, but she said everything was the same. So I thought maybe I was getting better . . . and then . . ."

And then my dad.

"I don't understand," she whispered.

"And you think some stranger is going to help you understand?"

"He's not a stranger, exactly. I've been talking to him," she said. "And now I have an appointment."

"You've already told him?"

"No. Not really. His study is on the idea that humans have the ability to sense pheromones, that our bodies can involuntarily respond to signals that typically only other animals respond to. But that it's gone latent or something. So I sent him an e-mail . . . told him I did. I said I'd had a brain injury. I said I had changed. He called and asked me to come. I told him I already had plans to be here."

This sounded like the equivalent of online dating, like she was meeting some stranger at a bar and had to cross her fingers he wasn't there for some other reason. I knew she was smarter than that, had probably done her homework, but it made me feel out of control. It made me feel like *she* was out of control.

Everything was out of control. Nothing like it had been planned. Not our plans. Not mine.

Her phone beeped, and she frowned at it, then silenced it.

She stretched her legs out in the grass in front of her. "Also," she said, "I have no clue what I want to go to college for anyway." Which was the most un-Delaney-like thing to say.

I shrugged. "You can do whatever you want." Whatever she chose to do, she'd be great at it. Nothing slowed her down. Not a coma. Not Troy. Not me.

"No, I mean, I don't know what I'm *supposed* to do."

"Well, from what I've learned from the majority of movies set in college, apparently we're supposed to be generally irresponsible and directionless. I, for one, am really looking forward to it."

She rolled her eyes at me, trying not to smile.

"You're thinking too hard," I said. "Do what you want."

"There's got to be a purpose, right?" she asked. "Because otherwise I'm just some tragic character from Greek literature."

"Okay, try not to freak out," I said, "but I actually know who you're talking about. That chick who could see the future, but nobody believed her, so she couldn't stop it."

She smiled. "Cassandra."

We were both sitting in the grass with our knees bent,

facing the river. But she was looking at me, and I was looking at her. And it was just us in this moment, with no history.

This would be the part where I moved closer, put my arm around her. "I miss him, too," she said.

And instead of moving closer, my head was between my knees and everything about being here, about living here, felt wrong. Like maybe I was leaving him behind.

"When in July?" I asked.

I just said it. No premeditation. Her whole body went stiff, but I had to know. It mattered.

"I'm not really in the mood to get yelled at," she said.

"One question," I said. Because there was only one that mattered to me right then. She stared at me, the air between us charged. "July Fourth. . . . Did you know?"

"No," she said. I felt the biggest sense of relief. Something uncoiling inside of me. "It was the next day."

The next day I had seen her at work, and she'd hugged me tight and buried her face in my shoulder, not letting go until our boss cleared her throat as she passed. I'd smiled at her. Kissed her. Thinking she'd meant something else. But everything she'd done that day, and in the month after, meant something else.

I could hear someone kayaking close to shore, but I couldn't see it in the dark. Just heard the dip of an oar, the sound of the boat skimming the water, and then another dip.

Listen.

"It freezes over," she said. Her eyes were wide when she looked at me. "I didn't know rivers could freeze, but they can. If they're slow."

The wind blew in off the water, moving her hair. Ever since Delaney fell through the ice, I felt like something was chasing me, right up against my back. It still was. *Move faster,* it whispered. *I'm coming.*

Even here.

I edged back from the water, but it didn't feel far enough. "We missed room check," I said, even though I wasn't sure if that was true. I needed her away from the water. I needed her *always* away from the water.

"I know," she said, squinting at the dark water.

"You know?"

She pointed to her phone, then stood up and brushed her pants off.

"You set an alarm for room check?"

She put a hand on her hip, just like she'd done the day my dad died, standing knee-deep in Falcon Lake. "Of course I set an alarm for room check."

And she knowingly missed room check.

I rubbed my hand over my face so she wouldn't see me smiling. And when she reached a hand down to help me up, I took it.

We walked back slowly, sharing the same space, in silence.

We ran into our advisor in the lobby, holding a clipboard. Apparently we weren't the only ones to miss room check. She didn't even look concerned. Delaney was starting to apologize, but she just waved us past. "Go," she said as she made a mark next to our names.

We took the elevator up together, too. She got off on the

fifth floor. She didn't ask me to stay. I didn't offer to. "Good night," she said as the doors closed behind her.

Kevin was in the seating area on our floor with a few other seniors. Everyone knew that, after check-in, we pretty much had free reign anyway. As long as you didn't make a scene. The waivers we signed said we had to check in to our rooms by nine; it didn't specify what we had to do after that. Justin's brothers said as long as you stayed in the hotel and didn't do anything illegal, you were in the clear. It was a big hotel.

Kevin jerked his head to the side, motioning for me to walk with him. "You are not going to believe this," he said, his mouth splitting into a wide grin. "We've been evicted."

"By who?"

"Justin."

"Bullshit," I said, walking toward our room.

"And Janna," he added.

I stopped walking. "No."

"I wish I was lying," he said, but he was still smiling for all he was worth. "Oh, trust me, I wish I was lying. I was in the room for check-in, which you missed, FYI, and then afterward, I went down to the bar to see if I could get served. Which you can't, FYI. And also, apparently, that's where the teachers hang out. Funny."

"And?"

"Right. And I come back up and someone is *in my bed* except it's *two people in my bed* and Justin's all, 'Shit, I thought you were out for the night.' And I'm all, 'How the hell did you get in here? And who the hell is that?' Justin was like, 'I took the key from Decker's wallet,' so you know, you might want to keep a closer eye on your shit. But anyway, she tried to hide, but it was totally her."

"Are you sure?" I asked. I had a hard time picturing Janna with Justin. Then again, it's not like I was paying all that much attention.

"The question you should be asking is, where do we sleep?"

We ended up knocking on the door of Justin and Parker's room a little after midnight. Parker looked somewhat confused, but he always looked like that, so it's hard to say if he was really thinking anything at all. Kevin stole Justin's bed, and also dumped Justin's shit out all over the bathroom, just because kicking us out was kind of a dick move.

I had to sleep on the freaking floor. Which seemed about right. I hadn't had a bed in over a month.

Screw you, universe.

Justin barged into our room—his room—before six. He saw me on the floor and said, "Ha." And something about that, about him sounding just like I pictured the universe laughing at me, filled me with anger. Or maybe it was the fact that, when I signed up for this trip, I pictured sneaking into Delaney's room. Not sleeping on some random floor. Alone.

I stood up and ran at him, even though I was half-asleep. I pushed him back against the wall. I'd guess we'd usually match up pretty fairly in a fight, but I had surprise on my side. And rage. I drew blood before Kevin pulled me off. Parker was sitting up in his bed, his hair like something out of an eighties horror flick, looking totally disoriented.

"Gah," Justin said, bent over against the wall, looking at the blood in his hands. "I have an interview, you asshole."

"Hope you slept well," I said.

I pushed past him out into the hall, the light too bright. Kevin caught up with me before we reached our room, which was good since I didn't actually have a key. He put his hand on my shoulder. Then patted the back of my neck. Looked at his bed, decided against it, and took a shower.

When his shower turned off, I could still hear water. Rain, like Delaney had warned me. I wondered where she'd be today. If there was any point to me going on any of these tours, anyway. I had no clue what I wanted to do here. I was here because I was following a girl. Her.

I looked at the clock, at the door, at the schedule.

I was still following her.

Chapter

10

Ten. That's what she'd said on the phone. Ten. Not ten at night. Ten in the morning. She'd probably leave around nine. No, this was Delaney. Eight thirty. I checked the clock and started getting ready. I was outside her door by 8:29.

She opened the door at 8:34, an umbrella in her hand, and did a double take when she saw me. "I forgot to pack an umbrella," I said.

She smiled, then stopped. Raised her hand to my mouth, still stinging from Justin's fist. She put her hand on my lip. "What happened?" Then remembered she wasn't supposed to touch me, definitely not my mouth, and pulled her hand back like I was an animal ready to bite.

I ran my tongue along my bottom lip, which was swollen and cut but wasn't bleeding anymore. "Fight. Not even. Skirmish."

She frowned at me, and I pointed to the bathroom door,

where I heard the shower going. "You know where Janna was last night?"

"I have no idea where she was last night."

"In my room," I said, and Delaney turned this horrible color, like she was going to be sick. She looked like she did when she heard Kevin talking about me and Tara.

It took until May for her to finally ask me about Tara. Not so much ask as assume. We'd been hanging out with Kevin, who was talking about Tara—about him and Tara specifically—and he'd turned to me and said, "Well, *you* know," without even caring that Delaney was right there. Like I said, he could be a real ass.

And Delaney looked like she always did right before she got sick.

"Uh, no, I don't," I'd said.

And Kevin looked at Delaney and said, "Oops."

She didn't say anything. Not until we were back in the car. "Okay, about that," I said.

"Don't," she said, and she put her hands over her ears like she did when she was ten. "I hate it, okay? I hate it. I don't want to hear it. And I don't want to . . . picture it."

My history with Tara was something I wished I could erase, but I couldn't. But I thought of my memory of Delaney and Carson on my couch, and I understood. I couldn't stomach thinking about it. So I didn't.

"It makes me physically sick. Like, I want to throw up. I hate that she knows you like *that*," she said, with her head against the window. It took me a second to realize what she meant.

"Oh," I said. "*Oh.* No. Uh-uh. We never. I didn't."

We were at a stoplight, and I cut my eyes to her for a second and added, "I haven't."

"Oh," she said. Then she put her feet up on my dashboard, and her whole body seemed to relax. The light turned green, and I thought the conversation was done. We were moving again when she said, "Do you want to?" I moved my foot to the brake, and the car behind me honked, jarring me back to reality.

I laughed. Turned the wipers on by accident when I was reaching for the turn signal.

"I mean," she added, "hypothetically. In general. Not, like, *right now.*"

And I thought: *Yes, right now.* I was watching the traffic. Watching the road. "Not in general," I said. "Yes, with you."

"Okay," she said, and I spent that night and the next three wondering what the hell she meant by that. Like okay, yes? Or okay, good to know. I should've asked her back. I should've put in all those nice-guy addendums, like, *if you're ready, when you're ready, but it's okay if not.*

I wondered how long it had been eating her up—the thought of me and Tara. How much it had hurt her, though she didn't mention it for months.

And now she was turning red, looking ill, like I was telling her about Janna to hurt her on purpose. "No," I said. "*No.* I wasn't there. Justin was. I had no place to sleep. And I was really freaking cranky this morning."

That at least got a ghost of a smile. And I thought, *we can do this.* I can talk to this side of her.

She stepped back into her room and came out with another umbrella. It was yellow. It had a duck for a handle. I turned it over in my hand. "Uh, trade?" I asked.

She shook her head.

I held the umbrella out to her again. "This is from second grade," I said. I remembered her carrying it at the bus stop.

She shrugged, smiled as she pulled the door shut behind her. "I told you to pack your own."

I loved that she knew I wouldn't.

It wasn't until we were in the lobby that she asked where I was going. "With you," I said.

She stopped walking and I said, "Can we please not argue about this. I don't want to argue anymore. About anything."

She was looking at me, trying to see what I meant, I guess, but I couldn't look her in the eye right then. She pushed through the door, not arguing. Except I could see every argument on her face, anyway.

It was hard to tell how much it was raining from inside the hotel. It wasn't like at home, where you could hear the wind rattle the windows or the rain beating on the roof or the ice bouncing off the walls. Here, everything sounded protected and sterile, and it was a shock to swing through the revolving door to a freaking deluge.

Delaney raised her black (nonembarrassing) umbrella over her head, the spokes directly level with my face, so I couldn't even hover under it if I wanted to. She twirled her umbrella and grinned at me—she was nervous about today, I could tell. Otherwise she wouldn't be twirling her umbrella and grinning at me. Delaney was decidedly not a twirler. "What's the matter?" she asked. "Your umbrella not working?"

It was too late anyway. My clothes were soaked through. I felt rain seeping through my sneakers to my socks. Felt it clinging to my hair, my eyelashes, everything. I grabbed her free hand. Let it go. Grabbed the umbrella instead. Watched her eyes widen in horror the second before the rain turned her blond hair darker and pressed her clothes to her skin. I watched her face break into the biggest smile I'd seen in months the second before she lunged under the umbrella, an inch from me, smiling up at me.

It was so easy here. Away. No history. I wished I could meet her here. I wished I could meet her here for the first time.

She was pressed up against my side, and I flashed back to months earlier, her doing the same, leaning into me and smiling while keeping secrets in her head, while my dad was starting to disappear. I felt myself pulling away. I handed her the umbrella and let the rain drown out the memories. "Let's go," I said, following the signs for the subway stop.

We were in a basement. Everything was labeled "lab this" and "lab that," but there was no getting around the fact that we were in a basement. And seeing as it was Saturday, most of the doors were locked, the rooms dark. The hallways were half-lit, and our steps echoed as we walked across the floor. My sneakers squeaked, leaving wet footprints behind, and I shook my hair out as I walked behind her. She read the numbers off as we approached. "LL3 . . . LL5 . . . here." We stood in front of an open door. Some guy who looked nothing like a scientist sat on a stool, perched over a lab bench with his back to us.

Delaney knocked on the open door, and the guy spun around. His hair hung in his eyes, and he had on a worn gray T-shirt and worn jeans. I bet he was the type who bought them that way to begin with. I didn't like the way he smiled when he saw her. Didn't like the way her body relaxed when she saw him smiling. "Delaney?" he asked, rising off the stool, strutting—yes, strutting—across the room. Scientists shouldn't be allowed to strut. He stuck out his hand and she took it.

"Sorry, I know I'm early. Nice to meet you, Dr.—"

"Josh," he said. *Josh.* Dr. Josh. Seriously? He looked like he was born about six months before us. And then he looked at me, like he wasn't sure if I was here with Delaney or just some guy wandering the basement, dripping wet.

"This is Decker," she said, waving her hand at me.

"Hey," Dr. Josh said, no hand extended. He did the whole guy-assessment thing. I wrung my shirt out on the floor. He cleared his throat, and Delaney made this pained expression. And then this guy masquerading as a doctor launched into a description of his research. He gave us a tour of the lab, and the one attached to it. He told us about the animals he'd been researching, of the way pheromones typically work. And about how humans have the parts necessary for receiving and processing these signals, but that the connection to the brain isn't active. That the organs are thought to be vestigial. Like an appendix.

But that Delaney, with the changes to her brain—neuroplasticity, he called it—might be an example of its functionality. He said that he was excited. Very excited. The dude was dripping excitement, practically drooling over her, leading her around the lab, and she was nodding and *uh-huh*-ing, but I could see her eyes glazing over. Her spine straighten. What the hell had she told this guy? I took a step toward her, put my hand almost on her back. Almost.

We went back to his work area, and he pulled out a second stool for Delaney. None for me. He rearranged a few beakers on the shelf, reaching behind them while standing on his toes before pulling down a pen. He winked at Delaney. "The undergrads keep stealing my pens."

He rested a yellow notepad on his knee and started asking questions. But it sounded like he already knew a lot. "So, after your brain injury, you soon realized you could . . . sense things that you couldn't before. Can you explain that a little more?"

Delaney cleared her throat. "Yeah, sure. I could tell when people were sick." She was choosing her words carefully.

"How, exactly could you tell? And what made you realize that?"

"It was like an itch, in the center of my brain. Like a pull I'd feel toward someone. I didn't know what it was at first. When they were really sick, my hand would start twitching. My doctor thought I was having a seizure, but the EEG showed no abnormal activity. But then I realized, my neighbor had emphysema. A friend with epilepsy . . ." She never said they died. Just that they were sick.

She was smart. She wasn't telling him everything.

I loved that I was the only one who really knew.

Josh swiveled from side to side on his stool. "Several animals have something like this, you know. The death pheromone. It's usually a signal to leave one of their own behind, for the betterment of the group. Or, in ants, it's a sign to remove them from the habitat."

"But it pulls her," I said, to show him that he was wrong. To show him I knew her better. Not a push. A pull. Not like animals. Not to leave them behind.

"Interesting," he said. "Tell me, are there any other pheromones you've been able to sense?"

"I'm not sure . . . I don't know what you mean," she said.

"There are danger ones, and sex ones." He said it so matter-of-factly, so scientifically, but Delaney turned red and cut her eyes to me for a fraction of a second.

Josh grinned. "I see," he said. But I didn't. Was he saying that Delaney was only interested in me because of pheromones?

"No," she said, like she could hear my thoughts. But he kept scribbling.

"Um," he said, tapping his pen against the pad of paper. "I'd like to show you something. We need the computer in the next lab."

"Okay, sure," Delaney said, but she said it slowly, like she wasn't okay or sure. She looked at me for a split second.

"Go ahead," I said. "I'll keep your seat warm."

Not the answer she wanted. Not even close. But I was standing, and I was taller than Dr. Josh, and I could see the glint of a metal corner on the shelf where his hand had just been reaching for a pen. Whatever else was up there was definitely not a pen.

They left the room, the doctor talking the whole time, Delaney shooting nervous glances over her shoulder. I waited until I could hear him through the walls of the next room, then walked over to the beakers where he'd gotten his pen. I ran my hand along the shelf, stopping at a cold metal rectangle. I pulled it down. It was one of those digital sound recorders that Kevin tried to use in class instead of taking notes once. And it was on.

I turned it off before stuffing it in the waistband of my pants and pulling my shirt down overtop. Then I strode over to the next lab, my muscles twitching in anticipation. I cracked my knuckles against the sides of my legs.

They were sitting on stools again, across from each other. The computer monitor was on, displaying a diagram of the human head, complete with random arrows and brightly colored regions. He had taken out this instrument, like the kind my doctor used to check for ear infections, and was holding it out to Delaney, like a question.

"Yeah, I don't think so," I said. They both looked surprised to see me. "I mean, do you have a waiver or something? Something for her to sign granting you permission to examine her and stating what you could use this information for?"

"I'm not really at the stage of research where I'm ready to publish—"

"Then what. The hell. Are you doing?"

He leaned back in his chair and scanned me slowly. "It's called *research*, kid. It's called *helping out your girlfriend*. It's called *asking questions to get some answers*."

Not for her. For *him*. Delaney stood up. "We actually have to be somewhere soon. College tours."

He smiled at her, like he didn't realize he was making her uncomfortable. "Will you be coming here next year?"

I wondered if she felt the same thing, something chasing her. Like she couldn't get away from it. Like it would find her anywhere. "Not sure," she said. "I don't think I could get into most of these places." And I wondered when she'd gotten so good at lying so effortlessly. She grabbed my hand as she walked away. I put an arm around her waist. Both of us, lying and lying and lying.

We didn't speak until the elevator opened on the ground floor. "Thanks," she whispered, and the word echoed through the empty corridor. "I never thought about all of that. Down there, you sounded so much like your dad." She shook off a chill as she pushed through the door and out into the rain, but we stayed pressed against the building, under the awning. "That was awkward. Crap."

"No," I said, "that was *creepy*." I lifted my shirt and pulled out the recorder.

Her eyes went wide. "Where did you get that? You stole that?"

"I *got* this from where he allegedly kept his pens. And yes I stole it. He was *taping* you."

Her mouth fell open. But then she closed it. "Because it's research . . ."

"No, it's *you*. It's *us*. And he has no right to it. You aren't research."

"Actually, I kind of am." Her eyes widened even further. "If that's his research," she whispered, pointing at the recorder in my hands. "There's probably more on it. Other stuff. *His* stuff."

"I don't care," I said. Couldn't she see? I only cared about *her*.

"He's going to know we took it."

"Still don't care," I said. And he couldn't ask us about it without confessing that he was taping us without permission in the first place.

"We need to give it back," she said. "It could be important."

"There's no way he's getting this back," I said as I slid the recorder into my back pocket.

"Just"—she was reaching for it—"give it to me. I'll delete my part, and I'll bring it back. Okay?"

"Yeah, no. *I'll* mail it back to him, after I delete your part."

She narrowed her eyes at me. "I promise," I said. "But you're staying out of it. He already has your *number*, Delaney. God, what were you thinking?"

And then I felt that thing that had been chasing us here, still. Not Falcon Lake. Not the water. Our past. Everything between us. And now it was here. "What I was *thinking* was that I needed to talk to someone. I was *thinking* I needed help understanding. I was *thinking* that I am, actually, something to research. I was thinking that maybe he could help."

"Oh, no, he can't. He's not interested in helping you. He wants to help *himself*. His research."

"It's not like I have a whole lot of options. Who should I be talking to, without my parents or my doctor thinking I'm losing it again?"

"*I* was right there. *I* could help you. Not him, *me*." Not my dad, me. Not this doctor, me. "You're supposed to talk to *me*."

She tilted her head to the side, closed her eyes. "Really?" she asked. "How about now, Decker? Who should I be talking to now?"

She nodded at me when I said nothing. She handed me the umbrella, held the duck from second grade over her head, and checked her watch. "There's still time to catch the one p.m. tours. Do you know where you want to go?"

I didn't, but it looked like she knew exactly where she wanted to be, so I nodded.

There must've been some school football game starting soon, because the street and the sidewalk flooded with people despite the rain. Drunk people, happy people, sad people. People. And suddenly I could see my future as clearly as she was seeing hers. I saw her disappear. I saw people come and go. I saw us swept in opposite directions. I saw her look for me for a minute, lose sight of me, and start moving.

I saw her leave.

*   *   *

We all slept in our regular rooms that night. I hadn't seen Justin or Janna all day. I didn't see Kevin until later at night, when we were going to sleep. I hadn't gone on any tours, just wandered the city, feeling lost. I told Mrs. Adams that I had a stomach bug, and since nobody else skipped, I guess she believed me.

The next morning, it was still raining, but our flight left on time. On the back of the shuttle from the subway to the airport terminal, I heard Justin saying, "But how can they fly in the rain?"

And a collective groan rose from over half the bus.

I smiled to myself.

Delaney was in the front row, sitting next to this girl, Tess, from her classes. After we got to the airport, as we were all going through security, I pulled Tess back by the elbow.

She scrunched her face and looked around. Yeah, we probably had never had a conversation before. "Are you sitting with Delaney?" I asked.

"Uh, yeah," she said, throwing her shoes onto the conveyer belt. "Unless you were planning on it?"

"She hates to fly," I said, ignoring her question.

"I noticed," she said.

"So this time how about you try to distract her or something." Then I threw my bag in front of hers and jumped her place in line.

I walked past Justin's row on the plane and said, "Hey." He had a cut on his bottom lip, but it didn't look too bad.

"Hey," he said. I slid into the row behind him. Conversation over.

Janna had a ball cap on and her hair flew wildly out of the bottom in every direction. I saw Justin grin at her, saw her eyes go wide, watched as she passed his row and slid in beside me instead.

I must've been smiling at her because she snapped, "What?"

"Nothing," I said.

She pulled the brim of her hat lower and slouched in her seat. "Shut up," she said.

Kevin slid into the seat beside Justin, but not before turning around and resting his chin on the back of his chair with a huge smile. "Hiiiii, Janna," he said. Justin punched him in the arm, and he turned back around.

"Don't get me wrong," I said. "I think he's a great guy, and I hear he's totally—"

"Shut. Up," she said. But it was too late. Kevin and I couldn't stop laughing, even though Justin smacked him over the head in the seat in front of us.

"You know what *I* heard," Kevin said. And that set us off again.

Joanne picked us up at the airport, and home started seeping in, straight to my bones. We arrived at her house, and I realized that this was it. The last time we'd be together. The last time I'd sneak over to her house or she'd sneak over to mine, or we'd sit on the floor of her room doing nothing or different things or the same thing. That next year, not too long from now, this will be done.

That she was going to leave. And maybe I'd go somewhere, be some guy that nobody knows. Never knowing the version of me before my father died. Never knowing the guy who once loved the girl next door. Or maybe I wouldn't go anywhere. It all felt the same anyway. I could go clear across the country, hear a drip of water, and be right back here again.

This place wouldn't change. But we would.

In a year, I won't be mad at her. I won't be so angry I can't look at her, won't feel the panic clawing at my throat. I won't feel any of those things because I will not see her at all.

I felt my breath coming fast, felt the panic coming on. I saw Delaney watching me in the rearview mirror. Because now she knew. She knew I was thinking about her. She turned around in her seat and said, "Hey," like she was reminding me that she was still here.

"I'm okay," I said, leaning my head back against the seat. But couldn't she see what was coming? She was still going to disappear from my life. And it would be because of me. She was going to be exactly where she said she'd be. But I wouldn't.

I promised her I would. Months ago. Even though I'd meant it when I said it, I wondered whether—like everything else between us—it now counted as a lie.

Chapter

11

July Fourth. I hadn't seen her for two days—my dad and I had been camping, and we'd been stuck in holiday traffic, so I didn't get home before we were supposed to meet up with everyone for the fireworks. She'd texted that she was going to wait for me. I told her to go. There was this field, two blocks past Main Street, and everyone, my parents included, took picnic blankets and hung out before and then after. I told her I'd meet her there.

It was dusk when I arrived, hours after I was supposed to meet her, and the fireworks were getting ready to start. I saw her standing with Kevin and Tara and Maya—this was right before Kevin dumped Tara and hooked up with Maya, but you could feel it starting already.

I saw her back, the way the breeze lifted her hair up off her back for a second before it settled back down. I saw her turn her face and smile at something Maya said. I pushed around people. Past people. She didn't hear me coming.

I was standing right behind her, and she was watching the sky, like she was waiting for something to happen. I brushed her hair to the side. Kissed her shoulder. Felt her melt back into me. She didn't turn around at first—I was embarrassing her, with everyone standing right there, watching. I knew I was. I didn't care. I wrapped my arms around her waist and kissed her neck.

Then she spun around, threaded her arms around my neck, pressed herself to me so hard I almost stumbled backward, and she kissed me. I mean she *kissed* me.

Guess I wasn't embarrassing her. Someone cleared their throat. We ignored them. She was still kissing me.

We were standing in the middle of a field in the middle of a crowd in the middle of an event and I didn't care. She didn't care.

"So, you missed me," I said, still so close that my lips brushed over hers as I spoke.

She pulled away from me for a second. Got this look like she was coming up with one of her epic plans, and I braced myself for her idea: maybe to climb a tree to get a better view, to run to the store and get snacks, to time the fireworks for some project I didn't understand. I'd say yes, whatever it was. I'd say yes.

"Do you want to go?" she asked.

I'd just gotten there. The fireworks were about to start. It took me a second to realize what she meant, with her fingers hooked into my belt loops, and the way she was pressed up against me, and the way I could tell she was blushing, even in the dark.

My stomach dropped. I thought, *Please mean what I think you mean.* "Yes," I said. "Yes. Yes."

"So . . . yes?" she asked. She was smiling, and she was nervous.

"I mean maybe, I don't know, let me think about it. . . ." But I was pulling her by both hands, and I was laughing. I was practically running.

Nobody watched us leave—they had all turned away; we were probably embarrassing ourselves. I didn't care.

She stopped in the middle of the street before we got back to my house and said, "I love you," with this really serious expression, like she hadn't said it before.

"I know," I said.

"No, I mean . . ." She waved her arms around like she couldn't come up with the word she was looking for.

"Delaney," I said, and my arm was around her waist, and my face was an inch from hers. "I *know.*"

I remember thinking I was the luckiest person on earth.

I told her I couldn't stand to be away from her.

I told her I'd follow her anywhere.

"Promise me," she said, with her arms wrapped around me.

I promised her over and over and over.

I looked at her now, sitting in the front seat of the car. That was only three months ago. I'd been so stupid to think that anything lasted forever. Not a promise. Not a life. Not us, either.

Not in the way we had been, anyway.

Joanne pulled the car into her driveway, but I was looking at my house. It was Sunday, so nobody was working, but I could tell there'd been progress. I wondered how much longer it would be before we could move in. I walked in the front door, and my mom tilted her head toward our house and said, "Shouldn't be long, now," like she could read my thoughts. "How was Boston?"

"Big," I said at the same time that Delaney said, "Crowded."

I'd planned to go to Boston for her. I was making every decision about my future for a girl. And one I wasn't even seeing anymore. I was a cliché. It had never even occurred to me to go to Boston before she mentioned it. I hadn't even attended a single tour. It wasn't for me.

"I think," I said, "I want to stay in Maine."

I knew Delaney heard me when I said it. I felt her pause. Felt the whole room pause. But it was true. In that moment, with my mom ruffling my hair, and looking at that house I'd grown up in, where my dad had lived, I wanted to stay.

Or maybe this was all part of the curse. It got a hold of my ankles, tethering me to the earth. Taking and taking, like I had taken from it, taking and making me watch: *everyone but her.*

I pulled the recorder out of my luggage after everyone had gone to bed and listened to the last recording. He'd started it after we entered the room, and Delaney's discomfort, his curiosity, my annoyance whispered around me. I hit Delete.

Then I went to the saved files and listened to the previous recording, to make sure I wasn't missing anything.

It was his voice.

"Delaney," he said. "A high school senior. Claims to have an affinity toward sickness."

Delete.

The one before it, I could hear Delaney's voice. "Ten? Yes, yes, I can make it." He had taped their phone conversation.

Delete.

And before that, another phone call. Dr. Josh was fishing for information. "Tell me about the accident that led to the brain injury."

"I fell through the ice," she said. "I was under for a long time."

"Where was this?" He was searching for something—he was searching for *us*.

"A lake. I was walking across a lake."

"And the EMS team managed to pull you out and revive you on scene? That must have made the news."

"No, no, I was in a coma. And no, not them. My . . ." I could hear her searching for a word. "My best friend rescued me."

"She must be very brave," he said. I winced.

"He is," she said.

The tape cut for a second, and then the doctor's voice was back. "The subject won't tell me who or where she is exactly, but her area code suggests Maine. The subject evades questions, and she has not told her personal physician. Which begs the question: Why?"

This whole recording was a study of Delaney. It was her story and mine. It was our history. I listened to the whole thing, everything that was left, three more times before wiping it clean.

I waited for her in my driveway Monday morning, like I'd been doing since last week. After being away from here, after being able to talk to her in Boston, it felt a little like sliding back to normal. The *normal* we had been before we were together. Before everything.

She seemed to sense something had shifted, too. She hopped in the minivan and held her hands in front of the heating vent. "Morning," she said.

"You know you have to wait for the car to turn on for that to work," I said.

"New idea," she said as I turned the key. "College in Florida."

I turned the heat up, ignoring the fact that she obviously wanted to talk about the whole staying-in-Maine thing. "Which school did you end up seeing?" I asked.

She bent and flexed her fingers in front of the vents a few times before speaking. "I was heading for Harvard, and then I got . . . I don't know. Distracted. Or overwhelmed. Both." She sat back in her seat and turned to face me. "I think I messed up," she said. "What if that guy comes looking for me? What if he talks to my parents, or my doctor?"

"Easy. You call him a lying pedophile and it's your word against his."

Out of the corner of my eye, I could tell she was giving me that *you're-being-ridiculous* look. "I'm serious."

So was I. "Delaney, do you really mean to tell me you skipped a college tour because you're worried about some sketchy guy?" Totally unlike Delaney, who did her homework in the hospital after almost dying so she wouldn't fall behind.

I thought of how the choice to leave her on the ice had changed me.

And that this choice had somehow changed her, too.

And I thought that maybe it *was* possible to forgive someone for anything.

"I don't know," she said. "I got there, but did you notice? Everyone in Boston walks so *fast*."

I bit the inside of my cheek to keep from laughing.

"So I wandered around," she said. She shrugged. "Maybe Boston isn't for me, either."

It was my turn to talk, but there was too much meaning in her sentence. Too many questions layered underneath.

When I parked, she said, "Thanks," then hopped out of the car. She paused for a second, I guess to see if I was going to walk with her, but I stayed in the car, watching her go.

I forgive you, I thought, willing it to be true. A mistake. A horrible mistake. A mistake that she can't take back, that would eat her up inside. Like me leaving her on the center of the ice.

Let's cut across, I'd said.

Your boyfriend's waiting, I'd said, harassing her about Carson. And then I left her there.

We don't have all day! I'd yelled. She slipped. She fell. She disappeared under the surface of the lake.

I could never take that back. But on the recording, she had only mentioned me saving her.

We are bigger than a fight, I thought. *We are bigger than a mistake.* And I resolved, right then, that the next time I had her alone in the same room, I'd forgive her.

"Hey," Janna said, tapping on my window. I rolled down the window. "Planning on getting out anytime soon? Or are you planning to stare at the school entrance for another five minutes?"

I got out of the car, and she kept talking. "I'm going to apply to BC. And Tufts. Did you go to BU? What did you think? I can't decide." She kept talking, but more like to keep me from saying anything.

Then she caught sight of something over my shoulder. Kevin's spare car pulled into the parking lot. His spare car probably cost more than 90 percent of the cars in the parking lot. Maya slid out of the passenger seat. Justin got out of the back. Janna cringed and made a beeline for the school entrance when she saw them coming.

"First-string car still in the shop?" I asked.

"Ha," he said. Then he got this weird look on his face, ran his hand through his hair, and said, "There was water in the engine."

"From the rain?" Maya asked. Her eyes were bloodshot, like she'd been up all night.

"Uh, no. Otherwise there'd be water in *everyone's* engine."

He was telling us something that Maya wouldn't understand. We heard him. Water in the engine. Water in my house. We'd all pulled her out of the lake. We'd all taken her back. It was coming for us all.

Kevin shrugged, like he was shaking something off. "Anyway. Should be fine. Just have to drive that hunk of metal for a couple more days."

I wondered if we were all seeing the same thing in the pause that followed. If we were all seeing different versions of the frozen lake, of me with the rope, of them pulling me up, of Delaney, still and blue.

Maya cleared her throat. "How does that happen, then?"

He shook his head rapidly. "It can happen if you drive through a big puddle or something."

But we all knew it hadn't rained that much. And we were all probably thinking of Falcon Lake. The silence was eating at us all, and Maya was looking between each of us, trying to put something together.

"You look tired," I said. But when she cut her eyes to me, I thought maybe I was wrong. Maybe she looked sad instead. And then I wanted to take it back.

"Got back late last night," she said.

"Speaking of," Kevin said, "I think your brother hates me."

"You were practically trying to grope his sister in the front yard," Justin said.

"In my defense, I had no idea he was on the front porch." He looked at Maya. "A little warning next time?"

"I pushed you away," she said. "How much more warning do you want? I told you he drove me back yesterday."

"You didn't tell me he was still here."

"Seriously? Use some common sense, Kev." It was the same way she'd spoken to me when she told me to grow up, and I could tell from Kevin's face that he had never seen this side of her before.

And before Kevin could respond, Maya turned to me. "Is Delaney here?"

"Inside," I said, as she brushed past me.

Justin hadn't been paying attention. He was scanning the parking lot. "Have you seen Janna?" he asked, a ridiculous smile across his face.

"Also inside," I said. "Avoiding you." Which did nothing to dim his smile.

There were blue and gold posters hung throughout the hall. And streamers. And anyone who played a sport was wearing his or her uniform. They would be wearing them all week, game or not.

The first week of October was traditionally homecoming, and it was traditionally the start of the weather getting cold, and traditionally it was fun. The best part about homecoming was that we didn't have the most traditional part—we didn't really have a dance. It was kind of the same: gaudy decorations and the school gym and music in the background, but it wasn't like a dance-dance. As in: we didn't have to dress up. Or pick dates or any of the stuff that took the fun out of most events. You just showed up each night, and a bunch of alumni came, and everyone hung out and ate food— and then we spilled over into the town.

We used to go to Justin's lake house, especially with his brothers home—they didn't go too far when they left for school. Most of us didn't. But Maya and her mom were in that house now, and apparently her brother, too. Kevin asked if she could have a party, and she looked at him like he was the biggest moron on the planet. He kind of was.

I didn't really have plans, and I didn't see Delaney in the parking lot after school, so I went back to her house, hoping to catch her there—but instead ended up doing homework, alone, in the dining room. So when Justin's car (full of Justin and his brothers) honked and then honked again outside Delaney's, I went. I was looking for Delaney—since she hadn't been at home, I figured she was here. At the school gym. But it didn't look like we were here to stay. We were on a people-gathering mission. We gathered Kevin, who gathered Maya, who had her phone pressed to her ear. And Kyle, Justin's oldest brother, gathered Janna, who turned red, but she said, "This sucks anyway," and came with us.

"Is that Delaney?" I asked, pointing to Maya's phone, but she shook her head, barely glancing at me.

"Have you seen her?" And this time I touched her arm so she'd pay attention.

She jerked away from me, cupped her hand over the phone. "Yes, I've seen her."

"Here?" We were heading outside, and I scanned the crowd behind us. She said a few words into her phone and hung up.

"Decker, if she doesn't feel like telling you where she is, I'm sure as hell not going to tell you."

She was right. I took out my cell phone and listened to it ring. Maya was watching me as Justin's brothers tried to convince Tara to come with us, but it didn't look like she was interested. I was standing in the middle of the gymnasium with a phone pressed to my ear, turning in a circle, trying to find Delaney.

It went to voice mail, and Maya leaned closer. "You just missed her."

"You could've just told me that," I said.

"She's my friend," she said. "And you're fucking with her."

"I'm not fucking with her, I'm—"

"Save it. You don't speak to her. You don't look at her. But you can't leave her alone. You're *torturing* her," she said, and I flinched. "And I don't get it, I mean, what did she even *do*? She won't tell me. I *know* there's not anyone else yet."

Yet?

"Maya, please tell me where she is."

We were out in the cold, moving as a group, and I had to walk fast to keep up with her. "She's meeting up with my brother, apparently."

I stopped walking, and Maya had to turn around. *"What?"* I asked.

"Wow, Decker, if I didn't know any better, I'd say you're jealous."

"What the hell is she doing with your brother?" I asked, ignoring the accusation.

She crossed her arms over her chest and narrowed her eyes at me. "Why do you care?"

She kept walking, falling into step with Kevin. "Shit," I mumbled, and called Delaney's number again. When she didn't pick up *again*, I sent her a text: *Going to clearing. You should come.*

Ten minutes later Maya was sitting across from me, on the hood of Kevin's spare car, laughing at a joke. I kept staring at my phone, willing Delaney to respond. We were behind the parking lot, behind the field house that I'd painted over—there's a makeshift road in case people need to transport equipment—right at the edge of the woods. There was something calming about this, about being with the same people I'd known my entire life. Plus Maya. Plus flasks. I'd be calmer if Delaney would show up.

Maya was practically sitting on Kevin's lap, laughing at something he said to her.

I put an arm around Janna, who was sitting unnaturally close. Not because she wanted to claim me or anything, more because she wanted to be as far away from Justin as possible. She was practically clinging to me. And judging by the way his brothers were looking at her, they knew why.

"He has such a big mouth," she mumbled.

"In his defense, you weren't exactly discreet."

With my free hand, I pressed the Call button again and held the phone to my ear.

"Who are you calling?" she asked, but I held up a finger until I got Delaney's voice mail again. Janna leaned across my lap to see the phone as I turned it off. "Tell me you're not obsessively calling your ex-girlfriend."

"Okay, I'm not obsessively calling my ex-girlfriend."

She rolled her eyes, grabbed it from my hand, and stuffed it in her bag. "I'm doing you a favor," she said.

"Janna . . ."

But she held her bag out to the other side, away from me.

Kyle stood up and handed his flask to Janna. "Little Levine, all grown up," he said, shaking his head and grinning at her. She blushed, refusing to make eye contact, then took a sip from the flask and passed it to me. Then she said, "This is funny, right?" And giggled.

"Is she drunk already?" Kevin asked.

No, I was pretty sure she was just about to flip out on someone. I was also pretty sure it wasn't me. I shrugged at Kevin. Janna stood in the middle of us all, closer to Justin than she'd been since Boston, and said, "Your brothers are very proud of you, huh?"

Justin looked at the hood of the car. He was trying not to smile.

"But if *my* brother were here, he'd kick your ass." And then she laughed once more—at least I thought it was a laugh.

Justin stopped smiling, and Kevin took a giant swig and said, "Shit." And the place fell silent.

I stood up, raised the flask, and said, "To Carson Levine, who right this second would be kicking Justin's ass." Then I tipped the flask over, watched as the liquid ran across the dirt, disappeared beneath the grass. Imagined, for a moment, Carson smiling. Laughing at us. Saying, *"It's about damn time, motherfuckers."*

"To kicking Justin's ass," Kevin added, dumping his flask over as well. Then he looked at Janna and grinned. "I'm sorry we dropped the ball on this." He handed the empty flask to Maya, stood, and cracked his neck.

"Stand up," he said to Justin. Kevin was grinning. Justin groaned. He slid off the hood of the car way too slowly. Kevin hooked him around the neck and dragged him to the center of the circle and took a cheap shot at his gut.

"Dude, that hurt," he said. But the side of his mouth quirked up.

Kevin hit him once more, then cracked his knuckles against the side of his leg.

Janna looked at me, eyebrows raised.

"Janna," I said, "I kicked his ass that night."

Kevin smiled. "It's true." Janna laughed and wiped her thumb under her eyes.

"Your turn, Janna," Kevin said, holding Justin's arms from behind. "For Carson." She waltzed up and decked him in the stomach, harder than Kevin had. Justin winced and coughed. And then she walked closer, stood on her toes, and kissed him on the mouth.

"She's definitely drunk," Kyle said, laughing. Even Maya was smiling. Kevin went back to her and whispered something in her ear, something that was meant for her alone, and she smiled some more.

I grabbed Janna's bag, looking for my phone.

We didn't hear them coming.

"Not to break up the lovefest . . ." Justin and Janna pulled apart. We were surrounded by a group of alumni, smiling at us. "It's time," the big guy said. Lance Cooper. Quarterback half a lifetime ago. He never missed a homecoming.

He used to go to parties, according to Justin's brothers, but it got seriously creepy as he got closer and closer to thirty. I'd figured he'd moved away since I hadn't seen him around in a while. But here he was.

I froze, and I think everyone else did, too. Even Justin's brothers, who weren't here last year when everything happened, knew enough to know that *this* part wouldn't go over well.

This part being the part where the alumni drag the senior guys down to Falcon Lake as some sort of initiation into alumni-hood or something.

"But . . . ," Justin said. I saw his throat move up and down as he swallowed. Wondered if any of us would have the guts to mention the curse. It sounded so ridiculous out loud, and I didn't think any of us really believed it. Not individually. Not Janna—she was like Delaney, all brains and logic. And Kevin was just aloof. Justin was the only one scared enough that he might say something.

"But what?" Lance said, homing in on Kevin. Kevin was the biggest. Kevin was the leader. Kevin would be his prize.

I dropped Janna's bag.

"Oh hell," Justin said, and he took off running. Kevin did, too.

I'm not proud to admit I did the same.

I may not be the biggest or the strongest, but I was definitely the fastest, and nobody was going to catch me. And nobody did. Not until I saw her, like a ghost in my peripheral vision, walking through the night like she was in a trance. Down to the fields surrounded by woods.

I stopped running. "Delaney?" I called. She turned and cocked her head to the side. Then her eyes grew wide as she saw something behind me. I turned just in time to see two ex–football players converging from both sides. "Oh, shit," I said. But it was too late. One took me down around the waist, and the air was temporarily knocked out of my lungs. I had this moment of panic where I couldn't breathe and wondered if I'd be able to take a breath ever again. I wondered if this is what Delaney felt under the ice. I wondered that a lot.

And then I was breathing again, and the guy who wasn't lying on top of me said, "Don't worry, pretty girl, we'll return him to you in one piece." Then recognition seemed to cross her face. Right, initiation. And then horror. *Right, initiation.* I saw her change directions and follow us back toward the parking lot. I was thrown in the back of a pickup truck next to Justin. Kevin followed shortly after. He tossed his keys to

Maya, who was watching the whole scene with complete confusion. "The lake," he said.

I saw Delaney arguing for a second with Maya, then Maya shrugging and them both getting in the car. I saw their head-lights shining on us as we drove to Falcon Lake.

Chapter
12

Janna was already there, standing beside Justin's brothers, with a cheering crowd of alumni clumped together on the shore. A bunch of cars and trucks had their headlights on, their beams pointing at Falcon Lake. There were already a bunch of seniors dripping wet on the edge, looking pissed. But then someone dragged a keg down the hill, and soon they were holding plastic cups and looking not quite as pissed. Just wet.

"Kevin Mulroy!" I heard as Lance dragged him out of the truck. Kevin waved and stuck his shoulders back, like he was in a freaking pageant. And then Lance dragged him into the water, pushed him down, and held him there as the crowd cheered. He pulled him up by the back of his shirt and Kevin shook his hair out. He looked around at the water for a second, then back to the shore and smiled.

"Hey, babe," he called to Maya as he high-stepped out of the water. But Maya did not run up to Kevin and lean into him, like she'd done the day he was in the dunk tank. She stared past him, at the dark water. I wondered if the curse could get a hold of her, too. How long it would take, living here, for you to sense something was off. For you to believe.

"Decker Phillips!" And then Lance was dragging me into the water as well. I wasn't scared of it. I'd been in it before. With Delaney. But it was cold and dark, and I couldn't see anything, only the headlights shining in my eyes, reflecting off the water. And when he held me under, the calm left. I pictured her on the other side of the ice, trapped. And I started flailing my arms. I heard them splashing above me. He pulled me back up. "Easy there, cowboy." I heard laughter. From him. From shore. I walked back toward the lights, looking for Delaney. Turned just in time to see Justin being dragged from the pickup.

"Justin Baxter!"

Justin, despite himself, resisted the whole way.

"No," I heard him say. He looked at Janna as he passed us, and she was biting her thumbnail. "Tell them," he mouthed to her. "Don't!" he yelled. But Lance kept pulling him, and everyone watched in horror as Justin screamed. This was a prank. This was initiation. He was acting like he was being murdered.

Then he was under, and he was struggling, and Lance held him under even longer because of it. He pulled him back up and Justin was coughing. Gagging. Retching. He sulked over to the shore and said, "It's in my fucking lungs." And then he repeated, loud enough for everyone to hear, "It's in my fucking lungs!"

"Calm down," I said.

"Calm down? *Calm down?*"

I put my hand on his shoulder. "Calm. Down. Tell him, Janna."

Janna reached for Justin's hand and pulled him away from the edge. "I'm not going to lie to him," she said.

Which only set off his panic even more. "See? I'm not the only one who remembers. This place, it isn't a joke."

"No, it's not," she whispered. Her eyes moved from Justin to me to Kevin. She looked at her feet, at the water lapping onto the heels of her shoes, and took a step closer to us. "There are towels. Follow me."

Kevin grabbed Maya's wrist to pull her along. Tara was with some of her other friends, and she was eyeing Kevin from down the path. She was eyeing Maya and Kevin, specifically. She didn't notice Lance behind her. Not at first.

"You get hotter every year," Lance said. He was dripping water, and he reached for her hair. She jerked back.

"Don't get me wet," she said. "I'm cold."

Lance grinned and tugged her by the arm. Tara didn't resist much, probably because we were all watching now. We were all about to watch her get dunked and stare at her as she stood there with her clothes clinging to her body, which had defied all rules of nature since she'd turned thirteen.

Which, to be fair, was exactly why Lance was about to dunk her.

And, to be fair, that was exactly why she was going to let him.

She was grinning but dragging her heels, and she was squealing.

They were up to their knees in the lake, and she said, "Holy shit, this is cold."

Their waists. "Wait," she said.

But Lance didn't wait. He pushed her legs out from under her and pressed down on her shoulders until she disappeared under the surface. Lance smiled and let her up right away. She busted out of the water, flung back her hair, and pushed him. Hard. He fell back, under the water, and a cheer erupted from the shore. Tara stood there with a giant smile and clothes clinging and everyone staring, and she curtsied.

Tara was almost back to shore, walking toward us. I wondered if she could feel Kevin's eyes on her. *I* could feel his eyes on her. And from the change in Maya's posture, so could she. Lance dragged himself out of the water and said, "Tara Spano, please tell me you're eighteen now."

She put a hand on her hip, turned to face him, and said, "Only if you round up."

Then she turned to me, stuck her tongue out like she was gagging, and mouthed the word, "*Yuck.*"

"Too bad I suck at math," Lance said, leering at Tara.

I walked up and slung my arm around Tara's shoulder. "Too bad she's taken," I said.

As we walked away, I let my arm fall off her, but she bumped her shoulder against mine as we walked to the pickup trucks with the towels. "Thanks," she said. "He's gross."

She started rubbing her hair with a towel, and I had to

actively remind myself not to look down. Kevin obviously didn't remind himself. Maya was probably pissed. No, Maya wasn't paying attention at all. She was staring at the water, her arms wrapped around herself, shivering like she'd just been dunked.

"I'm probably breaking guy code right now," I said, "but if you want Kevin back . . ."

"I don't want Kevin back," she said. She pulled another towel over her shirt, and I rubbed her upper arms as she shivered. I was also shivering.

"Sure seems like . . ."

"There's a difference," she said, shrugging me off, "between *wanting* someone and wanting someone to be *jealous*." She turned away from me, keeping herself covered with the towel. Then she looked at me over her shoulder. "You of all people should know that."

I hadn't been trying to make Delaney jealous. "Tara, that's not what I—"

"Oh, *please*," she said. "It's not like I *care*." She turned around. "I'm glad we're friends," she said. "I mean it. It's nice to have someone you can count on to save you from sleazy old guys."

"Intense," Kevin said, walking toward us. Tara flipped her hair again. I expected Maya to roll her eyes, but she was staring at her phone.

"Has anyone seen my brother?" she asked, keeping her eyes on her phone.

"Has anyone seen Delaney?" I asked, not caring that I was

being totally obvious. I stood in the back of the pickup truck and scanned the crowd around the lake, searching for her.

Maya scanned the crowd, too. "Or maybe he *did* see my message."

"Excuse me?" I said.

She shrugged. "He was on his way to meet Delaney. But she got . . . sidetracked." She narrowed her eyes at me, like she hated that Delaney still cared. That I wasn't worth it. "I told him we were heading to the lake." She looked toward her house, and I did the same. It was hidden in darkness.

"I don't get why he would want to meet Delaney," I said.

She put her finger on her lips as she assessed me. Assessed what to say, I guess. "Why wouldn't he? Is there some reason I'm not allowed to introduce her to Holden, Decker?"

She walked around the truck with Kevin. I saw his wet shirt on the ground. Heard her laugh.

"Holden," I mumbled. "What kind of name is Holden, anyway?"

Janna blinked at me. Justin laughed as he rifled through the stack of towels, searching for a dry one.

"Hey," I said. "Decker was my mom's last name. It has *significance*."

Janna smiled. "*Catcher in the Rye*? Ring any bells?" By my blank expression, I guess she could tell that it did not. She sighed. "Holden is only the angsty-est voice of discontented youth in all of recent literature."

Shit.

Delaney was going to love him.

In my head I saw Delaney talking to him somewhere in the woods. Him saying something angsty. Frowning. Her commiserating. Smiling. Justin shook his head, and when Janna turned around, he mouthed, *"Go, you idiot."*

"Janna, my phone?"

"Oh, right." She handed it over. I wandered away, and she called out, "By the way, Delaney called."

"What? What did she say?"

"Nothing. I said, 'Decker's phone,' and she hung up. I mean, what the hell? Can't even say hello?" Then Janna yelled, "She was the last person to see my brother alive, and she can't even fucking say hello?"

"Please," I said, backing away. "Why would she say anything to you? You're acting like she gave Carson epilepsy. Like she could've stopped it." I was breathing heavily, and everyone was watching us. And I stopped talking because I had basically just accused Janna of the exact same thing I had been doing.

"And you're acting like something isn't seriously wrong with this place," she said.

I almost flipped her off as I walked away, but I thought of Carson, and what he would do if he was here. What he'd think of me right now. What his death had done to her.

What it had done to all of us.

I tried calling Delaney back, but it just rang. I sent her a message, that it was me and not Janna.

I could see Justin's—no, Maya's—house from here, about a quarter of the way around the lake. Rather, I saw where it should've been, but right now it was just a black shadow. No lights. I was starting to shake. The towel was pretty much useless since my clothes were soaked through. My shoes, too. They squished with each step, and as the sounds from the initiation faded, my own steps grew louder. The light from the cars still cut through a few of the trees, lighting the way. But it faded as I rounded the next turn. I could still see everyone behind me, shadows in the light, but the area in front of me was in total darkness.

I walked by memory—there was a trunk coming up, a tree that the Baxters had cut down because it swayed too much in storms, threatening to come down on their roof. And when I reached the stump, I'd be able to see the backyard, sloping above me to my left. And then the sliding back door. There were no curtains on the back doors, then or now, but the inside of the house was pitch-dark. I tried Delaney's cell once more, listening for ringing in the silence. Nothing.

So I scrambled up the sloped grass and cupped my hands over my eyes as I pressed my face to the glass doors. The house was a ranch—but a big ranch. Huge, open living area, perfect for parties. A kitchen off to the side. A long hallway extending off the main area, leading to bedrooms. Perfect for parties. I could see a faint light coming from the hallway. I skirted the side of the house, peeking in the windows as I went. Like some sort of stalker. Great. I stepped away. None of my business.

There was a red car in the driveway. A car that normally wasn't here, that I hadn't seen since the day Maya moved in.

Holden's, I assumed. He was back at the house. He was here. Maybe Delaney—

None of my business, I thought again, but I pressed my face back to the window anyway. Nothing. The bedrooms all had shades drawn. But there was a light coming from behind one of them. My face was level with the base of the window, and I stooped down to try to see through the crack at the bottom. A shadow moved across the room.

My phone rang, breaking the silence. I fumbled for the Mute button. And then the window was all shadow, and the shades fluttered for a second, then pulled lower, cutting off my vision. They flew upward as I dove down against the base of the house.

Shit. I pressed my back to the wall, hoping whoever was in there couldn't see me. Hoping it wasn't her mother, scared of an intruder. Hoping they wouldn't call the cops on me. *Sorry, I was just checking to see if my ex-girlfriend was in there.*

Idiot.

I eased my way along the wall, toward the backyard, and nearly bumped into Holden's chest.

"Holy shit," I said.

"Holy shit, yourself," he said. "Maya's not here."

"I know," I said. I took a step back. Tried to calm my breathing. "Sorry, I was looking for Delaney."

He looked confused. Then his eyes narrowed, and he looked back toward his house. "Why would she be *here*?"

"I was just checking. . . ." *Because you're named after some angsty guy from literature. Because Maya said you wanted to meet her.*

"Did she *say* she'd be coming here?" He looked over his shoulder and then over my shoulder.

"No, Maya said Delaney went to meet you, and I couldn't find her. Sorry, this was stupid."

"She said she couldn't make it," he said. Which should've made me feel better but only made me realize they had talked. Who knows how frequently or what about. Holden was looking me over. "Were you swimming?"

I pointed to the lake. "Everyone's there. It's . . . stupid. Never mind. Sorry," I said, turning to go.

Holden grabbed my arm as he leaned forward, closer to the water. He took a step toward the lake. "What are they doing?" he asked. "What the hell is going on?"

"It's this yearly prank," I said, pulling my arm away. Trying to give him the quickest answer so I could get the hell out of there. "The alumni are dunking us." I held out my arms as evidence.

"I thought no one went in the water anymore," he whispered. So the curse *had* reached them. They knew. Maybe not the why, but they knew the what.

"Somebody forgot to tell them that," I said. Holden was still watching the lake when I turned to go.

I took off running, not once looking behind me. I walked behind the cars, still keeping out of the light, and checked my phone. The missed call had been from Delaney.

I called her back. "What is it?" she asked.

"I was looking for you."

A pause. "I had the ringer turned off. I'm home."

Because if she could walk to the lake house, she could also walk home. "Meet me at my house," I said. And after the silence that followed, I added, "Please."

I had this thought, that if we went back to this place where it all started, where everything changed, if we could talk, if I could forgive her, we could move on. It was the perfect thought.

She knocked. The electricity was still out, so it was dark. I had a flashlight, but that seemed weird. Still, I turned it on, set it on the table before me. "What am I doing here?" she asked. But she came, so she knew exactly what she was doing here. She was hoping.

"I thought you were with Holden. Maya said . . ."

"Yeah, not really in the mood to be friendly," she said, and I felt myself smiling already.

"You talk to him, though? You want to meet him?"

"Am I at an inquisition?" she asked. And then she sighed. "He has my number in case he can't reach Maya. For emergencies. And he called because he wanted to talk to me about her. Make sure she's doing okay or something."

"And he wanted to meet you in *the woods*?"

"I thought it would be awkward to talk about Maya *with her there*."

"Maya made it seem like she was setting you guys up or something."

She paused. "Is that a question? You called me ten times because I was meeting some guy, which, for the record, is the

first time you've called me since August. I didn't see him. I
don't want to hang out with him. Nothing happened. Am
I free to go now?"

"That's not why I . . ." I took a step closer. "You left and I
couldn't find you."

"Turns out I'm not really a fan of watching you hang all
over Tara Spano."

She had forgiven me for that, I thought.

"That's not what it looked like," I said. "That Lance guy
was being gross, and I was just—"

"I *know*," she said. "I know. Still sucks to watch. And I
couldn't think of any reason to stay."

She was standing near the door. I wanted her closer.
I wanted *her* to walk closer. "I wanted you to stay," I said. *Please
get what I mean.*

"I'm here right now," she said. And she was waiting. I
knew what she was waiting for.

I felt my clothes dripping water on the brand-new floors.
"I'm trying . . . ," I said. I cleared my throat and said, "I'm trying to forgive you."

She paused. I heard her shift positions. "You're trying, or
you're pretending?" she asked.

"I want to," I said. "I miss you," I added. Which seemed like
the biggest understatement.

I saw the shadows stretch over her. Thought she might've
been taking a step back. But she was coming closer. "You're trying. You want to." Another step. "But you can't, can you?"

"I don't know, Delaney. I *don't know.* I want to just . . .

move past it. Can we just skip this part?" She was standing so close that when she breathed, I could almost feel the air moving.

Close enough that I could kiss her.

"And pretend like this didn't happen?" she asked.

"Yes."

"Pretend like it doesn't exist?"

"Yes."

"How the hell are we supposed to do that? You can't even look at me right now," she whispered.

"I'm looking right at you." I reached my hand out to her arm, almost touched her.

She moved back. "We are standing in the *dark*. You invited me to a place without any light. You don't want to see me," she said.

I wanted to turn on the light. Prove it to her. Kiss her in the light. "I hate that he's dead," she said. "I hate it for you, and I hate that it hurt you. That *I* hurt you. I love your parents too, you know." I could tell from the waver in her voice that there were probably tears on her face. I wanted to wipe them away. I wanted her to stop talking.

"I don't know what to say," she said. "I'm not asking you to forgive me. I can't. Because it was horrible, and I hated it, but I did it. And if he asked me to do the same thing all over again, I'd do it. I'd do it for him."

Wrong thing to say.

"What about for me, though?" I said. Guess she was right. I couldn't just pretend like it didn't exist. "I thought that was kind of a requirement of being together, that you don't lie. What about *that* promise?"

Also the wrong thing to say.

"Yeah. That's what I thought. You don't forgive me. And you don't understand me."

"Don't say that," I said. I grabbed her by the arm as she spun to leave. If this was an insult-throwing competition, that would win. That *did* win. "Don't you dare say that."

"You keep things from me all the time," she whispered. "What people say about me. What they think. What they thought when Carson died."

I thought she'd forgiven me for that, too. But everything I'd done wrong was still living inside of her, forgiven or not. Impossible not to remember.

I was right. Something deeper than this was also broken.

I swallowed hard. I hated knowing that it was all still there. Something I couldn't cut out of existence. Forgiven. Not forgotten.

How did this whole thing turn into me wanting to apologize to her, and not the other way around?

"I'm sorry, Decker. I'm so sorry. But I can't exactly apologize for something that I'd do all over again, can I? And you can't exactly forgive me when you're still furious, can you?"

"I would've picked you," I said, and I heard my voice break when I said it. That's what killed me. Like it meant I cared about her more than she cared about me. I understood. I just would've made a different choice.

She couldn't respond to that. She almost left.

"It wasn't what that guy said, right? Not just pheromones, right?" I asked. I couldn't stand to think that everything between us was a lie, but I couldn't stand not to know, either.

She stood in the doorway, half out. "Second week of freshman year."

"What?"

"You were waiting at the bus stop." She paused. "Shut up about the pheromones." And she was gone.

Freshman year. Two years before the accident. I actually remembered that day because she acted so weird. She saw me, same as every other day. I smiled at her. She blushed. She didn't talk to me for the rest of the day.

I'd kissed her on a dare later that winter, but it was just an excuse to kiss her. And she got pissed. Because it was just a dare.

I tried to think back and remember the first time I wanted her, but I couldn't remember a time when I didn't.

And then she threw the door back open. "He was dying," she said. "That's why I picked him. I can promise you a million things. But that was the last promise I could make to him." She stepped outside. "I wish he hadn't asked me that," she said. And then she left.

I put my hand on the wall, leaned my forehead against it, shaking in my wet clothes. This was who she was. And the person she would always be. A lifetime of listening to the secrets of the dying. A lifetime of keeping promises to the dead.

Chapter
13

Two days later, Justin slid into his seat beside me in math and stared at me until I looked his way. "What?"

His eyes were red and his mouth was hanging open. "I'm sick," he said. And then he coughed to prove it.

I leaned away. "So go home."

"No," he said, coughing into his closed fist. "I'm *sick*."

I put my arm up over my face. "Yeah, could you maybe move back, man?"

Kevin took his spot in front of us and turned around. "Did Justin tell you about his cold of death yet?"

Justin ignored Kevin and leaned across the aisle toward me. "I inhale fucking lake water and now I'm sick," he said.

"Makes sense," I said, grinning at Kevin. "You did, after all, inhale water while you panicked."

"*Lake* water," he repeated.

"*Any* water," I said, speaking louder now, "in your lungs isn't exactly healthy."

Someone coughed in the back corner. "What about her?" I asked. "You think she got a cold from choking on lake water? Let's ask her."

Justin punched me in the arm. "Don't be an ass."

"Ditto," I said, taking out my notebook. But every time I heard him cough throughout class, each time I heard the rattle of his breath, I jumped.

I pictured him panicking in the lake, his arms desperately grasping at the surface. I pictured the water dripping off of him, inside of him, circulating in his blood now.

Not him.

I thought it quickly, in a whisper, as I cleared my throat and took out my pencil.

After class, Janna met us in the hall. I dealt with the fact that we'd had it out the best way I knew how. "Hey," I said, like nothing had happened.

"Hey," she said. And that was it.

Justin leaned in for a kiss—I guess they were together now, but her eyes went wide and she put a hand on his chest. "Keep the plague to yourself, thank you very much."

"See?" Justin said to me as Kevin waved Maya over.

"You shouldn't have gone in that water," Janna said. Then she pointed her finger at each of us. "None of you should've gone in that water. Don't you remember?"

"What is it?" Maya asked, and it looked like the panic had transferred straight to her. "Why can't you go in the water?"

"Because it's cursed," Janna said. "Everyone knows that."

Kevin forced a laugh and put his hand on Janna's shoulder. "Allow me to do Carson's job here." He cleared his throat, pretended to shake his hair out of his face, like Carson would've done, even though Kevin's hair was shorter. "Snap out of it."

She looked down at her shoes, but her face broke into a smile.

"Hey, my lungs are not a joke," Justin said. But Kevin waved him off.

"Anyone up for pizza? It comes with good news," Kevin said.

"How about just the news," Justin said. "I want to go home and die."

"Anyone else?"

"I'm not going to Johnny's," Janna said.

"News first," I said. "Pizza after."

"Fine," Kevin said. "Important stuff: since Justin's lake house is now Maya's real house and is no longer at our disposal, I went above and beyond and procured a new facility."

"Huh?" Justin asked.

"A place for Halloween. This weekend."

"Um, Halloween is in, like, three weeks," Janna said.

"Yeah, well, the *place* is available *this* week." He held up a set of keys. "Renters moved out this weekend. New lease starts in two weeks. Cleaning company comes next week. It's perfect."

His family really did own half the town. "Your parents are going to kill you," I said.

"They can add it to the long list of things they already want to kill me for. Anyway," Kevin said. "Costumes required."

"I'm not wearing a costume," I said.

"Costumes *required*," he repeated. "Now, pizza."

He hung an arm around Maya and nodded toward me. "Oh," Maya said. "I can't. My brother's home this week. Can you drop me off on the way?"

He stopped walking. "Come on, My, he's not your dad."

He didn't see the look that passed across her face for a brief second. "You're right," she said. "But seeing as *my dad* left when I was five, and seeing as my mom has been sick on and off since I was ten, and seeing as Holden will probably have to drop a class now, mostly because of me, and seeing as how he practically raised me and already took a year off school to help out with my mom, how about I don't make his life any harder than it already is? Some of us have more to worry about than driving a spare car, Kevin."

"I'm sorry," he said. God, we were all sorry.

We never went for pizza. I left them in the hall together, Kevin smoothing the back of her hair as he apologized over and over. I didn't want to be in that car. Didn't want to think about how one parent was better than none.

The ice started falling the morning of the Halloween party. It started as rain the night before, but I woke up after midnight to the sound of it pelting against the windows and the kind of darkness that meant no lights were working. Because, as usually happened during an ice storm, Delaney's house lost power.

I pulled the blankets up over my neck but couldn't shake the chill. This was ridiculous. My dad used to take me camping as early as April—the temperature always plummeted at night.

I imagined the blue and green material of our tent over my head. The smell of the earth, so close to my face. The sound of my father breathing on the other side of the tent.

Listen. Ice hitting the roof. Ice hitting the ground. And nothing, nothing, nothing coming from the other side of the room.

The heat was back on before I left the room in the morning, but Delaney was still bundled in about five layers of clothing.

"Good news, bad news," my mom said between sips of coffee. "The house passed inspection. But the electricity and gas company won't come out until Monday."

"So . . . not much different than last night, then?" Delaney said. She was huddled in the corner of the couch, like the cold was still in her bones.

I laughed, and when I turned back to my mom, she was grinning at me.

"You guys can go over, start setting Decker's room back up. Just take a flashlight."

It did not escape my notice that she said "you guys."

It apparently did not escape Delaney's notice, either. "Hey,

Mom, can I borrow the car today?" Delaney asked. "I need to go to the library for my history project."

And I guess that answered that.

My furniture was in my room, but it was in all the wrong places. Someone had removed it all to fix the drywall and the floors and then rearranged it themselves. Even the clothes in my closet had been randomly stuffed in there. I mean, it was kind of random to begin with. But this was random in the wrong way.

It seemed like a pain in the ass to move my furniture around without scratching the floors, which would piss off my mom. And honestly, there wasn't really anything *wrong* with the way it was set up now. So I fell back onto my bed.

I took a nap.

I slept like the dead.

Justin's call woke me up sometime in the afternoon. "Can you pick me up tonight?"

I yawned, trying to orient myself. "Can't Janna pick you up?"

He paused. "She's freaked out by the whole Cold of Death thing," he said.

"Speaking of . . . I thought you felt like death," I said.

"I did, but I took Kevin's advice and doped up. I feel excellent. I drove last time."

"Your brothers drove last time," I said.

"It counts," he said.

I sighed, because it did. "Fine. But I'm not waiting around for you." I wasn't really in the mood to go at all. But the house had no electricity yet, and I'd be lying if I said I wasn't cold out from under my covers. My mom was probably having dinner at the Maxwells'. And I didn't know what Delaney was up to. She didn't usually go to parties. I dragged her to one last year, and she walked in on me kissing Tara.

It was before we were together, but it sucked. Seeing her face, I mean. It really sucked.

I picked Justin up late, mostly because I was being an ass. I was still wearing the most nondescript clothes I owned, pretty much what I wore every day. Justin wasn't dressed up either. At least, not that I could tell. He slammed my car door and shook the ice off his coat. "I was about to call a cab or something," he said.

"Sorry. Couldn't decide what to wear." The windshield wipers cut through the sleet, like broken glass. "Have you been there?" I asked.

"No," he said. "It's only like three doors down from Maya though."

"I'm sure her mom will be thrilled," I mumbled.

"Should be perfectly awkward."

"Excellent."

And it was. Justin and I drove by his lake house—the lights were on, and cars were already overflowing down the street, bordering Maya's yard. Cars were stacked in front of the house

three doors down, in the driveway, off the driveway, anywhere they could find space. No secret what was going on
there. We parked along the street, directly in front of Maya's
place.

The house was weird, pretty much the opposite of Justin's
lake house. It was narrow and two stories, and it had been
taken over by purple. Purple couches and a purple throw rug
and purple paintings. "What the hell?" Justin asked as we
stepped inside.

Kevin saw us from across the room and pushed through a
group of people.

"Uh, your mom like purple much?" Justin asked.

"It was the renters," he said. "And I don't think they liked
purple, seeing as they left it all behind."

"You didn't dress up," Justin said. Not that we had either,
but still.

Kevin said, "Yeah, I was just trying to get you fuckers to
do it." He shrugged. Smiled. "Coolers out back. Later." And he
was gone, disappearing back into the crowd.

Someone waved frantically from the purple couch. Even
though she was wearing a blond wig and way too much
makeup, it wasn't hard to see Tara in the way her skirt was too
short and her boots were propped on a coffee table, crossed at
the ankle. I tapped Justin's shoulder and headed toward her.

Justin gestured that he was going to find a drink. Tara
scooted over to make room for me on the couch. "Who are
you supposed to be?" she yelled over the noise.

"Anyone," I said. "You?"

She ran her hands down the long hair that wasn't hers. Blinked slowly with long eyelashes that weren't hers. Put a finger on her bottom lip, a color that definitely wasn't hers. "Maine Barbie. Isn't it obvious?"

"Ahh, the fur boots. Dead giveaway."

"Hey," Justin had a can of beer in each hand as he walked toward us, big smile on his face. "Barbie, right?"

She turned to me. "See? Obvious." She scooted closer to me so Justin had room. I was wedged against the side of the couch, and Tara was practically in my lap. She took one of the drinks from Justin. "Thanks, babe."

I moved my arm out of the way, over the couch behind her, and she rested her head on my chest as she took a sip. "I mean, I don't get it," she said, like we were in the middle of a conversation.

"Get what?" I asked.

She nodded across the room. At Maya and Kevin. "It. Her. What does he see in her? She's so . . . scrawny."

Justin said, "Are you looking at her? Come on." Maya was wearing understated, tight clothes. The only way she dressed up was by wearing a mask over her eyes—it was black, with feathers—she could've been a bird, an angel, a demon. And Justin had a very solid point.

"Seriously, Justin? Way to kick a girl when she's down." And just in case the weight of her head on my chest wasn't a dead giveaway, her words let me know she was hammered. No way would Tara Spano admit she was down.

"But you're totally hotter," Justin said.

"Uh-huh."

"She's just . . . mysterious. Mysteriously hot."

I smacked the back of Justin's head.

"I'm not mysterious?" she said, scowling at him. No, she was decidedly not mysterious, with her short skirt and low-cut shirt and her hand on my leg.

"He's a moron," I said. "His loss."

She patted my leg. Turned her face to me. "Thanks, Deck." Her face was turned up, so I could smell the beer on her breath, see the sparkles she had applied over her eyes. "But you totally did the same thing."

I didn't. Not really. Tara and I were never a real thing, not something that would last, and she knew it. I was low, and she was lonely. But I didn't say that. Not when she was low. Not when I was lonely. "I'm sorry."

She sighed and rested her head back on my chest. "I forgive you." Then she tilted her face up so her breath, her lips, brushed my neck. "Want to get out of here?" she whispered.

I did. But not with her. "You're drunk," I said. "But I'll drive you home."

"Don't bother." She dropped her feet from the table to the floor. Smoothed the wig down over her brown hair. "I just want to know," she said, leaning forward and bracing herself on my knees so I could see straight down her shirt. Her fingers tightened on my legs. "I want to know if you're saying no to me"—and she jutted her thumb across the room—"or if you're saying yes to her."

I followed her thumb and saw her. Delaney was standing

across from some guy, nodding. Except she wasn't dressed like Delaney at all. She was dressed exactly like Maya. They'd probably gotten ready together. Tight black shirt. Low cut. And her hair was loose and wavy, and she wore that mask over her eyes, same as Maya, the elastic dark against her light hair. Her boots had heels, which made me think they definitely weren't hers. And some guy was standing way too close to her.

I felt my hands clenching into fists.

"So?" she asked. "Which is it? You don't want me? Or you *do* want her?"

"You're drunk," I said again. But what I really meant to say was *you're sad*.

"And you're an asshole," she said. She narrowed her eyes. "Her or me. Just say it."

I nodded. Looked at the jewels on the side of her eyes. Looked at her perfectly manicured nails on my leg. Closed my eyes. "I want her," I whispered.

Of course I did.

"Okay then." She pushed up off me, reached a hand out to the nearest body to steady herself. "Plenty of boys out there, right?" There was one who'd just walked in, in a generic drugstore plastic mask, checking her out already. She'd never have a shortage of guys.

Justin put his leg on the table to block her path. "Hey, right here. Boy." He pointed to himself and smiled.

"Aww," Tara said, bending over and kissing the top of his head. "You're sweet." Then she stepped over his leg and disappeared into the crowd.

"Dude," Justin said. "What gives?"

"Probably the fact that you're with Janna?"

"Tell that to Janna. It kind of depends on her mood. And right now, she's ignoring me," he said.

"Uh-huh," I said, but I was staring at Delaney. I was staring at the way someone else was staring at Delaney. "Hold on," I said.

"I see," Justin said.

"Be right back," I said.

"Sure you will."

I pushed through the crowd—a wing hit me in the face. An angel, I guess. Or a butterfly. She saw me coming. I pointed to her, then to the hall, even though I had no idea where it led. She blinked and turned her attention back to the guy who kept talking and talking.

I pushed past a witch and then a vampire and a few more costumes, until I was standing at her side. "I need to talk to you," I said, my fingers on her elbow.

She looked down at her arm. At my face. Up close, her mask had these pink feathers that perfectly matched her mouth. The guy she was talking to was staring at that mouth.

"Okay," she said. But she pulled her arm away from me as she led the way down the hall, weaving through people. The first door she tried was locked. The one at the end of the hall was closed, but unlocked. An office. No bed.

I closed the door behind us and leaned against it. "Who was that?" I asked.

"Who?" she shrugged. "The guy from my English class? Decker, what is it?"

"Are you trying to make me jealous?"

Her eyes grew wide behind the mask. "Yes," she said. "Obviously. That's at the top of my list of things to do. Make Decker jealous. I'm sorry, am I not allowed to speak to other people now?"

I shook my head. "What are you wearing? Why the hell are you dressed like that?"

"Because it's Halloween," she said. Her teeth were gritting together. "And today I'm someone other than me."

"No, you're exactly you. You're just the part of you that's supposed to belong to me."

"*Belong* to you? That's *hilarious*. The only reason you're even looking at me right now is because I *don't* look like me."

I squeezed my eyes shut and gritted my teeth together. "Because when I look at you," I said, and I felt my voice growing louder, "I can't remember why I'm mad."

She froze. I froze.

"I mean, I know why. But I don't care. How messed up is that?"

"Decker . . ."

"Tell me. How screwed up am I? I'm furious. And then I see you and I don't care." I was yelling. Just not at her.

Then she moved her fingers to the mask, lifted it up off her face. Let it float to the floor. There were lines around her eyes, where the mask had pressed into her skin. And a crease through her hair. I ran a thumb along the line on her cheek.

"I am so fucking mad," I whispered.

And then it clicked. In me. In her. I saw her get it. "Not at me," she whispered back.

"Not at you," I answered.

She stepped closer, then reached past me, for the door-knob. Turned the lock.

"Open your eyes," she said. I didn't realize I had closed them. I listened to her, and all I could see was her, nothing but her. And suddenly both my hands were in her hair, and my mouth was on hers. I was gone.

She pushed me back into the door, and the sound of us echoed through the empty room. And then the door on the far wall flung open, and Janna had one hand over her eyes, one hand in the air. "I'm sorry, I'm sorry, I'm leaving!"

Delaney started laughing into my chest. Janna kept talking. "I was in the bathroom and then you guys were here, and then I thought I'd just wait you out. . . ."

"You can open your eyes, Janna."

She lowered her hand but couldn't quite look at us. "Ugh. I thought you were fighting, but this encounter has taken an unexpected turn. And I'm sorry, I don't want to wait that out."

We stepped to the side as she hurried for the door. "*Really*," she said to me as she passed. She slammed the door behind her, and I looked around the sterile room. Empty room with cold furniture.

"Let's go home," I whispered in her ear. She nodded against my chest, her arms still wrapped around me.

I couldn't let her go as we walked through the party. Like this was a spell, and the moment we broke apart, it would be over. So she walked, and I walked behind her, my arms wrapped around her waist. I saw Justin standing with Janna now, and he caught my eye and shook his head. Guess he knew he'd be finding his own ride home.

"Jacket?" I asked her.

"I don't know. Maya took it, and she and Kevin are . . . who knows. Just . . . leave it."

I shrugged mine off and watched her slide her arms inside, the sleeves too long. She wrapped it around herself and smiled at me.

Gone.

We ran to my car—well, I tried to run, but with the heels on her shoes and the ice on the ground, mostly I just ended up half carrying her at nowhere near a run.

I kissed her against the side of the minivan. My hands were inside my jacket. On her. And all I could think of was the time I'd spent not kissing her. I felt her shudder.

"You're cold," I said.

"I'm not," she said.

But I unlocked her door anyway. Watched as she slid into the seat. Closed her door, feeling safe. Feeling like everything was back. Normal. The way it was supposed to be.

I walked around the van, closed my door. Smiled at her sitting beside me, rubbing her hands together. She folded her hands inside my jacket and leaned forward, toward the heater. I thought about turning the heat on and not going home at all. And since she didn't buckle her seat belt or anything, I knew she was thinking the same thing. I turned the key in the ignition, and the running lights lit up the edge of Falcon Lake.

I leaned forward and flipped the wipers on to clear the ice, thinking of all the places we could go to be alone.

The windshield wipers screeched against the window.

Her hands were gripping the dashboard, and she was leaning forward, and I could see the way her entire body tensed.

"What the hell is that?" she asked, leaning forward.

I leaned forward too. Saw a shape at the edge of the lake. Saw color. "Who . . . ," I said. It wasn't a *what* at all, but a *who*. It was bare legs on the rocks and blond hair floating in the water.

"Oh God," I said. "Get help."

I heard Delaney yelling before she reached the party, before I reached the edge of the lake. Before I pulled her by her fur boots, dragging her out of the water. Before I flipped her over and saw Tara's face. The wig attached by bobby pins, but her brown hair escaping from underneath.

Her open mouth. Stained red lips. Falcon Lake water dripping off her cold, still body.

Chapter

14

"Tara!" I yelled, shaking her by the shoulders.

Listen. Water lapping at my knees. Footsteps crunching the pebbles as people came racing. And nothing, nothing, nothing coming from Tara.

She had a cut on her forehead, and blood was dripping down the side of her face, mixed with the lake water.

I saw Delaney instead. Her blond hair floating in the water. The way her skin was blue when I pulled her from the ice. The way she didn't move. Didn't breathe. The gutting terror.

I couldn't take a breath. Couldn't focus on the girl on the side of the lake who needed help. I was useless. Someone pushed me back. Kevin, I think.

No to me or yes to her. Tara had asked me within earshot of the lake. *Her,* I'd said. *"I want her."*

Her for everyone.

"Is she breathing?" someone asked. But all I could hear

was someone asking that same question over my shoulder as I tilted Delaney's lifeless head back and put my mouth over hers.

"Can you feel her heartbeat?" someone said. But all I could feel were Delaney's ribs cracking under the weight of my hands as I tried to keep hers beating.

I heard myself counting in my head. I heard sirens coming, like they did that day, almost a year ago. I heard Delaney's voice in my ear. "Breathe," she whispered. I felt the air from her lungs against my cheek. Her hand on my chest as she knelt beside me.

I turned my face, and all I could see was her. Alive. "What's happening?" she asked, once she could tell I was breathing. "What the hell is happening?"

I didn't answer, because the question in her head became the only thing in mine: *What the hell is happening?*

I watched as everyone else watched Tara being loaded onto a stretcher, an EMT hovering over her so we couldn't see what was happening. I watched the police start to weave between us, searching for answers. I saw as everyone's attention shifted from the ambulance driving away to me, clinging to Delaney, on the edge of Falcon Lake.

People nodding in my direction as the cops asked them questions. The cops making their way to me, like I had any answers whatsoever.

I saw Tara in the water. That's what I told the young cop. I thought I recognized him from school. Not much older than us. "What were you doing when you saw her?" he asked.

I had stepped away from Delaney. He'd wanted to speak with me in private. "I was leaving," I said.

"Why were you leaving so early?"

I realized he was trying to see if I had been involved. "I was leaving with a girl," I said, keeping my voice low. Not wanting to bring her name into it.

"Care to point me in the right direction? Just to verify . . ."

I looked over my shoulder. Saw her watching me. "Delaney," I said, still looking at her. Then I turned back to the cop. "Delaney Maxwell."

He looked at her, like he was trying to place her. He knew her, of course. Or the story of her. He closed his notepad, took a step away from the lake. "You need to stay," he said. "Can't let anyone drive. We'll call parents soon."

"I haven't been drinking," I said.

"That's what everyone else said, too," he said.

Kevin was behind me, pulling on my arm. "Let's go," he said. "Maya's."

"We're supposed to stay," I said, trying to think straight.

"We need to *go*," he said. He turned to Delaney, gave her a look, and I felt her fingers sliding between mine. I felt her pull mc away, following Kevin.

We disappeared into the woods, picking our way over branches, grabbing onto one another in the dark whenever we lost our footing.

We walked in a silent, single-file line. Justin leading the way instead of Maya. It was his house first. When Carson died, Justin and Tara and I had spent the night at Kevin's because we didn't know what else to do. We didn't even talk. It was just a room filled with shock and grief, but it was better than being alone.

Justin let Maya pass when we reached the front porch. She looked over her shoulder and said, "You have to be quiet," as she turned the handle. The door creaked open, and our shoes echoed on the old wood beneath our feet. The house was exactly like I remembered it. A few sofas in the big, open area. A kitchen you could see into, with a second exit. A wood-paneled hall leading to a bathroom and three bedrooms, crammed together, with a third exit.

This was always built to be a vacation rental. There was nothing homey about it.

"Maya?" We heard a voice from the dark hallway, heard footsteps approaching.

"We have company," she called back. Holden stepped out into the living area, looking at each of us, then staring at Maya.

"It's not a good time," he said, looking back down the hall.

I felt bad, knowing their mother was somewhere down there, needing rest. "There's been an accident," she whispered, and a sob escaped Janna's throat.

Justin put an arm around her, and Kevin sunk to the floor with his head in his hands, like he'd forgotten until right that second.

"What happened?" Holden asked.

None of us could say it. "Tara," Maya said. "She drowned."

"She's not dead," Janna said. And Maya stared at her. "We

don't know yet." Janna glanced at Delaney quickly, and I knew what she was thinking. Dying and almost dying were nowhere near the same thing.

Holden put a hand on the nearest piece of furniture, and all the color drained from his face. He shook his head, like such a thing shouldn't be allowed. It's exactly how I felt when I got to the hospital and saw my mom waiting for me. "Who's Tara?" he whispered.

"Kevin's ex," Maya said, which was the least of what she was, but I guess that's the only Tara she knew. The one she'd taken something from.

Holden was still shaking his head. "Who are *you*?" Holden asked. He was looking at us like he was trying to place us. He knew Kevin. He knew me.

Maya did a quick halfhearted introduction of the rest. "Janna, Justin, Delaney," she said.

Holden stared at Delaney in a way that made me step closer to her. "This is Delaney," he said. As if he was expecting Delaney to say hi or that she was glad to meet him or something. She was holding on to me, or I was holding on to her, and she was definitely not acknowledging his existence.

"What the fuck is happening," Kevin mumbled. He looked up at me. "What the fuck was she doing in the water?"

"Shh," Maya said. "Stop it."

"Don't tell me to stop it when my—"

"Your what?" she asked. "Your *what*?"

This is how it starts. We'd all been here before. The accusations and the blame. They come first.

"Maya," Holden said, reaching for her.

"No, it's horrible, I know, but you're acting like she's yours," she said, waving off her brother.

Kevin looked at her like she was crazy. "She *is* ours," he said.

We belonged to one another. When things were on the line, we were protective of one another. To the outside world. And she didn't get that.

Kevin narrowed his eyes at her and continued. "And Janna is ours. And Justin. And Decker. And Delaney. Carson is ours, too, but you'll . . . never . . . know him." He spoke through clenched teeth. Janna started sobbing. He was acting like this was all Maya's fault. She was just a body. The closest thing he could blame.

"Stop. My mother," she whispered. Kevin stopped talking, but his shoulders were shaking.

"You all need to leave," Holden said, stepping closer to his sister. He put an arm around her and pulled her toward him. "Out," he said. "Now."

I was going to be sick. I started walking down the hall to the bathroom, and Holden called after me, "Where are you going?"

I raised my hand because I couldn't even answer. The bathroom was at the far end of the hall. I passed Maya's room on my right—all reds and browns—and then a room with a plain double bed, an old quilt, like it had been stitched by hand. The room was barren otherwise, probably because Holden kept most of his stuff at school. And a closed door on my left. I tried not to make any noise as I passed.

I shut the door behind me, put my hands on the edge of the sink, stared at the drain, and waited for the wave of nausea to pass. The bathroom already had the scent of sickness, like somebody had recently been ill right here, and my knees buckled as I tried to breathe through my mouth. My skin turned hot, and I felt beads of sweat forming at my hairline, which happens right before I hurl, usually. There was a knock but no pause before Delaney slipped inside as well, shutting the door behind her.

I couldn't look at her. Couldn't tell her how I'd rejected Tara to her face. Told Tara I chose Delaney instead. Imagined Tara lying facedown in the water while my hands were in Delaney's hair, while my mouth was on hers. My body, pressed against her, feeling entirely alive.

Delaney didn't say anything. She ran the faucet, put the hand towel in the sink, and then placed it across the back of my neck. I felt the water dripping under my collar, cooling my hot skin.

I saw her hands gripping the edge of the sink beside me, like she was trying not to be sick herself. And I remembered the way they had looked on the dashboard. Like she was gripping it to keep them still. The shudder that ran through her.

"You knew," I said, and her grip tightened against the sink.

"This place," she whispered, not exactly answering. "What the hell is happening?"

"Delaney," I said, because she knew, she *knew*. "Is she . . ."

She spun around, threw her hands up. "I don't know. *I don't know*. I don't know *anything*. Nothing makes sense."

She had her hand over her mouth and her eyes were closed, and I couldn't tell whether she was trying to keep something in or hold herself together. This is why she went to that guy in Boston. The not knowing would shatter anyone. The not knowing would irrevocably destroy a person who relied on logic, like Delaney. And it was.

I had my hands on the sides of her upper arms. "Tell me then."

We had never done this. I mean, she didn't *not* tell me. But she spoke vaguely. In shrugged-off events. In moods. I worried I was overstepping, that she wanted to keep it for herself. But from the way she was looking at me now, it was like she'd been waiting for me to offer. God, I was a moron.

"You were kissing me," she whispered. And she touched her fingers to her mouth for a moment. "Outside. And then . . ." And then I felt her shudder. "From nowhere," she said.

"Her body was starting to die," I said, and she nodded. Tara's body, giving off a signal. A Leave-me-behind signal. Only it pulled Delaney. Not a push. A pull. "Why didn't you say something?"

"I thought it wasn't real," she said. "Like a memory. Like a reminder of what I had done to you." And what I had done to her. "And nothing makes sense anymore. Like I'm standing right here"—she pointed at the closed door to the hall—"and I can't feel *anything*. Nothing makes sense."

I heard a door being closed in the hall. And then another. And then a knock on our door.

"Just a sec," I said.

"I'm driving you all home," Holden said.

Delaney opened the door and he looked at her. Looked at me over her shoulder. Like he thought we were up to something in here and not just trying to keep from hurling in his sink. "I'm getting my shoes, and we're leaving." Then he disappeared into the third room. The room that had the door shut. I mentally tallied them. Maya. The empty, quilted bed. Mom, behind the closed door.

Something was off. Delaney, not feeling anything. Holden, wanting us out. Holden, going into the wrong room.

"We have to go," I said to Delaney, grabbing her by the hand. She was confused, I could tell. But she didn't say anything.

Kevin was waiting by the door. "Holden is driving me to the hospital."

I shook my head at him. Something was *off*. "Come with us. We're walking. We'll make some calls."

"No. I'm going to the hospital." Holden was walking down the hall again. We had to *go*. And Kevin had that look like he was searching for someone to be angry with again.

"Come with me," I whispered.

He bumped his shoulder into mine as I passed. "We are *going* to the hospital to see Tara," he said.

He was staring me down, and Holden was coming closer. "Call me when you know?" I asked.

"You're not coming?"

I needed air. I needed to think. I needed to think *straight*. "We're walking." I pulled Delaney out the sliding glass door out back before Kevin could say anything more. We were moving way too fast, and I caught her as she slipped behind me down the embankment to the path. Our home was on the other side of the lake, but the path would take us all the way there.

I could see the police still picking over the edge of the lake a few houses away, and I put my finger to my lips as we walked. It wasn't until we were all the way on the far shore, where I couldn't see the cops in the dark, that she asked me, "What? What is it?"

"Their mom isn't there," I said.

Delaney looked confused. "Whose mom? Maya's?"

"Holden went into the only room she could've been in. For his shoes."

"Is there some reason his shoes couldn't be in there?"

I shook my head. "You don't feel anything because she's not sick. She's not *there*."

"Okay, so she's at the hospital or something . . . maybe that's why I don't feel anything. That makes sense."

Yes. No. I didn't know. My mind was mixing things up, like the way I saw Delaney in the water instead of Tara. I couldn't think straight. I was panicking over nothing. Over everything. Did I kiss Delaney tonight? Wasn't I on my way to be alone with her? "What the hell is happening?" I said.

She looked somewhere past me, I could hear the water

lapping against the shore nearby, and she shuddered. "We have to go home," she said.

It was weird to come home together. To the same place. To see our parents sitting on the couch together, having a drink. It was weird to see them all turn to us at the same time, with the same expression. A second of confusion seeing us together, seeing my fingers interlaced with hers again, before their faces turned momentarily up. Until they got a better look and saw the dirt on my hands. On Delaney's face. At our clothes, coated in ice and mud.

Joanne spoke first. "Where are your shoes?"

I looked down. Delaney was wearing only socks. Guess she left the boots at Maya's. I'd been dragging her through ice and dirt and she was barefoot. "Tara Spano was found in the lake," she said as an answer.

Then her hand left mine, flew to cover her mouth, and she ran up the stairs. Her slamming door shook the entire house.

"We're waiting to hear," I added.

"Oh my God." Delaney's mom was on her feet, heading for the stairs. I beat her to them.

"Decker," my mom said. "Let Joanne."

But I ignored her. I took the stairs two at a time and didn't knock. I threw the door closed behind me, slamming it just as hard as she had, house rules be damned. Then I fell beside her on her bed, in the empty space she'd been curled around. And I rested my face against her collar, hearing her heart, beating strong. A second later she wrapped her arms around my back, pulling me closer, and whispered the words I'd been waiting to hear. "It's okay. It's okay."

My phone rang a little while later, when I was stuck between wake and sleep. We both jumped up. I saw it was Justin, and my fingers shook as I pressed Answer. "She's not dead," Justin said, and I felt everything inside of me uncoil.

"She's okay?"

"Kevin called from the hospital, said she wasn't dead— unconscious from hitting her head is all. Took in some water and stuff. But her parents were taking her home. That's the last I heard. He's not answering his phone anymore. His parents are going to kill him. . . ."

"Okay," I said.

Justin started coughing. I heard him clear his throat and groan. "I gotta go," he mumbled. The phone clicked off.

Delaney was standing up in the pitch-black room. "She's alive," I said. She started looking through her drawers, and her breath was speeding up when it should have been slowing with relief. I stood up and walked toward her. Out from under the covers, I was shaking. My clothes clung to me, stiff and cold and dirty.

"Hey." I put my hand on her arm to steady her. "She's alive." I cleared my throat. "You saved her."

"I didn't," she said, yanking out some random pajamas and slamming the drawer shut. "I didn't do anything."

"But you saw her. You were looking and you saw her."

"That doesn't mean I *saved* her." She spat the word out, like it was vile. Her whole body stiffened. She cleared her throat. "I *saved* someone else once."

"You did?"

"A boy. Our age, I think. He was going to have a stroke and I told his nurse and they had him at the hospital in time. My doctor said I saved him, too." She shook her head, the saddest thing. "He's a vegetable," she choked out. "Do you think I saved him, Decker? Should I have said anything at all?"

I had no idea what to say. "I never know what to do," she said. "I never do the right thing. I tried so hard with Carson. So hard!" I realized in that moment that she'd never been allowed to grieve for him. Not with the guilt. Not with Janna pointing her finger at her. Not with the rest of us all caught up in our own grief.

"I know you did," I said. "But Delaney, Tara is *home*."

Her hands stilled, and she turned to face me. "She's okay?" she asked, her voice full of need.

I wasn't sure. I hoped I wasn't lying when I said, "She's fine."

I watched her face turn from hope to relief, I saw a ghost of a smile, I heard the breath she let out as a laugh, and all I could think was, *Please let it be true, please let it be true.*

I heard our parents' voices carrying from downstairs and knew ours were probably carrying as well. "I should go," I said.

"Oh." She held up her clothes, like she thought I didn't think I should see her get changed.

"I mean, I'm gross, and I'm messing up your bed," I whispered. "And your parents are going to kill me."

"You can wear my clothes," she said. I laughed.

"I'm not wearing your clothes."

She smiled, too. It felt like we'd beaten the curse somehow. Tara lived. Delaney found her, and I pulled her out of the lake and she lived. We were *smiling*.

"Decker Phillips: too good for my clothes and too good for my room," she said, which was her way of asking me to stay.

"For future reference, next time you're trying to lure a guy to your room, don't offer to dress him up like a girl. I'll let it slide this time." Which was my way of saying yes.

Yes, of course I would stay. "I should stay on the floor," I said, listening to the voices carry from downstairs.

She nodded and pulled out an extra pillow from her closet. She took the comforter off her bed and laid it on the floor. And while I was setting it all up, she got dressed, before I could see. She had on an oversize sweatshirt. Pajama pants. "Seriously," she said. "You need to change." She pulled at the bottom of my shirt. Lifted it up. Ran her hands along my stomach as she pushed my shirt up over my head.

We heard footsteps on the stairs. Her eyes widened, and I stepped away to the side of her bed. I lowered myself under the comforter on the rug. She got into bed. The door opened, but nobody said anything. We pretended to sleep. We pretended to sleep for so long, I *was* sleeping.

*   *   *

"Decker." I heard her voice, her fingers digging into my leg. *"Her or me,"* she asked. *"Her. Or. Me."*

I woke with a start, feeling cold. The comforter was around my waist. I looked up at Delaney's bed, but it was empty.

Then I saw her shadow in the open doorway. She padded back into the room and shut the door behind her.

I pushed myself up on my elbows. "Delaney?"

"Did I wake you up?" she asked.

"No," I said, my eyes adjusting to the dark. "I thought you left me here."

"Bathroom," she said. Then she padded across the floor and lowered herself beside me. "I wouldn't leave you."

She meant the words to be reassuring, I was sure— especially tonight—but they stung. Because I did leave her. And one day, she would too. "I did leave you," I said.

"Decker, it's—"

"No, I mean, before." There was something else at the core, and I was scared it was going to rise up again, when we least expected it. "I want to fix whatever is broken. I'm just not sure how. I can't undo it. And you can't forget it." I couldn't look at her when I said it, so I stared at the ceiling instead. This was the moment where she would see it, too. That we were unfixable, ruined by what we'd done to each other.

She slid under the covers, and I moved over to share the pillow. "Nothing's broken," she said. "It's just our life."

She put a hand on my chest, moved it down to my stomach. Put her head on my shoulder. "Go back to sleep," she said. My breath caught in my throat. And with her hand on

my stomach and her breath on my neck, there was no way in
hell I was going back to sleep.

I turned to face her, kissed her so she'd know it wasn't just
the clothes and Halloween and the party. That I loved her
even though she picked my father's wishes over my own.
Maybe even because of it.

Chapter
15

Everyone was in the living room by the time I got downstairs. I heard them all talking. "She hit her head," Joanne said. "She slipped and hit her head. She needed seven stitches."

"How long was she in the water?" my mom asked.

"Not too long, I guess. They stumbled upon her just in time."

I walked out from the stairwell, and Joanne said, "Ah, the hero awakes."

My mom gave me a look over her coffee. The look said, *I hope you practiced your apology because now would be a good time to use it.*

Delaney walked out of the kitchen. "I'm sorry," I said. Both her parents looked up. "I was upset. I wasn't thinking. And then I fell asleep." Part of the truth. Enough of the truth.

"All right," Joanne said. "Tara's okay." Ron shook the newspaper in front of his face, which was his way of disagreeing.

Joanne shot him a look—shot the newspaper a look, anyway. "It's okay," she mouthed, sending me an apologetic smile. As far as they knew, I slept on the floor anyway. Alone.

My mom was still giving me the look. "And it won't happen again," I added. And then I looked down at the state of my clothes.

Delaney stood in the entrance of the kitchen, leaning against the doorway, trying not to smile when she looked at me. I was trying not to smile at her. We were both losing. I turned away before someone would notice. "I'm gonna run home for warmer clothes," I said.

"Tomorrow," my mom said, "you'll have a home again." I walked across our yards—the ice had melted, but the ground was still wet, cold. I shook my head. I'd been waiting for over a month to move back in for good. And now I wanted to stay. To have an excuse to end up on Delaney's floor in the middle of the night. To see her first thing in the morning, with her messy hair and ridiculous-looking pajamas. To have her yell at me for drinking all the milk and putting the empty carton back in the fridge.

I pushed the shades in the living room apart, letting light—and hopefully some warmth—inside. I turned on the shower after stripping off my dirty clothes, but I had to keep the bathroom door open for any trace of light. The water ran completely cold—it was probably the fastest shower of my life, but at least it woke me up. *Tara was in the lake but she's alive. She's alive.*

What the hell is happening?

My phone was ringing when I stepped out of the shower. Justin. "Tell me," he said, in a raspy, tired voice. "Tell me that that did not just happen. Tell me that I was so doped up on cough medicine that I passed out and had the most fucked-up dream and you all brought me home while I was unconscious."

He coughed. Choked. "Tell me that Tara was not facedown in the goddamn lake. Tell me you didn't have to pull her out."

"She's alive," I said. "She's okay," I added.

"It's coming for us, Decker," he said, and I felt goose bumps form as the water dried off my skin. *Water in my house. Glass on her floor, like ice.*

I walked out of the dark hall toward the front windows and watched Delaney's house. "Stop. You're being ridiculous. It's a lake. It's water. It's rain. It doesn't do anything. God, listen to yourself!"

"Tell that to Tara," Justin said before he started coughing again.

"She was drunk. She fell. She hit her head," I said, reciting the facts, the things that were real. And when he didn't respond, I repeated, "She slipped and hit her head."

"She slipped. She was sitting there with us. Where the hell was she going? What was she doing outside?"

I didn't know. Maybe leaving. Maybe clearing her head. "What does it matter?" I asked.

"Are you a moron?" Justin yelled. I jerked the phone away from my ear. "Open your eyes. Carson. Tara. It's coming for us, Decker. It's coming for us all." His words dissolved into a fit of coughing and wheezing.

"Calm down, Justin. Calm. Down."

"I will not calm down," he said. And then he lowered his voice. "We rescued her and it's coming for us." Finally putting into words what we were all thinking. Delaney, cold and blue, on the shore of the lake. We had taken her back. "What the hell was Tara doing at the edge of the lake, anyway? The cooler was up on the patio. Thought she'd take a nice stroll? It was sleeting out, for fuck's sake."

"Calm. Down," I repeated, even though I had no idea what she was doing by the lake.

Water in Kevin's car. Water in Justin's lungs. In Tara's . . .

"Even Janna is freaking the hell out," he said.

"I'm gonna go see Tara," I said, forming the plans as I spoke, then realizing I needed to get my car, which was still parked on the other side of Falcon Lake.

The walk to the other side of the lake always seemed longer in the daylight because I could see how far I still had to go, how little progress I was making. It's why I made Delaney cut across the frozen surface last year. It looks pointlessly long when you can see the house directly across the way, a tiny dot on the opposite shore.

The farther I walked, the guiltier I felt about dragging Delaney back, walking barefoot over the wet, cold ground. And for what? Because I was disoriented and freaked out about the number of rooms in their house. And so what if their mom was home or not. Ridiculous.

Maya and Holden's house was silent and still as I passed it. But through the trees I saw a person sitting cross-legged next to the water in front of me. She heard me coming and stood before I got there. Maya brushed the dirt from her jeans and crossed her arms over her chest.

I held up my keys. "Just going to get my car," I said. As I got closer, I could tell her eyes were bloodshot and there were black smudges at the corners, remnants of her makeup from last night. I wondered if she was still waiting for a call. "Tara's okay," I said.

She released her breath. "Thank God," she said. "Kevin didn't call." She turned back to the lake as I passed by. But I remembered Delaney that day at Carson's funeral. The way nobody, not even me, stood up for her.

I paused behind her. I could see the minivan from here, through the trees, waiting for me. I cleared my throat. "It's not you," I said. "We've all been—we've had a lot to grieve about over the last year."

"And you think I haven't?" she asked, her voice wavering. "I used to be so jealous of you guys. You're all so close, and it seemed like you'd never just abandon one another. I wanted that." She laughed to herself. "But you're all so messed up. You're just too close to see it."

Time to go.

I heard the sliding door up the hill. "You okay, Maya?" Holden was staring me down, his arms crossed over his chest.

"Just getting my car," I said again. *And getting the hell out of here.*

"I'm fine," she said.

"Come on in," he said. She had to be freezing.

"Tara's okay," she said, ignoring his request.

She turned back to the lake, and Holden leaned against the door frame. I left them there and walked up the embankment, toward the road. Wondered if it would've been worse if I'd known about my dad beforehand. If I had spent the months leading up to his death grieving already, like Maya was for her mother. If this was why he didn't want to tell me.

Why nobody wanted to tell me.

As I drove back home, I saw Maya still standing at the edge of the lake. And for a second, I wondered if I really would've wanted to know what was coming.

I convinced Delaney to come with me. Delaney thought Tara wouldn't be thrilled to see her there, but I didn't really care. She took a deep breath as we pulled into the lot in front of Tara's house.

When I was younger, I thought Tara lived in the greatest house on earth. She literally lived over an ice cream shop with so much family it seemed like a never-ending party. The ice cream shop was the front of the first floor, and the top two floors were split down the center—her cousins' family on one side, Tara's family (complete with three younger brothers) on the other, and their grandparents on the top floor.

And we got free ice cream whenever we wanted.

Tara worked there during the summers, scooping out ice cream in a tank top even though it was probably freezing. She never ate it. Said she couldn't stand the taste of it anymore. As an only child, I was jealous of the perpetual noise in her house, of the fact that everyone was always climbing all over one another. Of the big family dinners. Of the fact that four extra faces never fazed them.

Now I could see why she always wanted to be out. This was a seasonal shop, and the season had just ended—the windows were boarded up, but the tables were still out front. Jared, her youngest brother, was sitting at one of the picnic tables with a portable video game in his hand. "Hey," I said. "We're here to see your sister."

"She's sleeping," he said, but he drew out the word "sleeping" endlessly. Like she'd been sleeping endlessly. Or maybe like she would be.

"She's not sleeping," Tony said, walking out of the woods with a stick in his hand. He was twelve and the closest to Tara's age. "We have to stay outside to keep it quiet, though," he told us. He pointed to the side of his skull. "Killer headache."

I took Delaney's hand and pulled her toward the steps— they were built up the side of the house, leading to a balcony on top of the ice cream shop, which is where the actual front door was.

Her mother answered the door, and before I had time to register what was happening, she pulled each of us in for a quick hug—first me, then Delaney. She was the complete opposite of Tara. Frumpy clothes. No makeup. Never seeming to care what she looked like. "Thank you," she said, and she tried to smile. "I'm not sure how much she's up for visitors— Janna was here for most of the morning. I think she may need a nap soon. But go on up."

She gestured to me because I'd been here more recently. Delaney used to come when she was younger, too, before it became obvious they weren't actually friends. Tara was the type to pop in and out of every social circle, never settling on just one.

We waited at the entrance to Tara's room. She was resting on top of the sheets, wearing the most anti-Tara clothes in the world. Baggy shirt. Sweatpants. A white bandage taped over her right eyebrow—I flashed to the image of watery blood running down the side of her face.

I knocked on her open door, and she squeezed her eyes closed before turning her neck slowly toward us. Tara's face didn't change. She didn't smile at me. Didn't frown at Delaney standing just behind me. Her mouth barely moved as she said, "I see that last night ended better for you than it did for me." Now would be the moment where she'd smile coyly or flip her hair. But she just lay there. Limp and un-Tara-like.

"We came to see how you were," Delaney said. She pushed me forward with her hand on my back until I was standing at the foot of Tara's daybed. The fact that her bed was also a couch was another one of those things that seemed a lot cooler when we were younger.

"Stitches," she said. She raised her right hand and touched the skin beside the bandage. Her fingers trembled as she traced the border.

"You tripped?" I asked. I had to be sure so I could tell Justin. She tripped and hit her head and almost drowned in the lake, but it was an accident. She was drunk and it was an accident. I hoped she remembered.

"Yeah," she said. "Not embarrassing at all . . ." I smiled when she said it, catching a glimpse of the Tara we all knew. She narrowed her eyes for a second and said, "Did you see?"

"You don't remember?" I asked.

"No, I remember that." She swallowed, and it seemed like it was painful for her. "I heard you pulled me out of the lake." She was out there because I pushed her away. I wondered if she remembered that, too.

"He did," Delaney said. She didn't mention that she was the one who saw Tara. That she was the one who saved her.

"Okay," she said, and her fingers started pulling absently at the comforter beside her. "I was just wondering if you saw . . ." She took a deep, shaky breath. "If you saw how I got in the lake."

I felt Delaney tense beside me. I couldn't move. Couldn't breathe. Even the room seemed to hold its breath. Tara's eyes were wide, and she was looking from me to Delaney and back again. Her hands grasped the comforter and she said, "How did I get in the fucking lake?"

I had to lean forward. Lean on something. Anything. I put my hands on the edge of her bed. "I thought you said you tripped and hit your head." The room was tilting around me. Or I was tilting. Hard to tell.

"I did," she said. "I fell off the patio. But how did I get in the lake? Tell me."

I couldn't tell her. The lake was a good ten steps away from the edge of the patio.

"We didn't see," Delaney whispered. "We didn't see how it happened."

"The doctor said I was disoriented after I hit my head," she said. "That most people don't remember the moments before. Or after." Except Tara did remember the moments before. "He said I must've stood up. Stumbled around. And fell again. Passed out cold. Bad luck," she said.

"Bad luck," I repeated, wanting that to be true.

"The doctor said it was good luck that you were there. Good luck that I didn't drown in the lake. Good. Luck," she said, her voice growing louder. Her mouth twitched. "That's funny, right?"

I flashed to the image of her, her blond wig floating in the water. Like Delaney, disappearing under the surface.

She was starting to panic. *I* was starting to panic. "How did I get in the water?" she asked. She looked at Delaney, her eyes wide. "How did I get in the fucking water?"

Delaney shook her head. I thought she was going to turn around and bolt, but instead she came closer. She put her fingers on Tara's head, just near the stitches. "You're fine now," she said. Tara's breathing returned to normal, but she was still glaring at Delaney.

She looked at me and said, "Janna thinks it's real." She didn't have to say what *it* was. We all knew. "Not just the lake, though. This whole town. She says there's something wrong with this place. That it makes us forget."

This is a place that wouldn't let me forget. Delaney in the lake. My father on the floor. Taking and taking and making me watch. "So, what," I said, "she thinks it *made* you get up and fall in the water?" I laced my words with sarcasm, so they would sound ridiculous. So we would believe they were ridiculous.

We heard footsteps creaking overhead. I glanced at the ceiling. Her grandmother lived up there. She told fortunes and sometimes held séances. We used to spy on her when we were little. Tara never believed. *"Smoke and mirrors,"* she'd told me last time I was over here. She saw me looking now. "I don't know," she said, "what she thinks."

I had a vision of Tara lying beside the patio, her forehead bleeding. I saw two fingers of water, snaking up from the lake, weaving through the rocks and the dirt, like I'd seen it trailing down the walls in my house, seeping across the floor. I saw the water circle her wrists and pull her down. Pull her to the lake. Trying to take her.

Tara's mother stood behind us, pushed past us to get to her daughter. "I'm so glad that you saw her. We really can't thank you enough."

She thanked me, like Delaney's parents had thanked me. Like I had saved her life too. Good luck that we found her. Bad luck that she ended up there to begin with. Good luck that Tara—and Delaney—lived. Bad luck that they almost drowned first. I was the hero who pulled them out. I was the villain who sent them both out to the lake in the first place.

Like Falcon Lake was trying to tell me something. Something about myself.

Listen.

"Do you need some rest, hon?" Her mom sat on the edge of the daybed, ran her fingers along Tara's forehead. Tara nodded. Closed her eyes. Turned her head away from us. The lake had taken something from her—she no longer seemed invincible. But she survived. I repeated it to myself as Delaney and I walked down the stairs to my car. *She lived she lived she lived . . .*

We were two streets away when Delaney started to breathe like she did when she was trying not to cry. She was looking out the window, and she was breathing slowly. Deliberately. I could hear the catch. I thought, *Don't cry don't cry don't cry,* and a tear rolled down her cheek.

Shit. I pulled over to the side of the road. Left the engine running. "Delaney?" I asked.

"Why her?" she asked, facing me. "Why her and not me? If it wants me, I'm right here."

I reached across the center console, across the cooler of snacks I kept between the seats, unbuckled her seat belt, and pulled her toward me. I held her awkwardly across the gap. "Stop," I said. "It's not real. You know that."

"Then how did she end up in the goddamn lake? How did she trip and hit her head and almost drown?" she asked into my shoulder. I felt her tears through my shirt. Goddamn kryptonite.

"Because people who have a blood alcohol content over .23 are six times as likely to have head injuries. And they're ten times as likely to drown."

"You're making that up," she said.

"I am," I said, and I felt her smile.

Her phone rang, and I laughed as she jumped, even though I had jumped too. She ignored the ringing. "We're okay?" she asked.

"We're okay," I said.

She smoothed back her hair, buckled her seat belt again, and checked her phone. "Who was it?" I asked.

She shrugged. "Wrong number." She put it back in her bag and leaned her head against the window like nothing had happened.

Nothing had happened.

I tried to keep my breath even as we started driving again, but every time I caught a glimpse of her beside me, I saw the blond hair floating in the water, saw a girl floating, facedown. Pictured myself pulling her out by her boots, flipping her over.

And pictured Delaney's face instead.

Chapter
16

Delaney's house was empty. She punched in the alarm code while I read the note on the kitchen counter. "Supply run for my house," I told her.

She was staring out the window, still thinking about what Tara had said, I was sure. This is how the rumor of a curse starts. If you let yourself believe. The fear eats away at you, piece by piece, until it doesn't seem irrational anymore. We couldn't let that happen again. "I'm gonna call Justin back," I said. "Let him know everything's okay."

She nodded. "Everything's okay," she said. We needed to keep saying that instead. Believe it enough so it became true.

I went into Ron's office so she wouldn't hear Justin freaking out on the other end. "Tara's okay," I said as soon as he picked up. "I saw her. She tripped and she hit her head. So you can stop freaking out."

I heard him breathing, or wheezing, on the other end.

"That's not what Janna said." He coughed and spoke clearer. "*She* said Tara has *no freaking clue* how she ended up in the water."

I heard the doorbell in the living room.

"Justin," I said, lowering my voice, "it's Tara. She lives for drama. She lives for attention." She used to, anyway.

I heard a man's voice in the living room. Guess our parents were back. "Hey, I gotta go," I said.

"I know I was all drugged up last night," he said, getting louder, "but was it just me, or did Tara look just the slightest bit like Delaney last night?" And the hair on the back of my neck stood on end.

Delaney's laugh carried from the next room. Alive. She was alive.

But that's what I'd been picturing in the car, driving home with her. Delaney, instead of Tara.

"Decker? You still there?"

"I gotta go," I said, hanging up.

Tara said the doctors thought she was disoriented.

But *I* had been disoriented. I saw Delaney instead of Tara when I pulled her from the water, her blond hair floating around her.

I saw Delaney.

"Delaney?" I called, pushing open the door. I needed to see her. I needed to talk to her alone. I froze just outside the office door. Holden was standing in the living room like he belonged here, and Delaney was smiling at him.

He did a double take when he saw me. "Oh, hey," he said.

"I didn't know you were here." He held up a plastic bag. "On a shoe-returning mission," he said.

Delaney smirked. "I appreciate it," she said. "But I borrowed them from Maya."

He let the bag drop. "You're kidding."

"Nope. Sorry to waste your time."

I went into the kitchen so she wouldn't notice that I was starting to panic. *Why her and not me?* Delaney had asked, like she could sense it, too. It was supposed to be her.

"Not a waste," I heard Holden say. "Hey, listen. I have to leave tonight. But I was wondering if you wanted to grab something to eat first?"

I pushed back through the kitchen door, panic or not. "Are you asking her *out*?" I asked.

He looked between the both of us. "I'm sorry," he said. "Maya told me you guys broke up."

I guess he could tell my thoughts on that from the look on my face. "But no," he said. "I just wanted to talk to you," he said to Delaney. But she could tell something was wrong with me.

"Some other time," she said. And she started walking for the door. Holden, thank God, got the hint.

After she closed the door and locked it behind her, she said, "What? Decker, what?"

"Describe Tara," I said.

She put a hand on her hip and looked at me sideways. "Please," I said.

She held up her hand and started listing opinions as she

tapped each fingertip. "Likes to be the center of attention. Flirts with everyone, especially you . . ."

"No, I mean, the way she looks."

Delaney paused, and I could feel the look she was sending me. I could hear it in the tone of her voice. "Tall. Big boobs. Dark hair. *Beautiful* . . . Decker? What's the matter?"

I had to close my eyes. Had to see her in my head, like I saw her last night. I had to breathe.

This was how I'd describe Delaney: taller than average, curvier than average, beautiful. Mine.

They don't look alike side by side. But Justin was right. Last night, Tara was a pretty blond girl draped over me on the couch. Last night, Tara fit Delaney's description perfectly.

"What?" she asked. She reached out and touched my arm.

"Nothing," I said, but it came out as a whisper. I fell back on the couch, my head between my knees.

I had to get out of here. *We* had to get out of here. Out of this town, away from whatever was happening here.

"Nothing?" she asked, almost yelling at me. "Don't tell me *nothing* when you're sitting on the couch trying to breathe and we just visited a girl who thinks the lake called to her when she was unconscious."

I couldn't catch my breath and when I tilted my head to the side to look at her, she looked like she was going to be sick too. I remembered saying the words to her in the bathroom. *"In my head, I see you die."*

I wondered if she was seeing it too. Whether the vision in

my head transferred to her, and she saw herself floating, just under the ice, mouth open, eyes open. Perfectly still.

"In my mind, you're still dead."

"It was supposed to be you," I said, immediately regretting it, like I had in the bathroom when I told her I saw her dead all the time.

"Excuse me?" she said. "You just said she was drunk. You just *said*—"

"I know what I said. But you don't know what I saw. Tara, I mean. In the water. She looked like you."

"So the lake was coming for me?" she whispered. "You believe it? That the lake wants me dead?"

"No, Delaney. Not the lake." I swallowed. Steeled myself to say the words. Make them real. "A person."

How to put to words the way I could feel everything connecting? The way we feel about the lake, the way we let ourselves fear it and believe—that it wants us. That it could hurt us. The way a person could use that fear. Could hide something inside of it. *It's just the lake; it's what it wants.*

Except it's not the lake.

It's what *someone* wants. *Someone* wants her gone.

I was mumbling to her, frantically trying to explain, using my arms and pointing toward the lake, at everything, at nothing. And she was following my hands, like they made more sense than my words.

"Who would want me dead?" she asked when I finished. Her hands were clenched between her knees, like she was willing herself to hold on. And she didn't ask me like it seemed so far out of the realm of possibility. She asked me in the saddest way possible. Like she was asking *which one*.

"No, wait," she said, shaking her head. Breathing a sigh of relief. "People know Tara. She might look like how you'd describe me, but she doesn't look like me. Someone would know it was the wrong person."

"It's not someone who knows you, then," I said, which didn't make sense either. "I mean, they know *of* you. They don't *know* you." I thought of the article after Troy drowned, of the picture of me, reaching off the page for something that didn't exist. Of her name, whispered around town like a legend. Of the way the cops looked at me when I mentioned her name. Everyone knew *of* her. But not everyone *knew* her.

"It doesn't make sense, Decker." Delaney was picking through the logic of each step. She didn't rely on the way things felt connected. The way I knew it made sense, even if I wasn't sure how exactly. "Because it's not too hard to find out who I am. And Tara fell. She fell and hit her head. Nobody pushed her."

My mind was racing, trying on possibilities, running scenarios, searching for one to fit what I felt. The truth wasn't facts. I mean, it was. But it was also something else. Something I could feel. The facts would fill in around it later.

This was how my dad and I were so different. Everyone thought we were the same, but he was more like Delaney, needing facts. Without facts, it didn't count.

This counted.

Someone was coming for her. I could feel it.

It counted.

My mom, Joanne, and Ron were unloading all the bags from their two cars directly into my garage. "Oh good, you guys are home," my mom said. "Few hours of daylight left . . . get moving."

Delaney and I started with my room. We worked in silence, moving my dresser where it used to be, putting clothes back in the drawers. We both knew this room by heart. She helped my mom hang the curtains downstairs, lay out a throw rug across the new, darker wood floors. Delaney's parents were cleaning the surfaces throughout the house—everything was coated in a layer of white construction dust.

But by late afternoon, the sun didn't cut through the windows at the right angle, and the rooms closed off, one by one, in darkness.

I was helping my mom clean the windows in her room when Joanne knocked on the door. The hallway was dark behind her. "Dinner in an hour, okay?"

My mom balled up the paper towel and tossed it in the trash bucket beside me. "I'm going to take Decker out tonight, actually."

"All right. Enjoy."

A minute later, Delaney called into the room, "Bye," as she passed, and she was lugging a giant trash bag behind her.

"Hold on," I said, and I took the bag from her in the dark

hall and swung it over my shoulder. She gripped the handrail of the staircase as she walked down the steps and pulled her jacket tighter around herself.

I tossed the trash into the bin in the garage, and she stood in the doorway, waiting for me. I thought she didn't believe me about someone being after her, but it looked like she did. "Don't be scared," I said, walking toward her. I shouldn't have told her what I thought. It was a mistake. She needed facts to cling to, not this feeling of dread that she could do nothing about. Something else to feel powerless over.

"Nothing to be scared of, right? Just somebody who wants me dead. No big deal."

"Don't," I said, and I ran my hand through her hair, tucked it behind her ear. Felt her hands on the bottom of my shirt, her fingers sliding through the belt loops at my hips. "Nothing's going to happen to you," I said. I was getting so good at saying what I hoped was true, I thought for a second that I might have the power to make it true.

And before she had a chance to argue, I ran my thumb across her bottom lip and said, "I missed you like crazy." She turned her face up, just slightly, and I said, "I'm such an idiot."

She smiled, and that dimple formed in her cheek. Her eyes drifted closed as she drifted closer, and she said, "Good thing you're my favorite idiot."

I meant just to kiss her good-bye. Just a second or two. Or three. But it turned into the type of kiss that, no matter what you do, you feel like you can't get close enough. When she pulled back from me, I leaned in again, kissed her one last time, and said, "I'll see you tonight. Text me when everyone's asleep up there, okay?"

She left through the garage, and I watched her run across the yard. As I shut the door behind her, I felt hope instead of dread. I felt every hour between now and then. I felt them slipping by.

And then I felt someone else in the room.

I glanced quickly behind me, saw my mom leaning against the wall at the base of the staircase, holding her own trash bag, one eyebrow raised. I cleared my throat and didn't make eye contact as I passed her on the way to the stairs.

"A moment, Decker?"

I cringed, wondering how long she'd been standing there. I put my hands in my pockets and rocked back on my heels. "Oh, hey, I have an idea. Let's skip this part."

"Since your dad isn't here, I feel the need to tell you something."

"I promise, he already did this. Like, three years ago."

"No, I think he missed a part."

I held my breath. Please let this be quick. Please let this not be happening.

"You're too close—"

I let out my breath, narrowed my eyes. "Yeah, he did this part. It didn't go over well."

But she didn't stop. "You're too close, and you don't see what she's doing. Or maybe you do, and you don't care. I can't tell."

"Excuse me?" Delaney wasn't doing anything.

"She's changing her life, Decker. For you. Joanne said

she's applying to colleges in Maine now, like she doesn't care about looking anywhere else anymore."

It didn't make any sense. We had only gotten back together a day ago. It's like she always knew that one day I would tell her I'd been an idiot, and she'd forgive me by saying that at least I was her favorite idiot. She knew it would happen. She never stopped believing it.

"And I was going to go to Boston for her. How is that any different?"

"It's not," she said. "And your father was going to talk to you about that. Or he tried to. I guess, as you said, it didn't go over well."

He didn't try all that hard. Probably because he realized the futility of his argument.

"You're so stubborn," she said. But she didn't say it like it was a bad thing. "But think of *her*. I mean *really* think of her. Not just about how you want to be with her. Think about how hard she's worked all her life, and what she's giving it up for. Do you really want that on your conscience? What happens if she starts to resent you for it? And Decker, look at what *just happened*. What happens next time you decide you're done with her?"

I felt a red-hot fury in my chest. How dare she? "I was never *done* with her. I was—"

"Pissed, yes, I got that memo. You were pissed at her. You were pissed at me. You were pissed at the whole damn world."

"No, Mom, I'm pissed at *him*." Which is why I realized I was an idiot—being angry at everyone but him. Blaming everyone but him.

Like Janna, sticking her finger at Delaney at her brother's funeral.

"Because he didn't tell you," my mom said.

Yes, that he didn't tell me. Yes, that was a betrayal. But bigger than that. "Because he *died*." He fucking died. And that felt like the biggest betrayal of all.

She winced. "Yeah," she said. "I'm pissed about that, too."

"And, yes, because he didn't tell me, like he saw me as a little kid who wouldn't be able to handle it."

"That's not . . . ," she started. "I think he wanted to remember you the way you were—not as someone scared of losing him, which was going to happen either way. If you could spare someone you cared about that fear, that added grief, wouldn't you?"

But I had a right to know. Only then I thought of Delaney. I imagined her smile, and not seeing it again, and her not joking around with me, harassing me about putting the milk in the fridge. Not smiling and calling me an idiot. Instead, everything laced with sadness and desperation and the way I felt in the hospital when I thought she wouldn't wake up, making bargains with anything that would listen. *Anyone but her. Everyone but her.* And yes, I'd spare her that.

My mouth hung open in response. "And also," she said, "if I catch you sneaking upstairs over there tonight, I'm taking your car keys."

Point: Mom.

*   *   *

By the time my mom and I got back from dinner, everyone was already upstairs at Delaney's. She sent me a text a little after midnight. *All quiet.*

I texted back: *Plans foiled. Mom put the fear in me.*

A few minutes later, there was a tap on the office door. I opened the door and she waved, but she didn't come in. I peeked at the staircase behind her. "Look who's the rebel," I whispered.

"It's your last night here. And there's no rule about watching television in the living room after midnight. I'm sure of it." She smiled. "So . . . want to watch TV?"

I followed her out of the room. "I'm trying to figure out if that's a euphemism for something, but I have a feeling I'm about to be seriously disappointed."

She flipped on the television, turned the volume all the way down, and threw a pillow in my lap from the other side of the couch. Then she put her head on the pillow and sprawled across the couch. She pulled the throw blanket from the back of the couch down around her.

"I see you get the good seat," I said.

"Shut up," she said, her eyes focused on the muted screen.

She was scared. Correction: I had scared her.

"You're right," I said. "I'm wrong. Like always." I put my arm on her side.

"Okay," she said, but it was like my thought, the vision in my head, had transferred to her. And whether she believed it or not, it was stuck there, becoming something. I ran my fingers through her hair until she fell asleep, and then I tried to rest my head on my other arm, but it didn't really work. I slept like I was on an airplane, jerking awake every few moments when my neck fell at an awkward angle. But eventually, I must've fallen asleep for real, because the next time I woke up, there was a hand on my shoulder.

I jumped, seeing my mom standing over me, and I jarred Delaney in the process. She woke slowly, and then quickly, processing the fact that my mom was standing over us.

"Oh God," she said, pushing herself to the other end of the couch. "It's not what it looks like."

My mom raised an eyebrow at her. "What it looks like is that you fell asleep watching TV."

"Oh. Then, yeah." She had lines in her cheek from the pillow impression, and she rubbed at them.

"Now get upstairs before your mother comes down here and has a heart attack." And Delaney nodded, already getting out of the room.

But my mom had frozen. And I was staring at her. "Did I just make a joke about heart attacks?" she asked.

"You did," I said.

Her hand covered her mouth, and she sat on the sofa beside me. "I'm a horrible person," she said.

"You are."

She shook her head. Then she refocused on me, still sitting on the other end of the couch. "I see you set up your defense already. *But I wasn't in her room, Mom.*"

"No defense," I said. "It was her idea. I pretty much just go along with her ideas." I rolled my neck. "Ow."

I waited for the argument, but none came. She got up off the couch, ran her hand through my hair as she passed. She backed into the kitchen. "You're going to have a really good life. I can feel it."

I wondered how she could possibly think something like that, when in the last year alone, I'd lost my father and Carson, and very nearly lost Delaney.

"Thank you, Fortune Cookie," I called as she disappeared through the swinging door.

Chapter

17

My mom may have felt that my life was going to be good, but she didn't see the way everyone was watching us at school that morning. Nobody wanted to be us. Nobody wanted to be *near* us. Like the curse was a part of us now, and we were contagious.

I walked Delaney to class, and people whispered as we passed. And I was guessing it wasn't just because I was holding her hand. I strained to hear what they were saying.

Listen.

Carson and Troy.

Tara in Falcon Lake.

It's coming for them.

"Decker? You there?"

"Here. Sorry," I said, turning to face Delaney. "Meet you at lunch?"

She forced a smile as she backed into her classroom, but

her eyes roamed the hall behind me. Everyone watching. Everyone talking. I wondered if she was listening, too. I wondered what this place whispered to her.

I passed Janna in the hall. She was fidgeting with the lock on her locker, unable to open it. She hit it with the palm of her hand and tried again.

"Here," I said. I knew her combination without even realizing I knew it. It'd been the same since freshman year. I felt something click inside the lock, and I slid it open.

"Thanks," she said. "I didn't sleep." She pulled out her book, and I heard her breath shake. She leaned in close to me, gripped my jacket with her free hand, and said, "Have you ever pretended something so much that it became real?"

Justin had mentioned that Janna thought the curse was real. Tara said so, too. "It's messing with your head," I said. "None of this is real."

She got too close in my face. "It is now," she said. "Oh God." She covered her mouth and looked at me with wide eyes.

The warning bell rang, and she grabbed her books and took off down the hall.

I didn't see Kevin until lunch. He was already at the table, uncharacteristically somber. He wasn't even eating. Justin sat across from him, his head resting on his folded arms.

"Hey," I said as I sat beside Kevin. "You guys okay?"

Justin raised his hand and grunted.

"Well, I'm alive," Kevin said. Then he cringed. "Shit, that wasn't funny."

"What says the mother?" I asked.

"The usual," he said as he picked at his burger. "Irresponsible. Epic stupidity. Grounded for eternity. No car. No phone. No life." He looked up. "Also, apparently I make poor life choices, and we should all be grateful that Tara's not dead because otherwise I could be charged or something." Then he looked at me, his eyes bloodshot. "As if *that*'s the reason we should be glad she's not dead."

Janna sat down beside Justin and put her hand on his forehead. "You don't feel so good," she said.

"Bronchitis," he said. "Already went to the doctor."

"God, has anyone talked to Tara?" Kevin asked.

"We did," I said, just as Janna said, "I did."

"We?" Kevin asked.

"Me and Delaney," I said as she slid into the seat beside me.

Kevin looked between the two of us and started laughing. "I can't believe I had one of the worst weekends of my life, and Decker gets the girl."

"Speaking of . . . ," I said. "Have you talked to Maya?" If Holden left, and Kevin hadn't called, then she was pretty much on her own over there.

He cringed again. "No. I don't know, it's probably for the best."

"It's just . . . when I saw her, she mentioned you hadn't called. She didn't even know that Tara was okay."

"But I'm guessing you told her?" he asked.

"Yeah, but maybe you can tell her you were just upset, that you didn't mean it."

He locked eyes with me. "You are not seriously trying to give me relationship advice right now."

"And maybe he *did* mean it." Janna looked up at me, her eyes wide and wild.

"Yeah, I'm trying to remember your exact words at the funeral, Janna," Kevin said. "Funny. Did Decker ever ask *you* to apologize for them?"

And suddenly, we were all back there. At Carson's funeral.

"Stop," I said, which I didn't say back then. But I should have.

Janna tilted her head to the side, watching Delaney. I'd heard it once. I couldn't hear it again. "You don't get to breathe goddamn water for eleven fucking minutes," Janna said. She'd said it last year, and she was saying it again.

"*Stop!*" I said.

And Janna did. But Delaney picked up where she left off. "'And stand here all fine at my brother's funeral,'" she continued. "'You don't get to stand there all perfect like nothing—'"

"Enough!" I said. "God, *look* at us."

Delaney pushed back from the table. "I tried to stop it, Janna! I called 911. I did CPR until the ambulance got there. I didn't want him to die either. What was I supposed to do?"

Janna stared at Delaney. The table was silent. The whole damn cafeteria was silent. "A butterfly flaps its wings and a hurricane forms halfway around the world, right?" she said. "One small change, and everything happens differently. You die, and Carson isn't in the car with you. You're not there, and he's not distracted. He notices something is wrong."

"He noticed," Delaney said, and Janna jerked back. "He knew something was wrong, and I called 911 on the way to see my doctor. So now you know." She stormed off, and I sat, gripping the edge of the table, trying to keep myself under control.

"Janna, what the hell?" Justin said. "Did you just tell Delaney she was supposed to die?"

I left my food on the table and took off down the hall. Please let her be in the library. Otherwise, I was going to have to be a creep and check the girls' bathrooms. Thankfully, I found her in the back of the nonfiction section, at the end of the aisle, leaning against some Save the Wildlife poster.

"Nobody else thinks that," I said.

"Isn't it enough that one person does?" she asked.

"We're all just . . ." "*You're all so messed up,*" Maya had said. "*You're just too close to see it.*"

Someone knocked on the metal side of the shelf at the end of the aisle, like it was a door. "Sorry." Janna stood at the end of the stacks. "I'm sorry," she said.

Delaney nodded, and we stood there in silence, in the back corner of the school library, like we were waiting to see what would happen next. "So am I," Delaney finally whispered.

Kevin and Justin were maybe twenty seconds behind. "See?" Kevin said to Justin. "Told you. Library."

Justin coughed, and it seemed to come from somewhere deep inside of him. Kevin looked at the three of us, standing apart through the aisle. "So, we're having a bad day," he said. Which actually made Delaney laugh.

The bell rang, and Janna jumped. We were all so on edge, wound tight with adrenaline.

We started walking back to our lockers. "What are we doing after school?" Kevin asked.

"I'm moving back home," I said.

"Oh, good," Kevin said. "Please let me help. My house is a freaking hostile environment."

"I thought you were grounded," I said.

"Of course I'm grounded." He smiled. "So I need a ride."

"I'll take you," Janna said, staring at me. "Justin? You in?"

Justin coughed again, doubled over, and nodded before slipping into the closest bathroom.

Janna parked right behind me in the driveway. My mom's car was missing, but all the lights in the house were on. "Power," Delaney said when I opened the door.

"*Heat*," I said.

"Whoa," Kevin said. "Your house looks . . . *different*."

Their steps echoed on the wood in the living room. "New floors?" Justin asked.

I smirked. "Never knew you had an eye for interior decorating."

He flipped me off.

"Seriously," Kevin said, "everything is different." He pointed to the light fixture over the dining room table. "Even the lights."

"Yeah," I said. "Well seeing as the entire house was *ruined,* we kind of had to." I pointed to the kitchen, which my mom hadn't started on yet. "Pick up a rag. I want to get this room done before my mom gets home."

Delaney's phone rang, her spine stiffened, and she silenced it, leaving it on the dining room table. Same as yesterday. She'd silenced her phone last week, she was ignoring the calls this week.

"Hey, do me a favor?" I said. "Go see if your mom has more paper towels."

"Sure," she said, and she left without taking anything with her, like I knew she would.

I went to her phone and checked her missed call log. Son of a bitch. I pressed Call Back and held the phone to my ear, and that guy from Boston answered on the first ring. "Thank you for calling me back," he said breathlessly. "First, please accept my apology."

"You're welcome," I said. "And no."

After a pause, Dr. Josh said, "Right. The boyfriend."

"Yeah, so here's the thing. She's not going to talk to you. And this is bordering on harassment. So you might want to stop before she does something about it."

I heard him breathing on the line, but he didn't say anything. I was about to hang up when he said, "Pass a message to her, will you? Just one thing. It's . . . it's part of the

Hippocratic oath. It's a promise, to others, to 'share such knowledge as is mine with those who are to follow.' She'll understand the importance."

Great. So he was going to lure her with medical text. "Wow, that's beautiful. Really. Like poetry. Yeah, let's go ahead and share. How about I go ahead and share with your fabulous institution that you were taping a minor, that you were attempting to examine a minor without a legal guardian present."

Please let those words mean something. They'd sunk in, like osmosis, over years at the dinner table with two people who worked in law and social services, when I swore I wasn't paying attention.

"She's not eighteen?" he asked.

I smiled into the receiver. "Only if you round up," I said. And then I hung up. Win.

Delaney came back through the door with two paper towel rolls under each arm and one under her chin. She dropped them all in a heap on the floor, and they each unwound across the room in different directions. "Well, crap," she said. She turned to me, cocked her head to the side, grinned at the expression I was giving her. "What?" she asked.

"You," I said. "Are perfect."

"Are you mocking me?" she asked, one hand on her hip.

"Never," I said.

I helped her reroll the paper towels, and we went back into the kitchen. Janna was scrubbing the counters, scrubbing the fine white powder from the plaster that had settled over everything like ash, and she was crying. She wiped her hand, and the plaster dust, across her face, trying to hide it.

"Janna?" I asked.

She rinsed her hands in the kitchen sink, looked for somewhere to dry them, and shook them over the basin. She spun around and said, "How did Tara get in the lake, Decker? Tara asked me that, like I might know. Why does she think I'd know? I don't know. I *don't.*"

I didn't tell Janna what I was feeling. What I really thought. "She's desperate," I said. "She asked me the same thing."

She looked around, at the brand-new floors under her feet. At the new lights. At the new everything. "I didn't know water could destroy a house," she whispered.

Which was a funny thing to say, since it could take a life or two or three. We feared it like it could do much worse.

"And a car engine," Kevin said.

"Oh, and FYI, it can really mess with your lungs, too," Justin said. His voice rattled as he spoke, like he was still trying to cough up water, a week later.

"What did the police say?" Janna asked. "About your house."

I shrugged. "At this point, we wouldn't be able to prove anything anyway. Still, I want to know. Freaks me out thinking about it. Not knowing. Like it could happen again."

One of Janna's hands slipped off the counter, still wet. She wiped it on the side of her jeans, just like my dad had done. And now she was standing exactly where he had been, right before he . . .

"What?" she asked. She lowered her voice. "Why are you looking at me like that?"

I felt my throat closing off, but not from panic. "My dad died," I said. "Right where you're standing. He was here, and then he was gone, and now we're cleaning up the fucking kitchen like it didn't matter. Like he didn't . . ."

Delaney was there before I could finish. Pressing my head down onto her shoulder, her arms tight around my back. What I should've felt those first days. What I should've done those first days. "He did," she whispered, so only I could hear.

Janna turned back to the sink, scrubbing her hands, like she couldn't get the remnants of plaster dust off. "I can't be here," she said, to Justin I guess, because he took her by the arm and started walking out of the kitchen. "I'm sorry, Decker," she choked as they left. "I'm sorry," she said, as Justin led her out of the room. "I'm sorry," I heard, from the living room.

"Uh," Kevin said. "There goes my ride. So . . ." He squeezed my shoulder as he passed.

Sometimes I dreamed that Delaney didn't exist and that was horrible.

But sometimes I dreamed that my dad still did. And in the second that followed, in the second I remembered, he'd have to die all over again.

Delaney left to do some project for one of her many AP classes when my mom came home with takeout. The house was looking like a house again—not exactly ours, but close enough. Same pictures on the wall. Same furniture setup. Same layout of the rooms.

Except my dad's office, which was empty and purposeless. My mom was standing in the open doorway, and I guess she felt me behind her, because she said, "What should we do with it?"

I didn't answer. Couldn't answer. She turned around, narrowing her eyes like she was trying to keep me from seeing what she was feeling. "An exercise room? A sewing room?"

"You don't exercise," I said. "Or sew." She grinned.

"A library?" I asked, like Delaney's family had in the spare room upstairs.

Now she was smiling for real. "You don't read," she said. She pulled the door shut behind her, leaving it as it was. And presumably, what it would remain. An empty, gaping hole in the house. In our life.

I called Delaney before going to sleep. "It's weird that you don't live here anymore," she said.

I laughed. "No, it's weird that I *did* live with you." And I got this flash of something, a picture of us in a room somewhere. Somewhere else. A year or two from now. Would we be together in college? One day, would we live together? I wondered if Delaney thought about that. About something that far in the future. Or, with our history, if it was stupid to think past next month.

"Pop quiz," she said, which was something we used to do when we were younger. "Sole survivor of the apocalypse. Go."

But before I had a chance to respond, she added, "I call cockroach."

We used to do this all the time, whenever we ran out of things to talk about. We could both argue any side. The winner was just whoever out-logicked the other.

We didn't talk about who might be after her or why. We didn't talk about Tara. We didn't talk about Boston or whether she was changing her life for me.

I heard her breathing on the phone, like she was sleeping, when I was in the middle of arguing my case for mosquito as final survivor of the apocalypse.

I hung up and lay back on my pillow. It felt good. Like a reprieve from everything. Like when we were in Boston and away from the lake, away from our past, away from everything that we had become.

But the last thing I saw as my mind faded to nothing was the black centers of faceless eyes, growing wider.

Listen.

Footsteps, creaking along the new wooden floor.

The doorknob twisting, slowly, slowly.

My heartbeat, pounding and pounding in my skull.

I was upright, staring at the door, completely disoriented and powerless. I saw a flash of blond hair caught in the moonlight from my window the second before Delaney let herself into my room.

I pressed the heels of my palms into my eyes. "You scared the crap out of me," I said. Then, focusing back on her, I whispered, "How did you get in?" We'd changed the locks.

She held up a single key, letting it dangle from a miniature silver house. "Your mom left a copy with my parents. For emergencies."

I checked the clock, stared at the numbers until they slid into focus. After three. "What are you . . ." I looked her over. She was in sweats. Sneakers. Her hair was in a ponytail. "What's going on? What happened?"

"What happened is that I couldn't sleep. And I figured I'd be dressed like this in case someone was up when I got back in. You know, from my morning run."

Perfectly Delaney. Seeing things three steps ahead. Worrying about things three steps ahead. "And you're here because?"

She raised an eyebrow at me, wandered over to my desk. "Isn't it obvious?" She ran her hand along the edge of my desk, pulled out the chair, and sat. "I'm feeling rebellious."

"You don't do rebellious. Actually, you're kind of a dork."

She leaned forward, gave me the smile I knew she saved just for me. "But am I your favorite dork?"

"Yeah," I said. "You're my favorite."

I looked at her closer. At the way her heel was bouncing on the floor. And the way her hands were now tugging at the end of her ponytail. And the way she was still sitting in that chair. And that she had snuck out in the first place.

"Is this a thing now? Not that I'm complaining." I sat on the edge of my bed, my elbows on my knees, leaning toward her. "But are you going to tell me why you're really here?"

Her eyes drifted to my phone, sitting on the bedside table. "I called you first," she whispered. "But you didn't wake up." She pulled out her notebook, which she'd brought over in a plastic bag. "I've been looking through this and thinking," she said. "I'm making a list."

"What kind of list," I said, but I had the sinking feeling I knew exactly what kind of list she was making.

"People . . . who might want me dead."

"Don't do that. I told you already," I said. "I'm wrong. It's totally possible that Tara hit her head and stumbled around and fell."

"A coincidence?"

I pressed my lips together. I knew what she thought about coincidences. She hated them. Said it felt like the world was playing a trick on her.

That notebook was full of death. Obituaries.

"These people," I said, trying to take the notebook from her hand, "they're dead."

She clutched the journal to her chest. Facts. Answers. "You were so mad at me, and you were my . . . you loved me."

"I'm sorry," I whispered. I had a long line of things I was sorry for.

Who would win in a fight? The past or the future? The past. Every time. It was relentless.

She was running her fingers across the pen marks on the

pages. "Don't," she said. "But don't you get it? If *you* could be that angry, imagine them. Imagine a stranger . . . did I say something? Do something? Hang around too much and give myself away? Do *they* think I did something?" Troy did things. He sped up their deaths, thinking he was being compassionate.

Delaney needed facts. Not feelings. Not guesses. "Tara tripped and hit her head," I said. "That's a fact. Nobody pushed her. Nobody planned to drown her. It's a coincidence. It has to be."

"Or maybe not," she said. I wondered when she had called me, exactly. How long she'd been working all this through. "What if . . . ," she said. "What if, hypothetically, you needed money. But you're not a thief or anything. But I'm walking in front of you and I drop a bunch of money, and you pick it up. I mean, it's *right there*."

"Like a message from the universe," I said. Or an answered prayer.

"So, Tara's unconscious on the side of the lake, and it's like someone was presented with this opportunity," Delaney said.

"Opportunity," I repeated, remembering the things my dad would tick off on his fingers when practicing for the courthouse. Means. Motive. Opportunity. He was always looking for the hole in one of them. "Tara was already unconscious. The job was half-done. Just drag her a few more inches." A shudder ran through me, and I whispered, "Bet it didn't even feel like killing."

"It must've looked like a sign, don't you think?" she asked.

Here she is, just for you. Money, spilling around on the ground, for the taking. A girl, unconscious on the ground, for the killing.

"Only it wasn't a sign," she whispered. "It wasn't even me."

"It could've been Tara," I said. "I mean, maybe I'm jumping to conclusions. Tara pisses off a lot of people. Maybe they were really after her. Everyone knows her . . ."

But there was that feeling.

I could see it so clearly. Footsteps approaching the body. The lake, right there. Like a sign, calling to us. The lake, covering for us.

She slammed the book closed. "Or maybe Janna is right. Maybe there's something wrong with this place. It makes us forget. It makes us forget ourselves."

"Or maybe Tara drank too much. And tripped. And maybe you saved her from a horrible, accidental death. Now go to sleep."

She opened the drawer to put the journal inside, back where it used to remain. But instead she pulled out the recorder that I'd hidden inside. "I thought you were going to return this?"

"It's blank," I said. I cleared my throat. "It was just you." *A lot more of you.*

"I think this makes you a thief," she said, but she wasn't upset about it. He'd been calling her. She'd been ignoring him.

And I thought of the words, worried that they were burned electronically somewhere. Her secrets. Her history.

"So be it," I said, pulling her to the bed, telling her to go to sleep. And then I kept lying. Filling her head with promises I wasn't sure I could keep. *You're fine. You're safe. Nothing will hurt you.*

Last year, death couldn't touch us. It was a thing that existed in some other world, some other universe. It happened when you were old. Or to other people in the paper. On the news.

I had summoned it here when I left her on the ice. It sunk its teeth in, getting comfortable, making itself at home. It slept in the center of that lake. And every once in a while, it would roll over and stretch, and one of us would get caught in its claws.

I wrapped my arm around her as she lay in my bed, and I thought it again:

Not her.

Chapter
18

She was gone when I woke. Always disappearing. But the panic subsided when I felt the imprint in my bed from where she'd just been. Still warm. She left the notebook with me again. Probably because she was half-asleep. No, it was after five. I'd lived next door long enough to know the Maxwell house got an early start to the day. If she was supposed to be out for a run, she wouldn't have her journal. That would be just like Delaney, keeping her alibi.

Or maybe the notebook had a mind of its own, taunting me, like the lake. *Look*, it said. *Listen*, it whispered. The black and white on the front drifting in and out of focus, like the center of someone's eyes.

I flipped it open. Names. Obituaries. Some I knew. Some I didn't. And all the people just off the page, the people who were left behind. I was reaching for something that didn't exist. Not yet.

And the last page, for Maya's mom. Delaney didn't even know her name. But these were the facts, etched into the page with dark ink, in bullet-point format: The date we met them. June 22. A corresponding number. A seven. Pretty high, considering she was still going strong, wherever she was.

And then on August 1, a question mark. Nothing more from the page. Because there was nothing, nothing, nothing coming from Maya's mom.

Like the lake had healed her. Like they had moved here for that very purpose.

Shit. Shitshitshit.

I picked up my phone, but Delaney didn't answer. I checked the clock. Her mom would be up. Making breakfast probably. I threw my clothes on and nearly ran into my mother in the hall. "Good morning to you, too," she said.

"Going for a run," I said, brushing by her, thankful I'd grabbed wind pants instead of jeans.

I ran down the stairs, slipped my sneakers on as I hopped from foot to foot on my way out the front door. I raced across our yards and rang her doorbell, my body pressed close to the door.

Joanne opened their front door, bleary-eyed, coffee cup in hand. "You're early," she said.

"I know, sorry, I left my homework here. With Delaney. It's due this morning."

"She left me a note that she was out for a run. Do you want to come in? I can't imagine she'll be that much longer."

But I was already backing away. Running, like I said I'd be doing. Running, toward the thing we always ran to. The thing that pulled us all together. Binding us all to one another and to this place.

"Delaney!" I yelled her name before I could see her. *Be there*, I thought, as the shore of the lake filtered into view. But she wasn't.

I ran down the embankment, scanning the surface of the lake first, like a horrible instinct.

And then I saw her. Just around the bend, darting through the trees, toward me.

"What are you doing?" I asked in the darkness. Sunrise hadn't happened yet.

She really had been running, it looked like. Just not where she should be. She shouldn't be anywhere near here. She bent over, resting her hands on her knees. "Running," she said. "Man, I hate running."

"You shouldn't be here," I said, looking past her, down the path disappearing into darkness. At the shadows on the other side of the lake.

"Why not?" she asked, staring straight at the water. "I stood on it," she said. "I was stupid. We were stupid. I almost died because I stood on the surface. The lake didn't do anything to me. It never has."

"I'm not talking about the lake," I said, keeping my eyes on the distance. Not the lake, a person.

I put my hand on her arm, started pulling her back toward our houses. I stood close, whispered with my face close to hers, so no one else could hear, could know. "A stranger, right? It had to be someone who didn't know you."

"Right. But then that makes no sense, because everyone at the party knew me."

I shook my head. Delaney was listening. She was smarter than me, I knew that. But she also knew I was good at stuff like this. Making connections without logic. Taking the jump. Things that didn't count in school. I'd spent years trying to out-logic her. "Someone *near* the party."

I didn't say anything in the silence that followed. Neither did she. We had to be thinking the same thing. About a person near the party who didn't know her until he did. Whose eyes bore into her in Maya's living room. Who seemed surprised. Who'd said, "This is Delaney," like he was confused. He had the means. He had the opportunity. He could've been at the party without us knowing. He could've been that guy in the mask watching Tara. He could've been *anyone*.

"He was in my house," she whispered.

I pulled her farther from the lake. From their house. *Not her.*

"He . . ." She shook her head. "What did I *do*?" she asked.

"Why does a person come to a place like this?" I asked. "In the middle of nowhere. With a sick parent. It's not closer to any major hospitals. It's not closer to anything. And it's . . . I mean, people think it's cursed. Why would someone move here?" I felt it this morning, while reading the last page of her journal.

I felt her know it in the silence. I felt her believe it.

She was so close. Too close. Almost too close to see clearly.

"To hide," she said.

A place like this. Far from everything. Far from anyone. With people who gave life to a curse. The perfect place to disappear.

"When's the last time you saw their mom. Why don't you feel her anymore?"

It was so obvious now. If we were really looking. If we weren't so preoccupied with our own lives. Delaney raised her fingers to her mouth, shook her head at me. "Because she's dead," she said.

I nodded. "You didn't do anything," I said. "You *know* something."

That's something the doctor from Boston didn't understand. Sometimes knowledge is *not* for good. Sometimes knowledge is dangerous. Sometimes it can get you killed, because it's not something that can be undone any other way.

"They're not who they say they are," I whispered. They could've been anyone. A life we never saw off the page. "What do you really know about her anyway?"

"I know . . . I know what she tells me. And I know . . . I know it's not all true. But I let her say it. It's like she needs me to believe it." She looked over her shoulder, at their house. "So I pretend that I do."

A chill ran up my spine. "Go home and get ready," I told her.

"For what?" she asked.

"For school. I'm taking you there. And then I'll take you home. You're staying with me."

We didn't have enough. An accusation with nothing behind it. It was Tara in the water, not Delaney. And there was no evidence that anyone had done anything to Tara, anyway. She had a head injury. There were no facts. Just a feeling. All the connections, all the layers, lining up and feeling true.

In my head, I saw Delaney disappearing in every way possible. In her red coat, under the lake. Or facedown, a year later. Slipping under the surface of the water while we were swimming, and never surfacing. Leaving for college. Leaving me.

"And then what? And then what?" she asked, her voice going higher. *And after and after and after,* I thought.

"I'll do some research," I said.

Delaney loved research. She believed it could make sense of anything. I saw her relax. Saw her cling to the idea that it could save her. "Meet you in the library after school?" she asked.

"Sure," I said, but Delaney and I had very different definitions of the term "research."

"Listen," I said into the phone, because Justin most definitely was not listening. He was losing it. Sinking in paranoia. Drowning in fear.

Or maybe that was me.

"I'm not going to take anything," I said. "I'm not going to do anything. I swear."

"I was sleeping," he said. Which was completely irrelevant,

but it's what Justin did when he was nervous about something. Grabbed onto any possible excuse. Then he started coughing again. I couldn't tell if he was faking.

"Wake up," I said.

"Why the hell do you need the key to the lake house? And even if I could get it, just because I have a copy doesn't make it legal. People live there."

"It's about Tara," I said. And I could hear the weight of his fear in the pause that followed. Him processing which he feared most: the curse coming after us all or getting in trouble for giving me a key.

"I'm not coming with you," he said. "And if you get caught, I'm gonna say you stole it from me."

"Thank you," I said. "I owe you one."

I walked Delaney to her classroom. Thankfully, she didn't have any classes with Maya, because Maya was a year behind us. Delaney's face would be a dead giveaway. She always sucked at poker. "See you at lunch," she said, and I made myself smile as she turned away.

I couldn't find Justin—not at the lockers, not hovering around Janna, not in his first-period class. I ran back to Janna before she headed to her room.

"Where's Justin?"

She held her textbook to her stomach and said, "Last I saw, he was still in the parking lot, leaning against your minivan. Said you guys had plans and he'd see me at lunch."

I smiled. I hugged her. Didn't mean to, but I did.

He was still leaning against my passenger door when I got outside. He shrugged and yanked on the handle. "I forgot to do my history homework. I'd rather take the skip."

We drove away as the first-period bell rang, and I smiled to myself for a second, thinking of Janna telling me that dead dad would get me out of a bunch of unexcused absences. I hoped she was right.

"What are we looking for?" Justin asked.

"Trust me when I tell you that you don't want to know."

"Easier for me to claim ignorance anyway," he mumbled.

Easier for me not to explain that I was looking for proof that the person renting his house was dead. I wondered if Maya was who she said she was. If she showed different sides to different people. I wondered why the hell she was here.

"So," Justin said as I drove slowly by their street. "Park over here." He gestured to the driveway two houses before theirs. I couldn't see their lake house through the trees.

I pulled half off the road so the van sat at an angle, tilted toward the lake. Two wheels off the pavement, two wheels on. "I won't be long," I said.

He handed me the house keys as I turned off the engine. "No," he said. "Leave it on." He cleared his throat, looked out the window. "It's cold." He put his hands in front of the vents and rubbed them together.

"Okay, sure," I said.

"Don't fuck up," he said as I hopped down from the car.

"Thanks for the pep talk," I said, closing the door behind

me. The sound carried over the running engine. Justin was right: it was cold. I could see my breath as I picked my way through the trees, checking to make sure Holden's car wasn't in the driveway.

Nothing but trees and rocks and packed dirt from here to the house.

I stayed in the trees, like Delaney and I had two nights before, making our way from the party back to Maya's place. I snuck to the side of the detached garage that doubled as a shed.

No car.

But there was something. Something through the dirty glass window on the side. A wheelchair. A pile of pill bottles across the dirt floor. Boxes that were never emptied.

Great. Now I felt like an ass. A creepy asshole. But I took the key from my pocket and walked across the yard and up the front steps anyway. I rang the doorbell to make sure nobody was inside, then looked around behind me, checking that nobody was walking in the woods or driving down the road. Then I slid the key into the lock and turned it.

I stepped across the threshold, officially a criminal. Wait, if I had a key, did that make me a criminal? Probably. Maybe somebody used a key to get into my house, too. I hated that I was doing the same to someone else. Except this was for a different reason. I wasn't here to destroy anything.

The house looked the same as it had the night of the party. Barely lived in. The same furniture we'd seen, and used, for years. And suddenly it didn't feel like trespassing. This place was ours. Our life. Our history. Like I could see our names carved into the walls: *Decker was here, Carson was here, Janna was here, Delaney was here, Tara was here. . . .*

I ran my fingers along the back of the couch and walked to the kitchen. I opened the fridge—saw the bare essentials. Juice. Milk. A box with leftover pizza.

I let it swing closed, and the sound of the door catching echoed through the kitchen. I ran my hand along the counter, stopped at a pile of mail. Saw a bunch of opened envelopes addressed to Katherine Johnson. For a second I wondered if this was who Maya really was, but then next to the pile of mail, I saw a check made out to Katherine Johnson from social security, and another one from some official-sounding company. Probably for disability, which backed up Maya's story. I wondered if this was what they lived on now. I assumed so. Though I hoped they got more than this, because not that I knew much about money and the cost of living, but I got checks bigger than this from working over the summer, and the money went fast.

I dropped the checks back on the counter. One landed upside-down, and I saw the messy scrawl of Katherine Johnson on the back. I fumbled to turn it the right way, hoping to leave no evidence that anyone had been in here.

I went down the hall to the bedroom with the closed door. The one Holden had walked into that night. I knocked, then turned the handle and pushed it open. There were half-unpacked boxes on the floor, the furniture this place came with, an old computer set up on the tiny desk in the corner.

The closet door was open, and I could see a few random pieces of guys' clothing hanging.

Definitely Holden's room.

I went back into the empty room with the quilted bedspread that I'd passed Saturday night. I reached for a drawer, to see if there were clothes inside, and heard the sound of the back sliding glass door.

I froze, tiptoed out of the room, back down the hall. I knew this house by heart. There was a second exit that cut out the side, down toward the lake.

I heard footsteps in the kitchen—walking *past* the kitchen—the sound of shoes being kicked off. I kept moving down the hall, slowly, silently, but the footsteps started moving again, toward the hall. Toward me. I was losing time, so I ran the last few steps in the hall and hoped for silence. No such luck. The floorboard creaked one step from the exit. I froze. The footsteps froze. *Please let them think it's the house, settling with the change in temperature.* I held my breath, my heartbeat pounding in my head.

"Holden?" I heard. *Maya.*

Shit. I flipped the lock to the door, the sound echoing through the empty hall, and reached for the handle as the footsteps started moving again.

I stepped outside and eased the door shut behind me, holding my breath, hoping she'd waste time checking the rooms first, hoping I'd have time to get away.

But the door flew open as I was darting down the hill toward the lake.

"Decker? What the hell are you doing?" I froze at the bottom of the hill. Turned toward her voice. Maya was standing in front of the door I'd just escaped from. She was in jeans and a sweatshirt and socks. No shoes. Her hair was back in a ponytail, and she looked like a kid. Like someone's little sister. Not someone who had Kevin wrapped around her finger for months, not someone who made everyone turn their heads. Not the person who gripped my chin and smiled meanly and told me to grow up. Someone people had to take care of.

"Shouldn't you be at school?" I asked. Deflecting accusations with accusations.

She laughed. "Who's going to make me go, Decker?" Then she pulled her phone out of her back pocket and held it up, like a threat. "Now tell me what the hell you were doing *in my house* before I call the police."

"Where's your mom?" I asked. I couldn't stop the accusations. Couldn't let her get a word in. "I saw the checks, but I know she's not here." Strong offense is the best defense, so said my dad. "Is she at the hospital? Is she with Holden? Was she ever even here?"

Maya narrowed her eyes, started stalking down the hill toward me. "Of course she was here. What kind of question is that? You think I just conjured up the existence of my mother? An entire person? That she was never here?"

No, I knew she had been here. Delaney said as much. Said she felt her . . . had seen her once. What I really meant was, *Is she dead?* But I couldn't bring myself to say it with her standing in front of me all alone.

"You break into *my* house. And you're asking *me* questions. Accusing me of inventing an entire person, like she doesn't even matter. So you tell me. What. The hell. Are you doing. In my house." And she was still waving that phone around as she spoke.

I swallowed. "Want to know why I'm in your house? Trying to figure out why the hell you're here," I said. "I mean, *here*. In this place. In this town." I thought of the windows in Delaney's house, the glass on her hands. Tara's body floating in the lake. They had to be connected. Nothing else made sense. "What the hell do you want with us?"

"What are you talking about?" Maya asked, folding her arms across her chest.

"You know what Tara says? Tara says someone dragged her into the water."

Maya's entire body stiffened. "And you're accusing me?"

"Or your brother," I said.

"How dare you! What right do you have?" But her eyes were flittering past me, searching, searching. I wondered if he was around here somewhere.

"You know what *I* think? I think he thought she was Delaney. *I* think Delaney knew something that Holden didn't want her knowing."

"You are out of your freaking mind, Decker. He would *never*."

"Why are you here, then? Why? Why did you guys come here?"

She shrugged, like it was obvious. Like I was the only one

who couldn't see. "My mother always wanted to live near the water," she said. "She said it's the one thing that brings us all together. That I can have my toe in the ocean off the coast of Maine, and a girl my age can have her toe in the ocean off the coast of Africa, and we would be touching. On opposite sides of the world." She looked at me with glassy eyes. "If you drown off the coast of Florida, you could wash up in England or something," she said. But I didn't think that was true. Currents. Animals. "She said it binds us all together." Maya dipped her toe in the lake and closed her eyes. It must've been freezing. I watched as her sock turned dark, the water seeping through it. Up it. But Maya breathed out slowly, with a sigh. I strained to see the far shore. Nobody else was touching it. Nobody else to feel connected to. Not at Falcon Lake. Not here.

"There are plenty of lakes," I said, trying to understand why here of all places. Why this one? I felt like Delaney would have. Coincidence: like the world was playing a trick on me. "Around here, I mean. Why here?"

"There's no place like this, Decker," she said. I wondered if there was something special to this place, that you had to come from the outside to appreciate it. "Where you can get a lake house in the summer for dirt cheap, and not by the week." Nope, not that special. Just a place. A cheap place. "We thought we were so lucky. Though now I understand."

"It's cursed," I said, meaning it.

The side of her mouth quirked up. "What's cursed? The lake? No, the lake is everything it's supposed to be. *It's* not cursed. *You* are. All of you."

She pulled her foot back out and took her sock off, freeing her foot, which was red from the cold. But she didn't seem to notice. Instead, she wrung the sock back out, over the water. Returning it to the source.

"How'd you get in my goddamn house?" she asked, but everything was moving in slow motion. Her words felt like they were moving through water to get to me. Like I wasn't quite understanding.

"I had a key." Part of the truth. Let her think it was from years ago. From another life.

She held out her hand. "Give it to me." I did. "And get the hell off my property."

I did.

I ran, though I didn't know what I was running from. I ran back to the side of the road, where Justin was waiting in the driver's seat, his hands already on the steering wheel. I hopped in and yelled for him to go, but I didn't have to. He was already driving.

"What happened?" he asked.

"Maya was home."

"The key?" he asked, and I could hear the panic in his voice.

"Yeah, bad news about the key."

"Shit. Did you at least get what you were looking for?" he asked. Her mom wasn't there, but we already knew that. I still couldn't prove anything else. Not that their mom was dead, not that Holden thought Delaney knew, not that he dragged Tara into the lake thinking it was Delaney.

"No," I said. "Drive faster." The curse is us, Maya had said. It lives in us. I wanted to get away. Away from Maya, away from the water. Or I wanted to get closer. Closer to those of us who belonged to this place. Belonged together.

I saw a flash of color through the trees as we drove away. Maya, down at the lake, able to believe she was touching something that didn't exist.

And suddenly I wished we had done something for my dad. Scattered his ashes into the wind so I could imagine them in China and Russia and Brazil. So I could imagine him anywhere and everywhere, conjuring him up at will. Not buried under the earth, kept in a box, connected to nothing. I wished, like Maya said, I could dip my toe in the water and imagine him on the other side.

Chapter
19

I waited for Delaney after class, before lunch. She looked around the hall, her eyes wide. "Have you seen Maya? She keeps calling me," she said.

"She's not here," I said.

"It's like she knows what we're thinking," she whispered, leaning close. "Like she's got some sixth sense."

"Yeah, not a sixth sense. She maybe knows because I maybe went to her house when I maybe thought she wouldn't be there."

"You *what*?"

"I thought she'd be at school, and I went there because I'm trying to understand," I said, like Delaney had been trying to understand by going to Boston. By giving too much of herself away. "I wanted to see the rooms. I thought I'd *know* if I could just see them."

She tapped her foot against the floor. Gave me her *you are such a moron* look.

"Research," I said, smiling. Trying to make her smile.

She wasn't smiling.

"There are checks," I said, showing her I *did* actually get *something*. "And they're endorsed. So either the mom *is* alive and has been there, but I don't think that's the case, or someone else is cashing them."

"So, basically," she said, "you know nothing. Did you ask Maya?"

"I asked Maya a lot of things," I said, putting my hand on her back and leading her toward the cafeteria. "But she was not all that forthcoming with information," I mumbled.

"Decker, I love you, but sometimes . . . sometimes being on the receiving end of your questions can feel a little bit like being on trial." She pulled out her phone again. "I need to talk to her."

"You don't," I said.

"Yes, I do."

I cringed, thinking of the way I had just shot questions at Maya. "She might need a little more time."

At lunch, Tara was sitting at our table. She still had a bandage over her forehead, and her shoulders were hunched forward, like she was hiding out with us. "God," she said as we sat down, "Everyone keeps looking at me." Any other day, every other day, that would've been just fine by Tara. I glanced around the room, and she was partly right. They were looking at her. They were looking at *all* of us.

At Kevin, who put a hand on Tara's arm, as a faint tremor ran through it. At Justin, who looked like death. At Janna, without her brother. And me, without my father. At Delaney, who almost died.

And at the center, the empty seat where Carson should've been, where Janna had carved his name into the tabletop with the edge of a fork. *Carson was here*, it said, etched into the plastic.

It's not the lake—any outsider could see that. Even Maya. It's us.

I knew, from the look on Delaney's face after school, we'd end up back here. Didn't mean I was happy about it. Didn't even mean I was okay with it. "But Holden is gone, right?" she'd said, like that was the only reason I'd want her away from there. But she was as stubborn as I was, which meant she would do this with or without me. I chose with.

"She's not going to hurt me," Delaney said, not for the first time. Her feet crunched the leaves as we walked along the edge of the street. The house looked unfamiliar, suddenly. Unpredictable. For once, I couldn't imagine Carson running in or out of that door. Couldn't imagine it had ever belonged to us.

She looked at me and frowned. "Three months, Decker. If she's dead, it's been three months."

Delaney wanted me to feel sympathy for Maya, and I guess I could, kind of. A girl who lost her mother but couldn't grieve. All alone.

But they didn't tell. And they kept cashing those checks. And for what, some money? Like that's what her life was worth to them?

We were halfway up the driveway when the front door flew open, and Maya stood there, eyes wide, already shaking her head. "It's not true," she said, before we had a chance to say anything. "Delaney, it's not true. I would never. He would *never* try to hurt someone," she repeated, which is what my dad did during trials, when he was driving home a point. Say it again until they hear it in their own head. A simple thing that feels right, whether it is or not.

Or maybe she only saw that side of him. The side of him that would never do anything to hurt her. Not what he might do to other people. She noticed me, standing there, as an afterthought. "You brought *him*," she said.

"He brought me," she said.

"You shouldn't have done that," she whispered.

I heard the sound of wheels on rocks, moving slowly off the road. Maya's eyes moved to the driveway next door, where there was a blue car pulling in. Not Holden, not yet. But Maya was expecting him. Because if she called Delaney in a panic, she probably also called Holden in a panic. "You shouldn't be here," she said to me, and I could see she was nervous.

"Maya," Delaney said. "What happened to your mom?"

Maya shrugged. She placed her hands flat on both sides of the door frame, trying to look casual, but she was blocking us out. Blocking our view. "She was here one day, and then she was gone." Part of the truth, skipping over the important stuff.

"Where is she?"

"Just let us be," Maya said. "Please let us be. What business is it of yours? We're okay."

Delaney looked past her, at the half-empty house, and the half-empty fridge, and this lonely, lonely girl who had no reason to show up at school at all, because who would make her?

And there were boxes on the floor, open and ready to pack. She was preparing for something. As if she was preparing for the end, like she could see it coming. Would it be better, I thought again, not to know?

She saw us looking, and she shifted her body to cut off my line of vision. "Tell me," she asked. "Did anyone notice I wasn't in school today? How about yesterday?" She smiled. "How quickly you all can pretend I never even existed. Hey, remember that Maya chick?" She was mimicking someone's voice. Maybe Kevin's. Maybe mine. "Long hair. Sick mom. Right?"

She cleared her throat. Now she was being someone else. Anyone else. She ran her hands down that long hair now. Fixed her eyes on Delaney. "Let me go," she said. "Nobody will notice. Nobody will care. It will be like I was never even here."

Like we had conjured her into existence for a few months, for fun. For Kevin and the backseat of his car when he got bored of Tara. Never letting her in. Never really here. But this house was starting to take the shape of her. The scent of her. I'd never be able to walk in here again without seeing her, her name carved into the walls with all of ours. *Maya was here.*

"Your mom is—" I started.

"She's *not*. She can't be. Not yet," Maya said, not letting me finish the thought. Not letting me bring it to life.

"You can't keep someone alive," I said. God knows Delaney tried. God knows I had, too.

"You can," she said, "if your family depends on it."

"On the money, you mean," I said.

She winced. "Other way around, Decker. The money is the way to keep her alive." She frowned. "There's nobody else."

And then I understood. "Holden could take custody of you," I said.

She laughed. "But then Holden has no money," she said. "Did you even *look* at those checks? If she's dead, her work disability stops." A Catch-22. It's what Delaney would think, and now I was thinking it, too. "He's in school. Should I take that from him, too? Make him get a job instead so he can support me while I'm in high school? Like he already took time off to take care of my mom? He's a year behind, and he's already paying his own way. After everything he's done for me . . ."

"He tried to kill Delaney," I said. "He almost did kill Tara."

She shook her head. Hard. "No, he would never. He wouldn't." She took a step toward Delaney. A step too close. "Why would he possibly want to do that?"

"Did he think Delaney knew about your mom?" I asked.

Delaney wasn't breathing. *I* wasn't breathing. Something was shifting. Everything was shifting. The corner of Maya's mouth twitched, and her eyes sharpened for a second, then relaxed. But in that second, I saw everything change. I saw her start to believe, and that was enough for me. "Let me go," she said. "Let us go. You'll never see us again. It will be like we never even existed." She didn't realize that what she was saying was impossible.

"If I see him here . . . ," I whispered.

"What? What will you do, Decker? I'm curious," she asked. She smirked at me. "You're all so *full* of surprises."

He was coming, and I didn't want to find out. I didn't want to know exactly what I would or would not do. "Get in the car," I said to Delaney, my eyes still on Maya.

"Maya," she said, and I thought, *Please, for the love of God, get in the effing car.*

"My mother isn't your responsibility, Delaney. She's mine. And Holden's." I understood, in the same way we were still bound to one another—to the memory of one another—even after death. *Carson belongs to us, too,* Kevin had said. Death didn't change that.

"Delaney," I said. Couldn't she feel how everything was shifting? How Holden was almost here, and Maya would do anything for him, and we were just standing there self-righteously, defenseless.

I understood, because it's exactly how I felt, standing on the other side, with Delaney.

I felt her fingers sliding between mine. She felt it. Or maybe my fear had transferred to her, becoming real. Either way, when I took a step back, so did she. We walked without talking all the way back to my car. The engine turned over, and I saw Maya still standing on her porch with her phone in her hand.

And as I pulled out of the driveway, I noticed that Delaney had her phone out, too. She stared at the blank screen as she held it in her lap.

"She's dead," Delaney said. "She could be anywhere."

"Not anywhere," I said. She was everywhere to Maya. Dip your toe in the water and feel connected. Sit on your back porch, like holding vigil at a tombstone. Staring out at the water, connecting us all. "She's in the lake."

Listen. "Decker." I heard my name. Delaney had called it as she fell beneath the ice. My dad's mouth had formed the word as he slid to the floor.

"*Decker.*" She grabbed my arm, her voice sliding into focus. "The lake?"

"Do you believe me?" I asked.

"Yes," she said. She took her phone out and called 911. "There's a body," she said. "In Falcon Lake. Maya Johnson's mother." The biggest leap of faith on a feeling. On me.

"*I want to know what you believe,*" she'd said, "*so that I can believe it, too.*"

I cringed when Delaney gave her name before hanging up, because I knew what would happen next.

They came to us first. A dead body wasn't exactly an emergency. It was a tip. A very questionable tip.

I was there. In her room. With the door open. Trying to convince her she'd done the right thing, ignoring the fact that there was a police car currently idling in her driveway. "But I shouldn't even know about it," she said.

The engine cut off.

"But you do," I said.

A door slammed shut.

"I feel like I'm messing with fate. Like there's a way things are supposed to happen, according to the choices we make, and I'm changing it all."

The doorbell rang, and then the front door creaked open.

"You don't believe in fate," I said.

There were footsteps on the stairs. And then Joanne was standing at the entrance to the room.

"Delaney," she whispered. "Why are the police here?" She moved her eyes from Delaney to me. "Decker?" Things like this were usually my fault. She knew that about me. "They claim you called them?"

Delaney stood up. "We know something we shouldn't, Mom," she whispered back. "Maya's mom is dead."

Joanne put her hand over her heart. "Oh, no. Poor Maya."

"She's been dead for a while," I added. Not *poor Maya*.

Joanne sat on the edge of the bed as I stood up. "Poor Maya," she repeated, like an echo.

I followed Delaney downstairs. Joanne stood against the wall with a phone pressed to her ear. "Your father should be here for this," she said, like she was worried that Delaney was about to get in trouble.

"Hey," I said to the cop, like we were old friends. He wasn't the one who showed up at our house; he was the one who questioned me when we found Tara in the lake. Who told me to stick around. Which I didn't.

He nodded at me and started writing. Then he looked up at me and said, "D-e-c-k-e-r, right?"

Maybe this was part of Intimidation Tactics 101. "Yeah," I said. "And Phillips has two *L*s."

Joanne cleared her throat. "I need to call his mother if you plan on questioning him."

He smiled. "No, that's all right. I'm here to speak with your daughter. Not a questioning. Just want to make sure we have everything right."

"I already said everything I know," Delaney said, but she was looking at her mom. "This is a waste of your time," she said, turning to the cop. I think she was starting to realize that she'd have to (a) lie; (b) lie to a cop; and (c) lie to a cop in front of her mom.

"You should talk to Maya," I said.

"Allegations like this," the officer said, making him seem much older than he looked, "are quite serious. If you make a statement that a person was killed—"

"*Killed?*" Delaney said, rising off the couch. "No, she died on her own. She wasn't killed."

"Tell me, then," he said. "Tell me how you know all this."

I could see from the way he was looking at Delaney that he knew the rumors. That he was a part of this town. That he believed. The curse. Delaney, safe in this house. A body, hidden below the surface. A trade.

"Did"—he consulted his notes—"did Maya tell you this?" he asked. He didn't make eye contact with her, like she could wield the lake's power. Decide who the lake would take in her place.

"She implied it," she said. *Careful*, I thought.

"We need you to explain how exactly she implied it. We don't go searching a lake on a whim, you know."

Joanne sucked in air. "You're saying that Maya's mother is in the . . ."

"She is," I said.

"Okay," Delaney said. "Her mother hasn't been in that house for months. She was sick, really sick, before . . . on disability. And now she's gone."

"And she told you her body is in the lake? Of all places? What on earth would possess a girl to do that to her own mother?"

Delaney shrugged. "I don't know what possesses anyone to do anything."

"We've just been by the house," he said. "She claims her mother has been getting treatment in Canada. Something they don't offer here. She said she's been there for months." Something hard to track down, something to cover our story. "She said that she and her brother are going to pick her up this weekend and bring her home."

I looked at Delaney, thought of the boxes. They'd be gone before those few days were up. Wiped from existence.

"If she's away in Canada, then how is she signing the backs of her disability checks in Maine?" I asked. And the cop looked up at me. "They're cashing the checks," I repeated. Because that was something that was illegal. Something that could be proven. "She's not there, and they're cashing the checks."

Something real.

Chapter
20

It began.

Two boats, out on the lake. A crowd of onlookers scattered along the shore. Whispers—rumors—about what they were looking for. They started near Maya's place at the first sign of light. We saw them out there as we drove to school.

"What's going to happen to them?" Delaney asked, her forehead pressed against the car window as we passed the lake.

I didn't know. We couldn't prove Holden had done anything to Tara, but we could prove this. This was a crime. And there would be some sort of justice, even if it was for something else. "This will stop," I said. "This will all stop."

I hoped the lake heard me as we drove past. I hoped it was listening.

* * *

We heard the rumors in the halls at school.

"They're looking for a murder weapon."

"The water is toxic, and they're searching for the source."

"A man walked straight into the water, and never came back up."

They watched Delaney walking down the hall, perfect and untouched. "I feel like we shouldn't be here," she said.

"Where else are we supposed to be?" I asked. But I knew the answer. We should be down at Falcon Lake, waiting to see what it would offer, and what it would take.

Justin, Janna, and Kevin were already grouped together in an alcove at the science wing. "Go to class," I said to Delaney. Until this is over, that was probably the safest place for both of us. "There's nothing else you can do."

She slipped away, into the rush of bodies.

"Did you hear?" Justin asked. His eyes were watery, and his voice had faded, but he seemed to have more energy. More life to him.

"I heard," I said.

"My parents said they're looking for a *body*," Kevin said.

"Whose body?" Janna gripped Kevin's arm, her fingers digging in so tightly that he winced and pulled his arm away.

"I don't know," he said. "I heard my mom on the phone this morning, but when I walked into the room, she left. And when I asked her, she ignored me. Naturally."

Justin's and Janna's eyes flitted around the hallway. I knew what they were doing. A tally. A check. Not one of us. *Not one of us.*

Justin cleared his throat. "Has anyone talked to Maya?" he whispered.

Kevin's eyes went wide. A body in the lake. It hadn't occurred to him it was someone we knew. If someone was missing, we'd know. It would travel through town and we'd hear it in the halls or over dinner or it would just appear in our mind, becoming true.

I saw the panic in his eyes. I saw it start to take control of his shoulders, his face. Panic and guilt, that all of this could maybe be traced back to him.

"It's Maya's mom," I said. "They're looking for Maya's mom."

They pulled up bones while we were at school, but they turned out to be a cat's. The news traveled through town, and we heard it in school halls and over lunch. Lots of secrets buried here. A graveyard of them. And then there was a large chest that they pried open with a crowbar, only to find envelopes, sealed letters, the ink long ago bled away.

We didn't make plans. Not out loud. But we waited for one another after school in the parking lot, like there was safety in numbers, and we drove to the site of the party—the house that Kevin's family owned. There were police cars at Maya's. And vans designated with acronyms I didn't even want to try to decipher. And there was Holden's car.

For all the commotion, for the amount of people either involved in the search or watching from shore, the lake was eerily, ominously silent.

People gathered around in clumps, watching as the boats moved slowly, two people in each, a long rope attached to a diver on the other end, moving slowly back and forth along the bottom of the lake. Yard by yard. Foot by foot. We couldn't see them through the murky water, just the rope as it stretched back and forth, but the diver came up about fifteen minutes after we'd been there, sending someone else down in his place.

Delaney pulled her jacket tighter, dipped her chin into the collar. Our neighbors nodded at us as they breathed warm air into their hands or pulled their hats farther down over their ears. But mostly we were all mesmerized by these men searching our cursed lake.

We all stood on the pebbled shore, watching the water, like we were coming to make our peace with it. Everyone negotiating the terms of their own deal. "What *is* that?" Justin asked, leaning forward. The diver had come up again, and the man in the boat was wiping black ooze off of him, off the rope, off everything.

"Just sludge," whispered the man beside us, whom I recognized as one of the neighbors here. There were people everywhere, dotting the shore all the way around, coming and going around work and school schedules. But most people didn't speak, or they spoke in whispers out of respect for whatever was buried below.

When the man beside me stepped back, I saw Maya sitting on the edge of the lake three houses down. He whispered, "She's been sitting in that exact same position since they started." Her legs folded beneath her, her chin in her hand, letting them drag up every secret buried in Falcon Lake before they got to hers.

"What's she still doing here?" Delaney asked. "And where's Holden? I thought they'd be gone. . . ."

Kevin looked over toward Maya. "Should I say something?" he asked. "I feel like I should say something." But he didn't.

I saw our cop—the one who came to question us yesterday—watching us from down the curve. When his eyes locked with mine, he started walking in our direction. "Heads up," I whispered to Delaney, and we stepped away from Kevin, Justin, and Janna.

When he stood beside us, he looked at Delaney, and then away from her. He cleared his throat. "Could you point us in the right direction?" he whispered. He understood. The way we were all tied to this place. Like she knew the secrets of Falcon Lake, was a part of it, heard it whispering to her in the dark.

"I wouldn't know," she said. "I only know what Maya told me." She folded her arms across her chest, and I thought of the recorder still buried in my drawer somewhere. Proof. Truth.

"Problem is, Maya says it's not true," he said.

"Her brother," I said. "Did you talk to her brother?"

"Holden?" he asked. "We called him this morning. He's sticking to Maya's story. He just arrived."

Delaney pushed past us, straight for Maya. Maya saw her coming, held her eyes like the betrayal didn't sting at all.

Maya watched us approach, and she stood before we got too close. She stuck her finger out at Delaney. At me. "You wouldn't be doing this to me if I was one of *them*." Then she extended her arm so she was pointing at Kevin, at Justin, at Janna.

"They never would've done what *you* guys did," Delaney said.

And Maya started laughing. "Wouldn't they?" And suddenly I saw the Maya that stood on my porch turning mean. No, they wouldn't. They pulled Delaney *out* of this lake. "You think they're not hiding things? Are you even *looking* at them? Can you really not see how scared Justin is?" she whispered. "Can you really not see how *angry* Janna is?"

I saw Delaney's gaze flick over to Janna. "There are things about our past that you wouldn't understand."

"Go," Maya said. And when Delaney didn't move, Maya yelled, *"Go!"* and Delaney jumped.

But she didn't leave. "I know what he did," Delaney said. "To Tara."

"Who?" Maya asked. "My brother?"

"He was at the party," Delaney said.

"He was at my house, after the party, where he had every right to be, since he was visiting."

"But I *know*," Delaney said.

Maya paused, looked past us. Made sure the cops were looking at the water, distracted, and not at her.

"That's the problem," she said, lowering her voice. "He's my brother, Delaney. I don't know what you expect me to do. But you can't prove anything. And he's all I have." Then she looked out at the water. "None of it matters."

She was right. We could prove nothing. In the courtroom, it meant nothing. But I'd know. They'd know.

"It matters," I said. "It matters that he tried to hurt—"

"Stop it," she said, glaring at me. "You don't know when to quit, Decker." Then she lowered her voice and leaned toward me. "Though I'm beginning to understand why someone might want *you* in the bottom of that lake."

I froze. Delaney froze. "I want to believe," Delaney said, "that you don't actually mean that."

Maya turned to Delaney. "And I want to believe that my closest friend in this hellhole didn't completely turn on me." She pointed at her. "This is your fault, you know. Holden knew this would happen. He warned me about getting too close, about letting people know me, know us. I promised I'd be careful, and I *was*. You kept asking and asking about my mother. I told him . . . I told him because we'd have to leave. And we were going to, just as soon as the lease was up. We didn't know what you knew. He was just trying to find out. And then I guess it looked like you were there, facedown, inches from the lake."

Like a sign.

She seemed to catch sight of something on the surface of the water, in the distance. A yellow buoy—they'd been sending up buoys every time they came across something suspect. "So you knew about my mother . . ." She turned to Delaney. Tilted her head to the side. "But what I can't figure out," she said, "is *how* you knew."

Careful.

I felt Maya grasping at the truth, like it was slipping across the surface of the ice, but she could see it—she could almost catch it.

"When someone dies," Delaney said, and I thought, *Please no*, "it always matters to someone." She looked away. Closed her eyes. "It mattered to you."

I heard the oars dipping into the water as the boats moved another yard away. The water lapping the shore.

"People can't just disappear," Delaney said.

And then the strangest thing happened. Maya sat back down, and Delaney sat beside her. Maya's breath shook, and I felt like I could see the air moving along with her, in the cold. "The last thing she said, before she stopped saying anything at all, was that the water looked so peaceful."

I didn't know how anyone could look at Falcon Lake and see peace and calm and beauty, when they had just pulled up sludge and secrets and bones. What side had the lake shown her mother? Or what had she wanted to see? All I saw was black water, churning in the wind, and the yellow buoy, bobbing along the surface.

I saw what it had made us.

Delaney sat next to Maya, watching the water, waiting for this to be over.

And suddenly I understood what that lab guy couldn't in Boston. Why she felt a pull and not a push. She couldn't help the dying. Mostly, she couldn't. But the people left behind— like me, like Maya—she could. She did.

Delaney looked up at me, and she gave me a smile, like she knew what I was thinking by the way I was looking at her.

But she was a better person than me. I looked over my shoulder, caught Holden's shadow in the sliding door. Hiding, like a coward. I stomped up the hill, straight for him. He closed the door but didn't lock it in time. I slid it open and stepped inside. "You think you're so smart," I said. "Manipulating your sister into pretending you had nothing to do with this. With any of this."

"You should probably go," he said, and I could see how furious he was. I *should* probably go. But there were people and cops and nothing was going to happen to me. Not here, and not now. "I know what you did. Even if no one else ever does, I know. Even Maya knows."

"Don't. Don't act like you care about Maya. Not when *you* have just ruined her life."

I looked around the house. I didn't see how I had ruined anything. She was living by herself, taking care of herself.

"You could just take custody of her. Maya said so. Couldn't you?"

"Oh, sure, I can probably get custody. And then what? I can barely afford to take care of myself. There's no way I can take care of another person without the disability from my mother's old job. I am twenty freaking years old. Most twenty-year-olds are at a bar with their fake ID, not working two jobs while at college, not driving back and forth every time their sister gets lonely."

He didn't see Maya standing in the open doorway, her eyes wide.

"I love my mom, and she fought hard for years to keep us, to keep us together, but asking me to take care of my sister? She's dying and she makes me promise. I don't know *how* to take care of another person. She told me I'd make it work." He let out a deep breath. "She told me *how* to make it work. So I'm trying." Was Holden saying his mother had told him not to report her death?

"But she would understand."

"Oh, she would? Tell me, how are you so sure? She's dead. How do you break a promise to someone who's dead?"

He heard Maya then, standing behind him, heard the noise that escaped from her throat. "Maya," he said, reaching for her. But she was already gone.

She was running down the hill, straight for the cop, with Holden chasing after her. "Wait," he said. "Maya, don't."

She grabbed the cop's arm, and she looked out at the lake. She narrowed her eyes against the glare from the setting sun, and she extended her arm forward, pointing at a spot in the distance. "There," she whispered.

She turned around and looked at Holden over her shoulder. "I'm sorry," she cried. "I'm so sorry." And then, back to the cop. "I didn't know what to do," she said between sobs. "I didn't want to be taken away. I didn't want to live with strangers. And I panicked. I tried digging a grave, but the ground was hard." She looked down at her tiny, useless hands. "And I thought of animals . . . so I found the chains and the concrete in the old garage, and it just seemed like it was telling me something. Like the lake was calling me. They used to bury people at sea, you know."

Chains and concrete. Oh God. The cop looked over at Holden, and Maya saw him looking. "When my brother got here," she said, "he tried to stop me. But it already looked like I was guilty of something. And I begged him. I begged him."

"And the checks?" he asked.

"I needed the money," she said. She looked back at Holden. "He had nothing to do with it. But what was he supposed to do? Turn in his own sister?"

He ran a hand through his hair and nodded, like he had a sister of his own and understood. "Don't move," he said as he stepped away.

And as he walked away, she whispered, "Where could I possibly go?"

Holden pulled her toward him, wrapped his arms around her back. "Dammit, Maya," he whispered as he held her close.

"What the hell just happened?" Kevin asked as another cop led Holden and Maya back into their home. "*Maya* said *she* did this?" That's the lie she was sticking to. But Maya hadn't done this. At least, not alone. But she was going to take the fall for it.

Nobody left, even though it was getting darker. Even though I didn't really want to see this part. More people showed up, like the whole town was holding some vigil at Falcon Lake. The buoy went up, near where Maya had directed the cop, and we waited. Nobody spoke. Nobody moved. They brought a body bag down, but it didn't come back up at first. *She* didn't come back up. She was not supposed to come up. She was *never* supposed to come up. So they waited, hooked onto the bottom of the lake, hooked onto what was presumably something that was supposed to remain hidden.

They got more equipment, more air, to force the cement blocks up as well—the weight and chains that held her to the bottom.

The crowd grew at the shoreline, and then there was a bubble from under the surface, like the lake was gurgling, releasing something—its secrets, its air, its life.

She came up, black garbage bags buoying to the surface, floating there while we all stared.

Kevin made the sign of the cross, then leaned over and put his hands on his knees.

"I've got to get out of here," Janna said.

Justin backed away with her. "Let's go," he said.

We all started walking toward our cars. We walked away from the lake, bumping shoulders. Closer than we normally walked. Kevin close to Delaney, close to me, close to Justin. Justin had his arm around Janna. "This place is so fucked up," he said. "How long till we get out of here?"

"Seven months until graduation," Kevin said. "If I'm ungrounded by then."

I reached out and took Delaney's hand.

"This place," Janna said, "is like living with ghosts."

I felt a chill run through Delaney, through her hand, straight to me.

Chapter
21

"What's going to happen to them?" I asked my mom. She'd made supper. Neither of us was eating it.

My mom pushed the food around her plate with the back of her fork. "They'll probably hold her on what they can until the autopsy is complete. Make sure her mother died of natural causes."

"What about Holden?"

"What *about* Holden?" she asked.

Holden could've killed Tara. Could've killed Delaney. "I find it hard to believe that he's remotely innocent in this," I said.

She shrugged. "There are things that are hard to prove. And there are things, to the court, that are not worth proving. You should know that."

"So they're just going to get away with it?"

What had happened to my house. To Delaney's house. Taking and taking and making me believe . . .

My mom fixed her eyes on me, stopped moving her food around her plate. "They lost their mother. And they did something stupid. The only thing that's going to happen is that Maya is going to have a place to stay and people to look after her. And personally, I'm more than okay with that."

But I looked at my house, and I thought of Delaney's windows and Tara in the lake. Holden had been around the night the windows were broken. He was obviously capable of it all. It had to be him. I shoved a forkful of food into my mouth, ground my teeth into it, and concentrated on avoiding eye contact with my mom so she wouldn't see it in my face.

I wanted Holden to pay. I wanted justice.

"I'm going to Kevin's," I yelled from my room.

"Don't you have homework?" she asked.

"Yeah," I said, digging through my top drawer and pulling out the stolen recorder. "That's why I'm going to Kevin's. Project."

I shoved the recorder into my pocket and took off down the street. Delaney's bedroom light was on. She was home, and she was safe. Maya was gone. Holden was leaving. And I needed proof, for her, for me.

There were tons of cops when we left—I was sure they'd still be combing through the shoreline, taking statements from people. But when I pulled up to Justin's lake house, into the dark driveway, I didn't see anyone. I set the recorder on the seat beside me and turned off the engine. I didn't hear anything. I didn't *see* anything. Just a light from the house, behind the cheap blinds. Just a light in the distance, through the trees, from the neighbor's.

Bad idea. Like standing on the middle of Falcon Lake. I turned the ignition, my headlights cutting through the dark, and something slammed into my door, shaking the van, shaking me. Holden's face was in the window, and his eyes were wild. A wooden plank was positioned over his shoulder, a bent nail near the top, catching the light from my headlights. Then he brought it down against the hood of my van and yelled, "Get out of the car!"

He tossed the plank aside—I heard it bounce off the ground. "Get. Out. Of. The. Car!" he said again.

This was the guy who wanted to kill Delaney. And for what? To protect his secret. Her life, for a secret. *Her life,* for nothing.

I opened the door, looked at the wooden plank, at the bent nail, and wondered how quickly I could get it in my hands.

Not quick enough. Holden pushed me against the van, once, twice, before I slammed my elbow in his face. "Who the fuck do you think you are?" he asked, running his hand over his jaw.

"Me?" I asked, regaining my footing and pushing off the door. "*I'm* not the one who tried to kill someone! *I'm* not the one taking a plank to someone's car."

My eyes drifted to the wood and back to Holden. We both dove for it, but I was faster. Got there a fraction of a second before him, had a better grip on the wood, felt the splinters digging into my palm, my fingers, as I wrenched it out of his hands.

Holden took a step back. "What the hell are you doing here?" I asked, and I hauled the slab of wood over my shoulder in one quick motion, weighing it in my hand, adjusting my grip.

Holden looked at the wood, took another step back. "Leaving," he said. "I'm just getting the last of our things and leaving." He was panting, and he was furious with me. "But the question is, what are *you* doing here?"

I felt the wood grains biting into my palm. Saw the dent in the door behind me. The hood of the minivan caved in. The recorder, just through the window, still off. And I didn't care. I dug my fingers into the wood, and I knew it wasn't justice I wanted. It was revenge.

"I wanted answers," I said. But even if I got them now, I wasn't going to have the proof. And now I wanted something more.

He laughed, still eyeing the piece of wood in my hands. "You already got them. Are you happy now? Our mom died. We lied. It's over now. So do me a favor, and leave me the hell alone."

"You're the one who just attacked my car," I said. Holden shifted positions, like he was deciding what to do. To run or to fight.

"I shouldn't have done that," Holden said, pointing to the car, breathing heavily. "I don't know what I was thinking."

I took a step closer. He took a step back. "You shouldn't

have done *that*? There's a lot of things you shouldn't have done. This is kind of at the bottom of that list. That night," I said, stepping toward him, "at the party . . ."

He shook his head at me. "It's this place," he said in a whisper. "It makes us do things. You understand?"

He was eyeing my grip on the wood because he wanted me to understand. He wanted me to believe it was *this place* that made him capable of the things he had done. He stopped moving backward.

"It made you destroy my house?" I asked. "Destroy Delaney's windows? You've been *tormenting* us."

"What the hell are you talking about?" he said.

"Were you just trying to distract us? Make us believe in the curse?"

"I don't even know where you live. I've got more important things to worry about than pretending there's some curse," he said. He sank back into the darkness, but I followed him.

He was admitting to Tara. But denying something far less. Saying we were all pretending.

The wood slipped from my fingers. "And now Maya's gone," he said. "And I'll be gone the second you turn away. So what are you gonna do, kid? What are you gonna do with that piece of wood and your pretty little girlfriend and your bright fucking future? What," he said as he took a step closer, like he could see me wavering, "will this place"—another step—"make you do?"

But it wasn't this place that made him lunge in my direction.

And it wasn't this place that made me swing the chunk of wood into the side of his ribs.

Listen.

I heard the crack of his rib, like I'd felt Delaney's break when I was trying to keep her alive. I heard the impact of his hands and his knees on the pavement. I heard him grunt and then laugh.

Holden was on the ground, and he was laughing as he grimaced. "See?" he said.

"Yeah," I said. "I see."

And I let him believe it. I let him believe that it was this place that made him capable of murder and me of this. That it was this place that made me capable of hatred. That it was this place that made everyone capable of dying.

Falcon Lake didn't take from us. It told us things. It showed us things about ourselves.

"Have you ever pretended something so much that it became real?" Janna had asked me in the hall after Tara ended up in the water. She was angry. She was so angry. Even Maya could see it. I started to get nauseous, tried to get my bearings. Remembered the fight Kevin had with Janna right before she went out to his car. Remembered the way I blew her off, didn't want to talk about Carson, before my house was flooded. The gasoline in the shed after I'd painted over Carson's name.

Like the curse. Coming for us all.

Holden turned over, looked up at me as I walked toward him, still holding that beam of wood.

"What else do you want from me?" he whispered, his

hands held out to show me he had nothing. I wanted to trade him. For my dad. For Carson. For everything that had been taken from us.

I wanted vengeance for every injustice, everything I couldn't change and couldn't stop.

But more than that, I wanted to believe in the future, like Delaney did, always planning for what came next. Like she could see it coming. Like she could see *us*. And even if I couldn't see it yet, like she did, I wanted to believe in it. I wanted that future, more than I needed revenge.

"I want to know what you believe," she had told me, *"so that I can believe it, too."*

And so I left him. I walked up to him, past him, as he tried to catch his breath. I dropped the beam of wood beside his head, and I went straight for my car. I pulled out of the driveway. I didn't look back.

But I didn't go home.

"Where are you?" I asked into the phone.

"Home," she said.

"I'm coming over," I said.

And after a pause, "It's about time someone did."

Home. We hadn't been to Carson's house since he'd died. It had never been Janna's house. It had been Carson's. She had just lived there, too. I drove the streets as if in a dream. Taking the turns by memory, pulling up in front of the brick home with the stone path and the blue curtains, always hanging open.

They were closed now.

Janna's car—Carson's car—was in the driveway, beside her mother's car. There was no sound coming from inside. The whole thing was like a tomb. A constant reminder that *Carson was here*, but now he's not. A person wiped from existence.

I rang the bell and heard footsteps coming down the stairs. Janna opened the door and frowned when she saw the expression on my face. "Hi," she said.

"You." I stuck my finger at her chest, same as she'd done to Delaney at her brother's funeral. But now, staring into her eyes, same as Carson's, I couldn't speak. Couldn't accuse. Couldn't even blame.

But it hung there—half-spoken—between us. She stepped outside and closed the door behind her. "My mom's upstairs," she said, though I didn't hear a sound from inside. How easily she could've been Maya—for all purposes, alone. Without us, alone. She walked off the front porch, around the side of her house, to the patio where we all used to hang out with Carson and whatever he could snag from his parents' liquor cabinet without them noticing.

She sat in a chair—not his—and crossed her legs at the ankles, leaning back, breathing out toward the sky. "Everything's gone to shit," she said.

I reached into my pocket, hit the Record button on the recorder that I never sent back. Like my dad, needing facts. Needing proof. *Getting* proof.

I couldn't prove anything else. Not that Holden dragged Tara into the lake, thinking it was Delaney; not how Maya's mom got into the lake; not what the lady in 2B was trying to tell me as she died.

"You're going to have to do better than that," I said.

"He'll be gone *forever*," she said, like I didn't understand the concept. Like I didn't dream about that very thing all the time. Delaney, disappearing. My dad, ceasing to exist. She took a breath in, but it shook. There were tears, but it was like they had always been there, just waiting for her to take a breath.

"My dad wanted to sue the doctors, like that would bring him back," she said. "But here's the thing: every time he went in for an appointment, they asked him a series of questions. About what he was feeling. *How* he was feeling. He passed the test." Then she laughed. "Probably the only test he ever got a perfect score on." She frowned. "It's not the doctors' fault."

"It came out of nowhere," I said. A sudden seizure, a sudden, unexpected death, and nothing that could be done to stop it. Some deaths are unstoppable. Delaney understood that, worst of all. "It's nobody's fault." Not a doctor's. Not Delaney's. Not mine.

She stared at his empty seat. Gritted her teeth. "I don't know, Decker. Sometimes I wonder if he just didn't say anything. If he felt the signs starting up again, if he just pretended he was fine." She stared at me. "Think about it. It's something he would do, acting like everything was great, like life was perfect. You *know* he would. You *know* him."

She buried her face in her hands, and then I was sitting. My legs weren't working. My mind wasn't working.

We could carve his name into a wall, into a tree, into our skin, but it wouldn't matter. It was true. Carson had always lived his life like he might not last as long as the rest of us, I could see that now. With a girl on the couch or cannonballing into the lake or saying what he wanted when he wanted. Not worrying about the future, in case it never came. Feet stomping over the earth, over all of us, shouting, *Carson was here, Carson was here, Carson was here.*

But he'd fight to live. He'd fight for us, and he'd fight for Janna. I knew him.

"How could he do that to me?" she cried. It's what I thought about my dad. That he died. That he left. Her fingernails scratched at the plastic armrests, and I could imagine her carving his name there, too.

"He wouldn't," I said. I was sure of it. He may have lived his life like he wanted to make the most of every day, but he would've tried to stop it if he could. He got in that car with Delaney because he wanted to live. "Janna," I said, "there's no way. It's not his fault. There's no one to blame."

But her eyes were dead. She wanted someone to blame. No, she needed it. "I hate it here," she said. And then lower, "I hate it everywhere."

Dead here. Dead everywhere.

I wanted to pull one side of her toward me and wrap my arms around her and tell her, *it's okay, it's okay.* But I was furious at the other side.

"My *dad* died, Janna. What the hell were you thinking? I mean, my *house.* My mom's house."

"It was a mistake," she said. I wasn't sure whether she was talking about Carson or what she had done. Probably both.

"You destroyed my house, Janna." Couldn't she see? My dad and then my house. And then everything. Becoming the curse. "You hurt Delaney."

"For what it's worth, I didn't know Delaney was home. Or you. And I didn't mean to destroy your house. It was just water. . . ." But water destroyed everything. It rotted the wood, shorted the electricity. Got in Justin's lungs. Ruined Kevin's engine. Froze over and trapped Delaney, suffocating and suffocating.

Breathe.

She was crying still, but I thought it was for Carson. Not me. "I thought you guys didn't remember," she said. "That you were letting Carson go. And he never would've let you guys forget me. *Never.*"

Carving his name into the wood. Showing us the curse. The trade. A reminder.

"But the curse . . . it made you all remember. You remembered everything that happened. What we lost. And why." She leaned toward me, across the gap between our chairs. "By then it was too late. It's like it was coming to life. Justin got sick. And then Tara . . . I can't stop it."

She almost smiled. "It's alive now," she said. "Everyone will remember."

"I never forgot, Janna." I closed my eyes, picturing Delaney in the hospital bed. Carson's funeral. I never forgot.

"Yes, you all did. You never talked about him before this.

You never wanted to. You never wanted to do anything for him. The only person you thought about, even after you broke up, was Delaney."

Maya was right, we were all too close to one another, too wrapped up, so we couldn't see. All the layers. The things we grieved for. The things we feared. No, *that* we buried in Falcon Lake. We gave our fears over to it. We gave it power.

"You're wrong," I said.

She shrugged. "Doesn't matter now. Everything has a price, right? They won't forgive me for this. I know that." She shifted in her chair, looking somewhere else. "I *knew* that."

"What makes you think *I'll* forgive you?"

"Oh, I know you won't," she said. "*You* won't, most of all."

I pushed back from the chair, the metal legs scraping the bricks on the patio as I stood. I walked away, turned the recorder off as I did. "You're right," I said before I disappeared around the corner. "Carson never would've let us forget you. But he *also* never would've let you become *this*."

Chapter

22

I didn't do anything with the recording.

That night, I sat and listened to it—listened to *her*—but mostly, I thought of Carson. What he would do. What he would want *me* to do.

I thought of all the mistakes I'd made in the past year. Of all the "almosts" that we escaped, escaping punishment or punishing ourselves instead.

That maybe justice and vengeance are not opposite sides of a coin, but more like the same side of a paper, folded in half.

And sometimes they didn't exist. There was really nobody to blame for Carson's death. And maybe Janna wanted justice or vengeance for that fact alone.

She found me on the way to lunch. I saw Delaney at our table, and I was ignoring everything but getting to her. Janna grabbed me by the elbow as I walked through the double doors of the cafeteria, pulling me back outside, pulling me close so I could hear her whisper. "Justin called this morning, wondering why I hadn't picked him up," she said. "You didn't tell them yet?"

"No," I said, and I shook her loose. "And I'm not going to."

Her eyes searched mine, and for a second I wondered if she wanted to be punished. If she needed it. But if she wanted them to know, she'd have to tell them herself.

She narrowed her eyes at me. "Do you mean that?"

"Yeah," I said, my fingers finding the recorder in my pocket. I'd brought it with me, unsure what to do with it. Proof. I had it. But Carson never would have told. He would've covered it up for her. No matter what. "But it's not for you," I said. I let her think I was doing it for Carson, but that was only partially true. Like Holden, I could become bound to the dead. Or I could be bound to the living.

If Delaney picked apart the logic—and one day she would—she'd revisit this months from now, a year from now, and she'd see the holes. If I let her think Holden had done it all—destroying my house, targeting her house—she'd find the holes. Why my house? Why try to scare her before trying to kill her? And did the timing add up? Right now, she was too close. We were all too close. But later, she'd come back to this, like she went back to Carson and the boy she saved and who knows how many other decisions she had to make. She'd sift through the facts and try to make sense of them, like she did in that journal of hers. And when she confronted me with the facts, the facts that made it count, would she understand it when I told her that I'd made an unspoken promise to the dead? And another to those of us left behind?

I hoped she would.

I was back in Delaney's room after school, and I was rifling through her desk, which she hated. "If you'll just tell me what you're looking for . . . there's a system . . . and you're . . ." She grabbed the papers from my hand and restacked them. "You're messing with the system!"

But I saw what I was looking for. I pulled out the stack of new college pamphlets and held them over her head when she made a jump for them. "Nope," I said. "You don't want to go here." All Maine schools. All the wrong schools.

"I can get a degree anywhere," she said, elbowing me in the gut so I doubled in half and she could reach the pages.

"You're a giant cliché," I said, "going to school for some guy."

"Ha," she said. Then she stepped back, gave up trying to stop me. "You know what your dad told me?"

"Not to go to school for me?" I asked, because that's what he'd implied to me.

She smirked. "I asked him, you know. When it got closer. I asked him what he'd do if he had one day left to live."

I grimaced. "You and that question," I said. I wasn't sure I wanted to hear the answer.

"Yeah," she said. She took a deep breath. "He told me he was already doing it." She smiled to herself. "He said his life was exactly what he'd hoped it would be." I had stopped breathing. "And I don't think he was talking about what college he went to."

"Delaney," I said, but I didn't know what to say after.

"So, I'm staying," she said.

"No, you're not." If she stayed, if we stayed, we'd never escape the pull. The reminder of the past and how our lives had woven together in unbreakable threads. Binding us to each other and to this place.

The lake was our excuse. For all of us. We hid ourselves in it, giving and giving and giving to it.

"We're leaving," I said.

"We?" she asked.

"Yeah," I said. As if it could've possibly happened any other way. "Maybe not to Boston, because, yeah, I noticed, like you said, everyone walks too fast." I smirked at her. "But somewhere. Someplace where you can do great things, and I can do . . . slightly above-average things." She punched my shoulder, but she laughed.

And then she was staring off through the window, like she could see our future.

There was a knock at her door, and then Joanne saying, "Open," as her footsteps continued down the hall.

"A year from now, there's not gonna be that stupid door rule," I said, turning the handle.

"A year from now, you'll probably be sick of me." I didn't think she really meant it, but maybe she wondered. Maybe she worried.

"Yeah, probably," I said. She hit my arm again, but she

was smiling, just for me. "Sometimes," I said, "you say the most ridiculous things."

I woke up before my alarm, sure I heard someone calling my name. It must've been part of a dream I couldn't remember. But just in case, I got up and checked on my mom. I smelled coffee. I heard her heels on the floor downstairs.

So I got ready for the day and stared at the clock on my desk. "Bye, Decker," my mom called as she left for work. Fifteen minutes to spare before I met Delaney out front. On impulse, I pulled the recorder back out of the drawer. I didn't listen to it again. I wiped it clean.

But that wasn't enough. I grabbed my bag and my keys and left the house, but first I walked in the opposite direction—to the end of our road, over the hill, kicking up rocks as I skidded down the embankment—straight for the water.

I felt the weight of the recorder in my pocket, pulled it out, tossed it into the heart of Falcon Lake. It was good at taking what we gave it. It was good at holding on to our secrets.

I watched the glint of silver disappear under the surface.

It keeps them all. Like a promise.

Was this justice for anything? Was it my dad's idea of justice? Was it my own? I wasn't sure. I wasn't sure if it was anything at all, other than my choices, my life.

I walked back up the hill, and then I stood very still, at the corner of my street, wondering if I could hear his ghost in this place that holds its ghosts so close.

Listen.

Nothing but silence and the wind, pushing me away from the lake.

It showed me things about myself, like it always had. That I left her, yes. And that I went back for her. That I let the ice break under my feet as I ran so I could get to her sooner. I'd fall, and fall again, for the chance to keep her with me.

I saw Delaney walking toward my car, and my stomach flipped like I was meeting her for the first time. She stopped when she noticed me at the far end of the street, and she raised her hand over her head, like I wasn't already on my way.

"Decker!" she yelled, and I could tell that she was smiling. She had called my name when she fell through the ice, too. And just like then, she didn't need to. It didn't matter.

I was already running for her.

Acknowledgments

Thank you to the following people who helped this book come to life:

As always, agent-extraordinaire Sarah Davies, who championed this idea when it was just a few sentences in an e-mail and provided perfectly creepy suggestions along the way as it developed.

My thoughtful and brilliant editor, Emily Easton, who pushes me to become a stronger writer every time I sit down at the computer, and who always sees just what I'm trying to do and shows me how to get there.

The fantastic team at Walker/Bloomsbury, who are also so much fun to work with, including: Laura Whitaker, Patricia McHugh, Jenna Pocius, Nicole Gastonguay, Katy Hershberger, Erica Barmash, Beth Eller, Linette Kim, and Bridget Hartzler. Also, Rebecca McNally, Natalie Hamilton, Emma Bradshaw, and the team at Bloomsbury UK and Bloomsbury Australia. I am so lucky to work with you all!

Jill Hathaway, Elle Cosimano, Ashley Elston, Megan Shepherd, and Marilee Haynes: my ridiculously talented critique partners, who do so much more than critiquing. Thank you for the brainstorming sessions, the honest feedback, and the friendship.

My husband, for his endless support.

My parents, for an endless list of endless things, which would take up far too many pages.

And to the readers. This book exists because of you. Thank you.